By Valerie Wolzien
Published by The Ballantine Publishing Group

Susan Henshaw mysteries:
MURDER AT THE PTA LUNCHEON
THE FORTIETH BIRTHDAY BODY
WE WISH YOU A MERRY MURDER
AN OLD FAITHFUL MURDER
ALL HALLOWS' EVIL
A STAR-SPANGLED MURDER
A GOOD YEAR FOR A CORPSE
'TIS THE SEASON TO BE MURDERED
REMODELED TO DEATH
ELECTED FOR DEATH
WEDDINGS ARE MURDER
THE STUDENT BODY
DEATH AT A DISCOUNT

Josie Pigeon mysteries:
SHORE TO DIE
PERMIT FOR MURDER
DECK THE HALLS WITH MURDER
THIS OLD MURDER
MURDER IN THE FORECAST

MURDER IN THE FORECAST

VALERIE WOLZIEN

FAWCETT BOOKS • NEW YORK
The Ballantine Publishing Group

ISBN 978-0-345-49033-9

146673257

For two fine women, Lisa Dropkin and Sandy Mellion
—their caring helped make this book possible.

ONE

Weather forecasters in Florida are keeping an eye on a tropical storm forming in the middle of the Atlantic. They're saying Agatha, the first big one of the season, could hit us sometime this weekend. And you know what I say, boys and girls, who knows what will happen tomorrow—party hearty now! This is WAVE radio: the voice of the shore.

"**C**ARA, I AM worried about little Urchin." Josie Pigeon placed her coffee mug on the kitchen counter and looked over to her landlady standing in the doorway. "Isn't it a bit early for you to be up and dressed?" she asked.

"In an emergency, I am like the Boy Scouts. I am prepared. That is, I will be prepared. Today I go off island early to shop for supplies."

"What emergency?"

"The storm they talk about on the radio."

"I wasn't really listening," Josie admitted.

"There is a storm coming. A big storm. I am stocking up on food, batteries, water, candles. And I worry. What are you going to do about Urchin?"

At the second mention of her name, a small brown cat,

1

busy absorbing the first rays of sunlight as they came through the window of Josie's apartment, turned her head and stared at the two women. They were an unlikely pair. Josie was dressed for work in faded jeans, a worn chambray shirt, and brand-new work boots. Her unruly red hair was barely controlled by a frayed green cotton scrunchy; her freckled nose was sunburned and peeling. Risa, her Italian landlady, had unique ideas of what to wear when grocery shopping: layers of iridescent silk formed her skirt, and instead of a shirt, she wore an embroidered poncho, which kept slipping off one elegant shoulder. She had on espadrilles and carried a voluminous straw bag. As always, her long dark hair was impeccably groomed, and she looked chic and sophisticated.

Urchin wasn't impressed. The cat yawned, stretched, and got back to the serious work of staying warm.

"Why should I do anything about Urchin? She's fine," Josie insisted.

"Now she is fine. Now the sun is shining; there is no rain, no wind. But in a storm, she will be a problem. And not a happy problem. You read the evacuation procedures notice that was with the mail I brought up to you a few days ago?"

Josie glanced over at the pile of unopened bills, notices, and flyers that was threatening to fall off the tiny dilapidated table by her front door. She had been too busy to pay attention to anything other than the infrequent postcards her son, Tyler, sent from the computer camp, where he was spending the summer. And, since she wouldn't have any extra money until the next installment on Island Contracting's summer job was paid, she hadn't bothered to look at the bills.

Risa followed the direction of her gaze. "If you'd read those emergency instructions, you would know that if we are evacuated, you are supposed to let Urchin out of the house. All alone. To fend for herself," she added ominously.

"Urchin's not an outdoor cat," Josie protested.

"That's what I'm telling you. I worry all night long. And then I come up with solution to your problem. Evacuate Urchin now."

"Evacuate Urchin?"

"So she will be okay when we are ordered to leave the island," Risa explained patiently.

"Why would anyone order us to leave the island?"

"Because of that storm. The storm they talk about on the radio!"

"Risa, there's no reason to pay attention to those guys on the radio! They have to talk about something. Every year the weathermen blab on and on about storms coming up the coast, and every year those storms either go out to sea or hit an island in the Carribean or Florida—"

"Not always. Sam says—"

"Don't pay any attention to Sam." Josie sighed and ran her hands through her unruly hair. "He's spent the last month reading books about storms: *The Hungry Ocean*, *The Perfect Storm*, *Isaac's Storm*. He's obsessed with storms. And he seems to think I should be, too. He passes the books on to me as soon as he's done." Two of those books were still on the coffee table, where Sam Richardson, retired prosecuting attorney, current liquor-store owner, and Josie's significant other, had left them over two weeks ago. The third sat, unopened, on the nightstand in her bedroom. "But just because he's reading about storms doesn't mean a hurricane will hit the island this summer."

"But the emergency evacuation directions—"

"Risa, you know those things come out every few years or so. All the rental properties on the island have them posted someplace—usually on the refrigerator right next to the DPW schedules for garbage and recycling pickup."

Risa gathered her various layers of silk closer to her body. "I still shop today. Supplies will last for long time if this storm hit someplace south. There will be other storms. There always be other storms. And you, Josie, will think about Urchin. Tyler not be happy if something happens to his little cat."

Risa was tripping down the staircase before Josie could think of a suitable reply. Oh, well, she had to get down to the office anyway, Josie realized, getting up and stretching. Island Contracting was scheduled to start a new project in a few days, and there were many details to be checked out before then, and, with an entirely new crew for the summer season, most of the checking would be left up to Josie, as owner of the business.

Josie knew she should get going, but she poured herself another mug of coffee. "I feel like shit today," she announced to the cat.

If Urchin was at all interested, she hid it well, not even bothering to move. Josie yawned and then coughed. She sure hoped she wasn't catching a cold. She didn't have time for a cold. She didn't, in fact, have time to sit here drinking coffee. She slid off the stool next to the counter that separated her kitchen from the living area of her small apartment, feeling an unaccustomed pinch as her big toe hit the front of her new boots.

"Oh, good, a summer cold and a blister. This just isn't going to be my day," she muttered. But she took the time to empty a packet of cat food into Urchin's bowl and to pat her head before starting off to Island Contracting's office, a few blocks away.

She flipped on the radio as she drove, but the obsession with heavy winds south of the Bahamas seemed to be universal. By the time Josie had found a station playing her preferred music, she was at work.

Island Contracting's office was a small fishing shack that hung out over the back bay of this seven-mile-long barrier island. The company's founder, Noel Roberts, had remodeled the building, and one of Josie's joys was keeping it in tip-top shape. She jumped out of her truck and glanced up at the roof. Last winter, she had given the building a Christmas present—a copper weather vane in the shape of tools. A hammer pointed north and south. An old-fashioned handsaw indicated east or west. As she watched, a slight breeze caused the vane to move, and sunlight glinted off its brilliant surfaces. Josie smiled and tripped over a large oblong box blocking the wooden pathway to the front door.

She picked up the box and studied it. J. PIGEON—ISLAND CONTRACTING was printed in large block letters on the front. There was no indication of the sender's identity. She tucked it under her arm and headed down the boardwalk to her office.

Island Contracting, besides being one of the best building contractors in this wealthy seaside community—Josie's opinion—was the unofficial kitten adoption agency. A basket of calicoes had been dropped off anonymously the week before, and Josie plopped the package on the large desk in the center of the room before taking the time to provide the mewing creatures with food and fresh water.

Then she opened the package.

"Hudson House." She said the words aloud. Why had someone sent her a sign for someplace called Hudson House? A very expensive sign, she realized, running her finger along its edge. The mahogany was smooth and, she suspected, had been sanded by hand. The copper letters were forged and had been inlaid instead of merely nailed on. "Hudson House . . . Who the hell sent me this?"

"What is it?"

Josie looked up and saw Betty Jacobs standing in the doorway. The last time she'd seen her friend Betty was at the woman's wedding to a prominent New York City lawyer. That was over a year ago, and the passing time didn't seem to have done Betty any harm. Her blond hair was, perhaps, a few shades lighter. And she was certainly better and more expensively dressed than in her days working as a carpenter for Island Contracting. In fact, Betty was positively glowing.

Josie rushed to the door to give her friend a big hug. "Betty, I can't believe it's you! Why are you here? How long can you stay? Where's your husband?"

"He dropped me off and went up island to find Sam. We want you two to join us for breakfast at Sullivan's. Don't tell me you're busy. I've been craving greasy fried eggs and hash browns for the past month."

Josie hesitated. She did have things to do.

"And we have to go back to New York tonight—"

"No, not so soon! We have so much to catch up on."

"So say you'll go to breakfast with us."

Josie laughed. "Okay. I will. But why aren't you staying longer?"

"It's that overprotective husband of mine. Ever since he heard about the storm, he's been saying we have to get back to New York. . . ."

"Oh, damn that storm. Betty, you grew up here. How many storms were predicted and how many actually arrived?"

"I know, but I've been here longer than you have, Josie. And we did have some whoppers when I was a kid. And I remember my parents talking about the big one that hit back in the sixties. There were miles of sand dunes before that storm. And you know how few are left now."

"Speaking of sand dunes . . . You'll never guess what building Island Contracting is going to be remodeling this summer!"

Betty, who had been Josie's best carpenter before she moved away, picked up the excitement in Josie's voice. "What?"

"The Point House!"

"You're kidding. When was it sold? Who bought it? What have you been hired to do?"

"It's a complete remodel. Fabulous job. I've never done anything so big. The blues are here. Do you want to see?"

"Of course I do!"

When Sam Richardson and John Jacobs arrived a few minutes later, the two women were stooped over massive blueprints, which completely covered Josie's desk.

"I guess you can take the girl out of the carpenter's shop, but you can't take the carpenter out of the girl," John said affectionately.

"Honey, wait until you see this. Josie's remodeling the Point House!" Parted for almost half an hour, John and Betty embraced for a few seconds.

"What is the Point House?" John Jacobs asked, his arm still around his wife's shoulders.

"It's the biggest house on the island. Up in the dunes, on the point up north. You know it!"

"The big gray monstrosity that we used to see when we jogged up to the inlet?"

"Exactly."

"Wow. It's gonna take someone a whole lot of money to fix up that place."

"Cornell Hudson seems to have it—hey, Hudson House! That's what the sign must mean!" Josie said.

"What sign?" Betty asked.

"That one." Josie pointed.

"Where did that come from?" John asked, looking in the direction Josie had pointed.

"Why don't you tell us over breakfast," suggested Sam, who knew Josie's indirect method of conveying information.

"Good idea. I've been dreaming of food cooked on Sullivan's griddle for the last few weeks. I'm going to have bacon, eggs, sausage, and potatoes," Betty said enthusiastically.

"Watch out, you'll gain weight," Josie kidded her weight-conscious ex-carpenter.

"Well, I will anyway," Betty said, smiling up at her husband.

"You? I can't imagine you with an extra pound. You've been thin all your life. Why would you suddenly put on weight?" The light that clicked on in Josie's mind showed on her face. "Betty, don't tell me you're pregnant!"

"Yes, I—"

"When?"

"When did I find out, or when is the baby due?"

"Either! Both!"

"I found out last week, and the baby is due in February. February twenty-sixth is the doctor's prediction."

"Are you going to find out ahead of time if it's a boy or a girl?"

"We haven't decided yet," Betty said, smiling at the beaming future father.

"Have you thought of names?"

"We—"

"I hate to interrupt, but I'm famished. Why don't we all go to Sullivan's in one car, and we can catch up during the drive?" Sam proposed.

"I really think I'd better take the truck," Josie said. "I should stop at the hardware store on the way. I need to check on a delivery, and it will only take a minute."

"Oh, I want to go with you!" Betty cried. "I'd love to see all the guys who work there."

Sam and John exchanged looks. "Okay. Betty and Josie in the truck. Sam and I will take his MG," John said. "You'll drive slowly, won't you?" he asked Josie.

"You know there's a twenty-five-mile-per-hour speed limit here on the island," she answered, grinning.

"And Josie doesn't get along with the local cops, so she has to stay within it," Sam added.

"We'll be five minutes in the hardware store. No more," Josie promised.

But they arrived at Sullivan's over half an hour later.

"Where were you?" Sam asked as John leaped from the booth and embraced his wife.

"At the hardware store. I told you."

"But why did it take so long?"

"It seemed like everyone on the island was there."

"And I wanted to say hello," Betty explained.

"It was amazing! Would you believe they've sold out their entire supply of lanterns, flashlights, and batteries?" Josie added, sliding in next to Sam.

"Agatha—," he began.

"Oh, that damn storm," Josie interrupted him. "It's all anyone's been talking about ever since I got up this morning. Why is everyone so sure it's going to hit here?"

"No one knows what a storm is going to do. They're just being prepared."

"An entire island of Boy Scouts. Who knew?" Josie muttered.

"Hey, at least you're getting your delivery extra early,"

Betty reminded her. "That probably wouldn't happen if everyone didn't think the storm was on the way."

"Yeah, it's a first."

"Josie, what sort of delivery?"

She looked up, surprised at the serious expression on Sam's face. "What do you mean, 'What sort of delivery'? It's the stuff I need at the beginning of a project . . . lumber, Sheetrock, plumbing supplies. They usually come separately, but this is a huge project. It's a monstrous order. And, for once, everything will be on site early!"

Sam frowned. "You know, that might not be such a good thing in this case."

"In this case? Oh, you don't have to worry. I've already deposited the first payment. I'm paying for everything with cash."

"But what if the storm hits?" Sam asked.

"I . . ."

"I see where you're going," John said to Sam.

"What do you mean?" Betty asked.

"Josie, who is responsible if something happens on the work site—something happens to your equipment, your supplies, whatever?" Sam asked.

"I am, but nothing's going to happen."

"And what if your supplies are damaged or destroyed before they are delivered?"

"That would be the problem of the supplier, of course. Sam, you know this. Why are you asking me these questions?"

"Josie, I know you don't want to worry about the storm, but think for a second. If Agatha does hit and if it is a dangerous storm, where would you rather all the lumber and such was located? On your work site or awaiting delivery at the lumber company?"

"There's not going to be a big storm," she insisted, getting up.

"Where are you going?" John asked.

"To make sure that Island Contracting doesn't get that delivery too early—just in case . . ."

When Josie returned to the booth, Basil Tilby had joined them. Basil, flamboyant owner of the island's three best restaurants, had just finished telling a story that had his companions laughing loudly.

"Josie, you'd better hear this! It has to do with your son," Sam said, moving over so she could sit down beside him.

"Tyler!" Josie looked around as though she might actually see her seventeen-year-old son burst into the room.

"He's got some sort of new scheme," Basil explained. "According to my sources, he's been calling a lot of his old friends on the island and telling them to get prepared in case Agatha hits."

"What are they going to do?" Josie asked.

"That's just it," Betty burst out. "Basil was just explaining. Apparently no one knows. All Tyler is saying is that it has something to do with the hurricane. But everyone has faith in Tyler, and a bunch of kids have already agreed to mobilize when he tells them to."

Josie frowned. She knew her son, and his harebrained schemes regularly came to fruition. "How do you know about it?" she asked Basil.

"One of my new busboys was recruited," Basil responded, getting up from the chair he had pulled over to their booth.

"Can't you stay for breakfast? We haven't had a chance to visit!" Betty protested.

"Come to dinner at the Gull's Perch tonight. In fact, why

don't you and Josie come, too, Sam? As my guests, of course. We'll have a prestorm party."

"John wants to leave this afternoon . . ." Betty glanced at her husband instead of finishing her sentence.

"Okay, we'll spend the night. But don't expect to get a lot of sleep. I plan to keep an eye on the Weather Channel all night long. And if that storm starts moving closer, we're going to head back to the city whether it's the middle of the night or not," he warned her.

"Where are you staying?" Sam asked.

"The Island Inn."

"How is it?" Basil paused to ask.

"We just arrived, but so far so good. We made reservations a few days ago and were promised the moon—luxury room with a view of the beach, satellite TV, spa, indoor pool, the whole bit."

"You'll find everything is as promised. It really is a world-class resort," Josie said. "I just wish the owners had hired Island Contracting to do the remodeling job."

"Who did the work?" Betty asked.

"Some company from off island." Josie, still annoyed that such a big and prestigious job had gone to a competitor, looked around. "I'm starving. How come we haven't even seen menus?"

"As though you need a menu here," Betty teased.

"Besides, I ordered for you while you were out—your usual," Sam explained. "And here it is."

Josie looked down at the plate the waitress put before her. Eggs, bacon, sausage, and French toast were piled high. "There's more food here than normal, isn't there?" she asked.

"The cook is trying to use up supplies before the storm hits," the waitress explained, putting identical plates in front of the others.

Josie picked up her fork, a smile on her face. If an extra large meal was the result of all this hurricane panic, it couldn't be all bad.

TWO

WAVE radio, the voice of the shore, is pleased to cooperate with the local humane society and make the following announcement: In case of a mandatory evacuation of our island during Hurricane Agatha, don't forget the pets who enrich our lives. Leave ample food and clean water out and provide high ground within your home for animals who may have to leave the first floor during flooding. Remember, pets will not be allowed in shelters, so they will have to take care of themselves here.

Now back to our regularly scheduled programing. Boogie on the Beach . . .

"WELL, THE PLACE I'm renting is a dump, but at least it's a second-floor dump," Renee Jacquette commented, picking up her long blond ponytail to let the cool breeze reach her neck.

"Would someone please turn that damn radio off for a moment!" Josie yelled her request from the deck hanging over the bay at the rear of Island Contracting's office.

"Do you think you could take care of Bitsy for me if we're evacuated?" Sissy Gilpin asked plaintively, ignoring her boss's request. "My place is on the first floor. It's near the beach, so if we're evacuated and there's flooding, she might be in danger."

"Can't you just put her cage on top of the refrigerator?" Ginger Luntz didn't even bother to look up to ask the question. Like the other two women, she was hunched over sheets of paper, writing with an annoyed expression on her face.

"But that's the worst place for her. What if there's an explosion from a gas line leak? What if the apartment catches fire? What if the entire building collapses down on top of Bitsy?"

"Cats have nine lives," Renee reminded her.

"Bitsy's not a cat. She's a rat." Ginger stated flatly, flipping over one sheet and starting on another.

"She's not a rat! She's a Russian hamster! She's very rare!"

"What's very rare is that a rat would find a sucker who'll give it a home instead of calling an exterminator to get rid of the damn thing."

Josie came into the room in time to hear Ginger's statement—and see the hurt expression on Sissy's face. She sighed. Sissy was young and naive, and even Josie sometimes found her more than a little irritating. But Ginger was a major pain in the butt. She was older than anyone else Josie had employed and had once owned her own contracting company. Consequently, Josie had expected maturity, competence, and a bit of understanding. But if Ginger felt sympathy for anyone in any situation, she managed to keep it to herself. As she had told Josie on the day they met, she didn't believe in giving in to weaknesses.

Josie had been running Island Contracting for five years and working as a carpenter for over a decade before that. She knew that crew members who got along made for a pleasant job and, frequently, a more efficient workplace. She also knew that a crew's ability to get along was a result of serendipity. She could do little to force it to happen. But she could stop Sissy from tearing up—she hoped.

"How's it going?" she asked, leaning against the door-jamb and pulling a handkerchief from her pocket.

"They want an awful lot of personal information," Renee answered, frowning. "Stuff that doesn't have anything to do with health issues, it seems to me."

"Goddamn insurance companies. They think they can do anything," Ginger growled.

"In this case, they can. If we don't get these forms in before the end of the month, they can cancel our policy. And no one wants to work without health insurance."

"When this happened to me, I called the company and told the guy who answered the phone he could stuff his forms you know where. Never had any problems with that company again," Ginger muttered.

Josie heard the implied criticism and tried to keep any anger from her voice. "Well, I just want to get these forms out tonight. I'll fight the guys in the office when they refuse to pay up on a legitimate claim." She glanced down at her watch. She was supposed to be meeting Sam, John, and Betty in two hours. She had hoped to get home in time to change. . . .

"Done!" Sissy flipped over her form and looked up, a big smile on her face.

"Yeah, me, too." Ginger's announcement lacked enthusiasm.

"I will be in a minute," Renee said, writing furiously.

"Okay. Okay." She looked up. "Here it is." She handed her form to Josie.

Josie glanced down at the sheets. She didn't have to look at the names to know who had filled out which form. Sissy's writing was cute; she still, Josie noted, made little circles instead of dots over each and every *i*. Ginger wrote in large block letters. And Renee, who claimed to be an artist as well as a professional carpenter, had filled out the forms with handwriting that was bold, artistic, and almost completely illegible.

"Aren't we going to see the house?" Sissy asked.

"I'd planned on it. I want to drop off some supplies, too." Josie answered. "Why don't we all drive over in our cars, and we can go straight home from there. It's going to be a long summer. I think we can knock off early today."

"Sounds good to me."

"Great."

"Anything you want."

Finally, Josie thought, blowing her nose, something they could agree on.

The Point House was a local landmark. One of the oldest and largest homes on the island, it was located at the northernmost point, where an inlet connected the bay on the west to the ocean on the east. A shingle-style house, for the last few decades it had been owned by an elderly couple from Philadelphia, who opened it sometime after Independence Day and stayed until about a week before Labor Day. From the outside, it was obvious to everyone walking up and down the beach that it needed major work. From the inside, it had a charm Josie found difficult to resist. Unfortunately, the new owner didn't agree with her assessment. Fortunately, he was going to pay Island Contracting a lot of money to tear down age-darkened chestnut paneling, hand-laid oak parquet floors, and an intricate, if well-worn, stairway leading to the second floor—and then to replace everything with a modern, open floor plan created by one of the East Coast's leading young architects.

Josie pulled a pile of drop cloths and her trusty toolbox from her truck and waited for her crew to gather on the cement slab, which was where the macadam driveway winding through the dunes ended. The outdoor shower, to the left of the entrance, was dripping, and she frowned. She had assumed the house was unoccupied, but she hadn't noticed that leak the last time she was here. . . .

"This is awesome!" Sissy said as she climbed out of the small beat-up Nissan wagon she drove.

"Not bad," Renee agreed, walking up the driveway, having parked her green Jeep at the bottom of the drive.

Ginger arrived last. "Hope you put in a realistic bid. These old places can have lots of hidden problems. Could cost a hell of a lot more to remodel than you think," she commented.

"The bid was a good one," Josie said flatly, rummaging in the pocket of her jeans for the key to the door. Used tissues fell on the ground.

"I can't wait to see the interior."

Sissy didn't have long to wait. Josie found the key, and the four women, carrying Josie's supplies, tramped into the small mudroom. The left wall was hung with old oilcloth and plastic rain slickers. Fishing equipment leaned against the walls on the opposite side of the space. Someone hadn't been terribly careful about cleaning up, and the unmistakable aroma of dead shellfish permeated the air. About a dozen plastic flip-flops were piled in the corner, and shells covered an ancient wooden bench.

"The kitchen's through here," Josie announced, leading the way.

"Good Lord." Ginger piled the paint-spattered drop cloths on the butcher block by the kitchen door and looked about.

"This place was built in the days when people came to the island with their staff," Josie explained. She wasn't surprised by Ginger's reaction. She had felt the same way when she first entered the huge, white, tile-covered room. A massive old enameled stove had been set in a disused brick hearth. Identical (and ugly) refrigerators and freezers stood guard on either side. A chipped soapstone sink had been placed under the only window in the room, and a gigantic maple table surrounded by a dozen mismatched chairs stood in the center of the room. Lamps hung from the ceiling by old-fashioned cloth-covered electric wires.

"Well, that's not code," Ginger commented.

"It's going. Everything in the room is going, except for the fireplace. We're going to sandblast that—"

"A miserable job," Ginger interrupted.

Josie resisted the urge to tell her that it was hers to do and just continued. "It will be fabulous when we're finished. Come this way. The rest of the house is in better shape."

But, somehow, seeing it with the critical Ginger diminished some of the charm Josie had discovered previously. The paneling was hand-wrought but scuffed and dirty. The floor seemed to have coughed up wooden tiles. The banister was shaky and the stairs creaky. She noticed cracked windowpanes and tilted doorways. By the time she had taken her crew through the eight bedrooms and two tiny, underequipped baths, she was apologizing for the place.

And then they walked out on the deck built over the large veranda facing the sea, and everyone stopped to appreciate the view.

"Fabulous," Sissy said.

Renee walked straight for the rail as though drawn by the late afternoon sun sparkling on the waves. "This is perfect. I could paint this," she muttered almost to herself.

"God, too bad you gotta be rich to get a view like this one," was Ginger's opinion.

"It's going to be our view for most of the summer, and we're not rich," Josie reminded her.

"Maybe I could bring my watercolors and work up here during lunch," Renee said, staring at the whitecaps out at sea.

"No reason why not," Josie said. "Except for possible chimney repairs, we're leaving the outside as is. The roof was redone a year ago, and these cedar shakes are in great shape.

"So, everyone be here tomorrow before eight. First day of a new job, I'll provide coffee and doughnuts for morning break."

"Great! See you all then!"

Ginger, possibly pleased to discover that they were being released close to half an hour early, didn't even bother to make a disparaging comment about Sissy's perkiness and followed her down the stairs.

Josie joined Renee, still staring out to sea. "Did you say you painted with . . . in watercolors?" she asked, not sure of the proper term.

"Yes. I used to think of watercolors as on old fuddy-duddy type of work. You know, little ladies doing simple flowers stuck smack in the middle of the page or dull landscapes. But then I started playing around with the medium, and something about it really appeals to me. I don't know why I didn't see the potential before. A lot of famous artists prefer the medium. Well, I guess I just missed the point. But I've been working in watercolor for about three years now. . . ."

"Maybe you'll let me see your work sometime," Josie suggested, starting for the door.

"Of course . . . Oh, I'm keeping you here, aren't I? I'm sorry. It's just that this place is such a surprise . . . it really would be wonderful to paint that view," she added quickly, moving toward the door.

"Do you like painting woodwork and walls as well as working on canvas?" Josie asked the question mainly to make conversation. Her crew would do what needed to be done whether or not they liked doing it.

"Yes, although paper rather than canvas is used for water-color work. But what I love is finish carpentry. All the fussy details that most other carpenters hate. And I'm fast, too," she added proudly.

"Really? Remind me to show you the plans for the woodwork around the new windows. The architect's draw-ings are sketchy, and I had some ideas myself—"

"I love inventing things!"

"Everything must be approved by the owner," Josie re-minded her. "And I have no idea yet how this owner will react to suggestions or changes in the architect's plans."

"Probably badly," Renee said. "At least that's how things usually work out for me," she added quickly.

"I only met the owner twice. The architect's been my main contact."

"What do you think of him?" Renee asked.

"The architect?"

"The owner."

"He seems—" Josie paused. "—nice. He seems nice. And what he's doing is more than nice. He bought this house for his family. Not like his wife and kids—he's old, and there's no mention of a wife. He might be divorced or a widower. He's building this house for his grown-up chil-dren and their children. The house is being remodeled to accommodate three families at the same time as well as himself. One master bedroom and three suites. It's a clever design."

"Is he going to be around a lot this summer?"

"No. He plans to stay in the city. The last time I spoke with him, he said the architect could just fax any possible changes to him for his approval. I have the blues here, and I'd be happy to show you, but I have . . . plans for this evening."

"And I'm keeping you! Oh, my goodness, I'm so sorry!"

"No, that's okay. Really!"

But Renee had rushed past her, down the stairs and out of the house before Josie had time to explain that she really wasn't in a hurry.

She heard Renee's car start up as she was locking the back door. She sighed and walked over to see why the shower was leaking. Maybe she should call a plumber. . . .

". . . but all I had to do was turn the knob. I wonder if I should give the Rodneys a call and tell them that someone has been hanging around the Point House while the owner is away." Josie took a sip of the wine Sam had poured for her.

"How do you know that it wasn't the owner himself?" Sam asked.

"Actually, I don't. In fact, I'll bet it was! Sam, Hudson House! That's what the sign is for. It's for the Point House. I'll bet the owner dropped it off at my office! He probably was in town for a few days."

Sam asked the obvious question. "Why is he naming a house on the ocean after a river?"

"The new owner's name is Cornell Hudson! I'll bet he's renaming the house after himself!"

"He may hang up a sign and probably all his city friends who come to visit will say they're coming to Hudson House, but people on the island will refer to it as the Point House for decades—at least," Sam said.

"That's probably true." Josie looked around the restaurant. "This place sure is empty tonight."

"It's the storm. There are cancellations all over the island. Business at the store is down by almost a third." Sam owned the island's most upscale liquor store.

"Really?"

"Yes, and it's probably better for me than a lot of businesses. Some customers are stocking up—buying liters of gin and rum and mixers. I get the impression that they're planning on riding out the storm drunk."

"But the storm may not touch land here. And, if it does, it might not do any damage. Why is everyone acting as though the worst is going to happen, canceling vacations, stocking up on supplies, making plans for their pets in case an evacuation is ordered?"

"A lot of lives have been lost because people didn't listen to storm warnings," Sam said, a serious look on his face. "This is the smart way to act under these circumstances."

Josie glanced over his shoulder. "Let's talk about something else. Betty and John are here. I don't want John to drag Betty home because some weatherman in New York has nothing to do but blab on and on about a storm that may or may not arrive." She frowned. "Look at the expression on Betty's face. I'll bet John's pressuring her to leave."

"Hi, guys!"

To Josie, Betty sounded just a bit too perky. "You're leaving, aren't you? John, why—?"

"It's not just John, Josie. We were watching the Weather

Channel. It looks more and more like the storm is going to hit here—possibly as early as tomorrow night. I can't take a chance with my baby. We're heading home right after dinner."

Josie sighed. "I guess I can't blame you. . . . But everyone is going to feel really silly if this storm heads out into the Atlantic or zips up to Maine."

"We're keeping our room at the inn. The second the island is out of danger, we'll be back," John said, sitting down and picking up a menu.

"That's right," Betty agreed. "Let's go ahead and eat. With any luck, the storm will pass us right by, and in a day or two we'll be lying in the sun on the beach, laughing about all this unnecessary traveling back and forth."

THREE

Good morning, Islanders. The storm is coming closer and closer! Forecasters are predicting landfall sometime around midnight. We at WAVE radio are pleased to bring you this live announcement from Officer Mike Rodney, son of Chief Rodney and organizer of the island's emergency planning. Tell us, Officer Rodney, what can we expect this day to bring?

"Besides rain, wind, and general mayhem . . ."

J OSIE SMACKED HER clock radio so hard it flipped off the nightstand and smashed on the floor. It might be a terrible day. Hurricane Agatha might hit. She might be ordered to evacuate. The island she loved could be flooded, ripped apart by wind, permanently altered by the damaging storm. She couldn't do anything about any of that. But she sure as hell was not going to start the day listening to that idiot, Mike Rodney.

She rolled over and peered out the window. The sun was up with only a few puffy white clouds marring the perfect blue of the sky. "What the hell are they talking about?" she asked Urchin.

The cat jumped on Josie's pillow and rubbed against her shoulder. Josie smiled. That's what she liked about pets— they rarely argued with their owners or predicted storms.

It didn't take her long to dress. She expected to arrive at the bakery right as it opened.

Except that apparently the opening was going to be delayed while the owner, bakers, and sales staff covered the store's windows with plywood. Josie parked by the curb and hopped out of her truck.

"I think you'd better stick to baking," she said, walking up to the owner.

"I do, too," he answered, turning around and displaying a swollen red thumb. "Being a carpenter can be dangerous."

"It would be easier if you drilled starter holes first. . . ." Josie flinched at the sound of good wood splitting. "Why don't you just hold the pieces in place, and I'll put in some screws—they'll cause less damage to the woodwork."

"If you have the time, I'd sure appreciate it, Josie."

"No problem. I have what I need in the back of the truck."

"And I have what you need in the oven."

Fifteen minutes later, Josie was on her way to the Point House with two large boxes of doughnuts and a slab of crumb cake. All the bakery's windows were protected, and she had explained to the owner how to shut off the gas to the huge professional ranges at its source.

There were four parallel north-south roads on the island. East to west, they were Dune Drive, Ocean Drive, Beach Boulevard, and Bay Avenue. The bakery, and most of the island's businesses, were located on Ocean Drive. Josie traveled north on Ocean, observing that almost all the businesses were either in the process of covering their windows or had already done so. She turned left and headed to the bay.

Even if she didn't believe the storm was going to hit and thought all the preparations were unnecessary, she couldn't ignore the precarious position that Island Contracting's tiny office was in, hanging right out over the bay, exposed to wind and water in a manner unknown to these inland buildings. An image of her office floating out to sea washed over her, and she frowned. She didn't think the storm would hit here. She really believed all these people were acting foolishly, but if a few sheets of plywood and some nails would protect her beloved office from possible harm . . .

The day's plan was for Josie to meet her crew at the Point House, so all the cars parked in the street surprised her—as did the crowd waiting outside her office. She parked her truck and got out, recognizing friends as well as clients in the group.

She hated to ask, but she really had no choice. "Anything wrong?"

Marge Crane, the wife of the biggest Realtor on the island, answered. "We're all here for your help, Josie."

"What can I do?"

"Some of us need supplies. . . ."

"The hardware store is out of plywood. . . ."

"There isn't a sheet of wood left on the island. . . ."

". . . wouldn't know what to do with it if we had it . . ."

"Josie . . ."

". . . be happy to pay for your time, of course."

"Wait a second!" Josie yelled the words. "You're all having trouble covering your windows?"

"Trouble isn't the word. My husband broke two panes in our French doors. . . ."

"How was I to know—?"

Josie had a feeling she wasn't going to get any work done today, but that didn't mean she had to resign herself to listening to family squabbles. "I have some wood out at the Point House. You make a list of what you'd like me to do, and I'll call out there, tell my crew to collect it and meet here, and we'll see how we can help."

"We don't want to take you away from your own work, Josie. If the Point House windows need to be covered—"

"Nope." She didn't bother to explain that she didn't believe there was going to be a storm. "Every window in that house is going to be replaced. No reason to protect them."

"What about here?"

"I was going to put wood over these windows," Josie explained, deciding to do just that. "And put away all the furniture on the deck. We don't know if the storm will even hit land, and anyway, it will come off the ocean and so the bay is protected . . ."

"Nope. The storm can hit from any direction. That's one of the things that makes a hurricane different from your ordinary storm—it's a circle."

Josie thought about the large swirls on the televison weather maps and glanced at her office. "But, if it travels

over land, it will be weaker," she suggested, trying to remember if this was exactly what she had heard.

"Not necessarily. Storms get weaker when they travel
over cold water—which is what the water is this time of
the year. But they can pick up speed when they hit land.
Besides, this is a big one. They were calling it the storm of
the century on the radio last night."

"The century isn't all that old," Josie reminded the
speaker, but she glanced at her tiny office building. It
looked so sweet—and so vulnerable. "Look, someone
make a list and give it to me. I don't have a whole lot of
wood, but maybe I can improvise something. I'll call my
crew. You go on home. Do what you can, and I'll try to
send someone to help out as soon as possible."

Everyone agreed with Josie's suggestions and she
headed down the narrow walkway to her office. She'd call
the Point House. She just hoped someone there would answer the phone.

It rang once.

"Hello? This is Josie Pigeon," she began.

"Josie! This is Renee. Why are you calling? We're all
here waiting for you."

Josie decided she would talk with Renee about answering the client's phone later. "There's been a change of
plans. I need everyone to come back to the office."

"Now? Right away?"

"Now. Right away."

"Well, okay. See you in a few."

Josie looked up as someone walked in the door. Marge
Crane looked tired and embarrassed. "Josie, I know we
dumped all this on you, but we're pretty desperate. I was
awake half the night worrying about this storm."

"You know you don't have to worry about asking me for

anything," Josie said. "Island Contracting has gotten more than a few jobs on the basis of your recommendations."

The woman smiled. "I tell people you're the best because you are."

"I guess that's how we got the Point House job," Josie said, glancing out the window. The crowd was leaving.

"The Point House? You're doing the remodeling?"

"You sound surprised."

"Sort of."

Josie heard the reluctance in her voice. "I thought you recommended us. I gather that's not true."

"Oh, I recommended you. I talked about Island Contracting and what you could do to the house as soon as I realized we'd made the sale, but, frankly, I got the impression that he wasn't listening. I mean, there was no doubt that the place needed major remodeling, and Cornell Hudson apparently has the money to do it. Heavens, he paid cash for that place."

"Cash?"

"Yes, how is he financing the remodeling job?"

"Cash."

"That's a whole lot of cash."

"It sure is."

The two business owners looked at each other. Josie knew neither of them would share this information with very many people. She also knew that they were both wondering exactly where all this cash originated.

"I understand he owns his own business," the Realtor said slowly.

"What sort of business?"

"Construction."

"He's a contractor, and he hired Island Contracting to remodel his house?"

"That's what I was thinking. That's what he told me when

I said something about Island Contracting, and that's why I didn't say very much. I assumed his company would do the work. I gather he didn't mention his business to you?"

Josie thought for a moment. "I know he mentioned Hudson Brothers more than once, but he didn't say anything about contracting or building or anything like that. I would have remembered." She frowned.

"And thought it was unusual?"

"It's not just unusual, it's odd. I babbled on and on, explaining all the petty details of remodeling. If he can afford a house like that and complete remodeling, he must be very successful. Why did he let me talk about things he knew perfectly well and not say something? Frankly, I feel like a fool."

"Why?"

"I suppose I was trying to impress him with how competent and successful I was."

"But not successful enough to afford a house like the Point House."

"No way."

"Perhaps Hudson Brothers doesn't work on private homes."

Josie considered that possibility. "That's feasible. Or maybe the other Hudson does all the work and Cornell Hudson is the financial whiz."

"There isn't another Hudson. I asked. Cornell Hudson took the name Hudson Brothers because he found it more impressive. At least, that's what he told me."

"Apparently you two talked about all this a lot."

"Not really. I didn't get to know him as well as most of our clients, in fact. He only looked at one house, so we didn't spend as much time schmoozing as usual."

"He only looked at the Point House?"

"Yes, and he barely looked at that. My feeling was that he was one of those rare buyers who knew exactly what he wanted and had the money to pay for it. I felt lucky that he had wandered into my office instead of someone else's. The commission on that sale is more than I've made some summers."

"Maybe now you can afford to hire me to build that deck off your bedroom that you've always wanted."

"Maybe I will, but, Josie, you don't have to drum up business. If this storm is as big or as destructive as predicted, Island Contracting will be busy putting the island back together for years and years."

Josie's crew joined them before she could explain that she wasn't interested in getting work that way.

Sissy, perky as always, needlessly announced their arrival. "Well, here we are."

Ginger and Renee just leaned against the doorjamb. "You've changed your mind about the day?" Ginger asked, managing to turn the question into a criticism.

"We're going to spend the day protecting the property of some of Island Contracting's clients and friends," Josie said, wishing Ginger didn't make her feel so defensive.

"That's a good idea, because I was listening to the radio on the way over, and they're saying that Hurricane Agatha will hit the coast here around midnight tonight." Sissy sounded more excited than scared by the prospect.

"I'd better get going. I know you won't be able to get to everyone on that list, and I'll understand if you . . ."

"Ginger can go with you and . . ." Josie looked down at the list. "Get your windows protected at the office and at your home. Then, if you could just direct her to—" Josie rattled off a list of a dozen other businesses located nearby.

"You want me to put huge pieces of wood up alone?"

"Nope. I want you to help the homeowners do it. I know these people. Just tell them I sent you to help out. I guarantee they'll all pitch in.

"You and Renee can take my truck. Go out to the storage sheds and get all the wood you can fit in it, bring it back here, and leave it next to the road—"

"Gonna get stolen," Ginger said.

"No, it won't. I'm going to be here. I'll do what I can to protect this place and take calls and see what we can do to help out. If the storm comes, we'll be as prepared as we can and we'll have helped others to do the same. If it goes out into the ocean or touches down someplace else, at least we'll have accumulated a bit of goodwill in the community. Now, where is that list?"

She reached out, but a gust of wind blew it to the floor as she was about to touch it. Josie glanced out the window. Was it her imagination, or were there really more clouds in the sky?

FOUR

Now, kiddies, your friendly DJ, Shore Time Solly, has heard rumors that some of you are dusting off your surfboards, hoping old Aunt Agatha is pushing some boffo waves in your direction. So let's play some old Beach Boys tunes to get you all in the mood. . . . And all you old fogies can just keep time with your hammers. . . .

D APPLED CLOUDS HAD appeared on the horizon, and with them, the pace of life on the island had shifted from panicked to frantic. Josie had run out of sheets of wood about an hour ago and was now using scraps of lumber to hold double layers of plastic, Homasote, and anything else she could find to protect fragile glass from the elements.

After checking on her crew, which was busy making houses and businesses as storm-proof as possible, Josie had headed up the island to work on Sam's house in the dunes. Then, together, they had driven to Josie's and taken over from a nervous Risa, who apparently had decided she would spend this emergency doing what she did best— cooking.

"What are you going to do with all that?" Josie asked. There were over a dozen large Tupperware containers lined up on the kitchen counter.

"I take them when we evacuate. The instructions say we should take bedding, change of clothing, medications, and food. This is food."

"I don't think anyone expects you to feed everyone else in the shelter," Sam suggested gently.

"In car, we should have first-aid kit, bottled water, warm clothing, tiny radio with fresh batteries . . . and many other things in case there is a problem on way to shelter," Risa continued despite the interruption. "They not say it, but I think boots, too. Big, ugly rubber boots like Tyler used to wear when he little. What do you plan to bring?"

"My hammer," Josie answered. "That's about all anyone is interested in today."

"Me, I am interested in your arms. We carry some things from here up to your apartment."

"In case of flooding. That's a good idea," Sam said, nodding his approval. "Why don't I help you with that. Josie can start outside."

"I remembered that wood in the garage that we were planning to turn into shelves in the upstairs hallway," Josie explained. "I just hope there's enough to protect the windows of your sunroom. That lumber may be the last left on the entire island."

"Risa and I will start moving things. Call me when you need help."

"I will," Josie promised before hurrying to the garage. She was in excellent shape and spending hours hammering was nothing unusual, but the muscles in her neck were beginning to ache, her lower back felt like hell, and her sniffles were getting worse. She stretched her arms above her head. It was tension, she decided, looking at the sky. There were more clouds, and they weren't puffy and white. The air was hot, more like the middle of August than the end of June. And the humidity seemed to be increasing. She'd turned off the radio hours ago, tired of the relentless and repetitive reports about Agatha. The last Josie had heard, the storm was stalled somewhere off the coast of North Carolina, and the North Carolina Division of Emergency Management was talking of a mandatory evacuation. Josie failed to understand how a storm off the coast of that state could threaten anyone or anything this far north. She lifted Risa's garage door and began to remove the lumber stored inside. She was carrying the last load around to the front of the house when Sam appeared.

"How's it going?" he asked, picking up some wood that had fallen.

"I think there may be enough to cover most of the glass,

but I'm worried about the woodwork on the sunporch. It's not in great shape. More holes won't do it any good."

"Neither will one-hundred-mile-an-hour winds."

"A hundred miles an hour?"

"Josie, last I heard, Agatha is a Category Two hurricane. That means winds between ninety and one hundred and ten miles an hour and a possible eight-foot storm surge."

"Boy, you sure know about this stuff."

"If she stays stalled over warm water, she could well pick up power and speed. Then we're talking Category Three. The wind could be one hundred and thirty miles an hour."

"Good thing there's no such thing as Category Four," Josie said, lifting the largest sheet of plywood and heading to the house.

"There is. Winds up to one hundred and fifty-five miles an hour. And there's a Category Five also. Hurricane Camille was a Category Five. There were winds clocked at one hundred and fifty-six miles an hour, and the storm surge was over eighteen feet. A storm that violent could cover this entire island with water. In 1969, Camille killed two hundred and fifty-six people."

Josie stopped and looked at him. "Really?"

"Josie, the biggest storm we know about hit Galveston, Texas, in 1900. There are historians who believe over eight thousand people were killed."

"Sam, what are the odds of a storm being that violent this far north this early in the summer?"

"It's never happened. But that doesn't mean it won't."

"I know. It's just that we had such a great job scheduled to start today. Now we're preparing for a storm that may never arrive. I know it sounds stupid, but remodeling the Point House is the best job on the island, and I was really looking forward to it, and now—shit!" She dropped her load on the ground.

"What happened?"

"Splinter." She sucked on the palm of her hand. "I lent my gloves to one of the cashiers down at Sullivan's and forgot to get them back. I stopped in to buy some Kleenex—one of the few items they still had on their shelves. Although there was a huge selection of suntan lotion—what's that?"

Sam put down his end of the wood and listened a minute. "One blast on the fire siren. That's the signal for a hurricane warning. I guess Agatha's started to move in our direction."

"They've been warning us about Agatha for days—"

"This is different. This is an official statement of the state's emergency management guys. It means there is a very real possibility of Agatha affecting this area."

"Then I guess I'd better get these windows covered."

"Batteries. Water. Where's your Walkman?"

"With Tyler. His broke last spring. And, since I don't have my Walkman, I don't have batteries for it. And you know I'm not one of those fancy people who drinks bottled water."

"Josie, I'm not talking about Pellegrino and Perrier. I'm talking about jugs of water to drink and buckets of water to use to flush your toilet in case the power goes off. And gas. It takes power to run gas pumps. Are Island Contracting's trucks' and Jeeps' gas tanks full?"

"I—"

"And what about your important papers? What sort of flood insurance do you have on the office, and what does Risa carry on your apartment—and where are the policies?"

"Sam, the storm isn't here. There hasn't been any damage yet. Why are you talking about insurance policies?"

"Because if you can't find your insurance policies, it's going to take a longer time to get any claims settled. They should be in your truck."

"My truck is more likely to be washed away than my apartment," she argued.

"Not if you're smart. Look, Josie, I love you. I don't want anything to happen to you, but I know how stubborn you can be—and how busy you've been helping everyone else all day long. You need to prepare your apartment, your office, and your truck if this storm hits. Now I'm going to help you with Risa's windows, and then we're going to get organized. Basil offered to garage the MG and any of your vehicles—"

"Where?"

"There's a huge barn behind the tavern he bought over on the mainland, remember? He says it's at least twenty feet above sea level and reinforced. It's not perfect, but I know our vehicles will be safer there than on the island. And the MG, at least, is completely impractical when it comes to evacuation. I was hoping, in fact, that you would let me take the newest of Island Contracting's Jeeps."

"The newest is five years old," Josie reminded him. "But, of course, you can take it. It's certainly higher if you have to go through water—"

"Josie! You never, ever go through water in a hurricane! Water can rise faster than you can possibly imagine. You could be in a flood. You could be washed away in a flood . . . killed . . ." He grabbed her shoulders. "You're not taking this seriously. You're not prepared."

"I . . . " She looked up at him and sneezed in his face. "Thank you," she said, accepting the handkerchief he offered. "You're right. I'm not. But I will be. Listen, what is going to happen next? I mean, it's still possible the storm isn't going to hit the island, right?"

"Right."

"And if it doesn't, will the fire whistle blow again?"

"No, if you hear that whistle again, it means the storm is coming and, I'd imagine, that an evacuation is being ordered. That's when the police will start to patrol the island, telling everyone to leave and distributing information about various shelter options. But, if you want up-to-date information, you'd better listen to the radio or local television stations. I—"

"Okay. You help me here and then take care of your precious car. Come back here. . . . No, come to the office. If I'm not there, I'll leave a note telling you where I'll be."

"Okay. But if there's an evacuation ordered, Josie, we should leave immediately. There are only two bridges off this island, and one is a drawbridge. I don't want to get stuck in a traffic jam."

"No problem," Josie assured him.

It was an elated crew that returned to Island Contracting's office. Television reporters were swarming over the island looking for people to interview. Attractive young women, working hard to protect buildings from storm damage, were just what they were looking for.

"You should have seen us!" Ginger gushed, wiping a filthy hand across her forehead. "For a while there, Sissy had four different men fighting to interview her."

"Well, not fighting exactly," Sissy protested.

"The guy in the huge, yellow slicker damn near decked the one with the beard who was wearing a blue plastic rainsuit. I call that fighting," Ginger insisted.

"I wasn't the only one. The man wearing the Weather Channel slicker spent a whole lot of time talking to you,"

Sissy reminded her. "And what about the man from the local TV station? . . ."

"Don't mention him to me. I felt like an idiot, he was asking such stupid questions."

"Like what?" Josie asked.

"Like was I covering the windows to protect them from Agatha, and was I prepared to evacuate if ordered to do so. I said yes and yes—not exactly thrilling dialogue."

"There isn't a hell of a lot to say, in fact. Either Agatha is going to hit the island or she isn't. Either we'll evacuate or we won't. The story is the storm and that hasn't happened, so there's not much to say," Renee stated flatly, leaning against the wall.

"That's true," Josie agreed. "Did anyone ask you anything original?"

"Renee didn't talk to the reporters," Sissy said.

"I was busy. Besides, I didn't want to sound like an idiot," Renee explained.

"Oh, I thought maybe you didn't want to be on TV," Ginger said.

"I—"

"I hope I do end up on television!" Sissy interrupted. "I called my parents right after my first interview. They turned on the television before I even hung up the phone. They're dying to see me—my dad was going to call all my relatives from home and Mom was going to run right next door to a neighbor's house and phone all their friends. I just hope some of the snotty kids I went to high school with see me—the ones who were in a college prep program and thought I'd never amount to anything because I was going to be a carpenter. Like that nerd Danny Rogers—he was always bragging about being on the *Today Show* as though they had invited him in for an interview when all he had done was stand outside the window and make faces at the camera."

Josie had other things on her mind. "Listen, you guys were great to pitch in. I've been thinking, though. If we are ordered to evacuate, heaven knows when we'll be allowed to return. But, when we do, I'd appreciate it if you'd all check in here as quickly as possible."

"Here?" Ginny looked around the tiny office.

"Do you think this place can withstand strong winds?" Renee asked.

"What should we do if this is . . . blown away or something?" Sissy asked, a worried expression on her face.

"Where this building is . . . Here, intact or not, here is where we meet," Josie said loudly, unwilling to consider anything else.

FIVE

Raindrops keep falling on my head. . . . Well, kiddies, we're not afraid of a few raindrops, are we? WAVE radio isn't afraid of old Agatha. Not us! Now let's hear what the Stones say about stormy weather. . . .

JOSIE HAD DONE it all. Her home and office were as protected as she could make them. Urchin was provided with food, water, a clean litter box, and a soft bed at the highest spot in Josie's second-floor apartment—the top shelf in Tyler's closet. Risa had left hours ago, her car full of excellent food and exotic clothing, apparently confusing a mandatory evacuation with a cocktail party. Sam had traveled off island with Basil after extracting a promise from Josie to join them as soon as possible.

But she wasn't leaving without her tool belt. Her tools were irreplaceable, many of them inherited from Noel Roberts, the man who had trained her, mentored her, and left her Island Contracting in his will.

She'd last seen it at the Point House, and she drove there down deserted streets. By the time she turned up the winding drive into the dunes, she had started to imagine that she was alone on the island. But an excessively large white Ford Expedition standing at the top of the drive convinced her otherwise. She parked her truck beside it and hopped out. The rain, combined with sand and flying pine needles, slashed at her face, and she didn't hesitate for a second; when the back door blew open, she hurried inside and pulled it closed behind her.

"Hello? Anyone here?" she called loudly.

No one answered. The noise level inside the house was only minimally lower than outside. Not wanting to surprise her employer, Josie tried again. "It's Josie Pigeon. Your contractor. Hello?" She pushed open the door between the kitchen and the dining room as she spoke. Curtains had been pulled, and the room was dark. Josie continued on toward the living room.

"Hello? Anyone here? I'm looking for my—" She stepped into the living room, gasped, and took a step backwards. She could hardly believe her eyes. . . .

"Just who are you looking for, Miss Pigeon?"

Josie spun around. "I—"

"You know you're breaking the law, of course."

"I—"

"I could arrest you, you know. There was an all-island evacuation ordered by our governor over two hours ago. By being here, you are breaking the law." The chief of police repeated his previous statement.

"I . . ." Josie didn't know what to say. She was working hard to resist the urge to look back over her shoulder into the living room. She couldn't let Chief Rodney see what she'd just found. . . .

"No chatting, Miss Pigeon. I have orders to clear this island, and clear this island is what I'm going to do. I'm ordering you off and then I'm going to get the hell out of here myself. They're calling Agatha a killer storm. And I sure as shit don't want to be one of the ones killed."

"You're right, Chief. Let's get going." She was moving as she spoke.

A branch crashing through an elegant bay window provided the only extra motivation necessary. Josie and Police Chief Rodney picked up their feet and dashed out of the house and back into the rain.

"Get in the police cruiser!" he yelled, turning his back to the wind.

"No way I'm leaving my truck behind!" Josie screamed her answer, pulling open the door to the driver's seat and climbing into her truck.

"Don't be stu—Oh, hell, follow me!"

The scrub pines were bent to the ground, and her truck was being sandblasted by the wind. Josie slammed the door, started her engine, and followed the police cruiser down the driveway as fast as she dared.

The wind felt even stronger once they left the protection of the dunes. Broken wires slashed through the air; water splashed up out of drains instead of following the demands of gravity. Josie squinted through the rain, trailing the police car north, toward the newest and sturdiest bridge connecting the island to the mainland.

The flashing lights on top of the cruiser were unusually comforting. Josie didn't have a friendly relationship with the island police force, but it was good to know that she wasn't alone, that if something happened to Island Contracting's unreliable 1966 Chevrolet pickup, help was nearby.

More important, if Chief Rodney was in front of her, he wasn't investigating the dead body lying on the living-room floor back at the Point House—or identifying the murder weapon.

Rain pelted across her windshield, heavier and harder than her old-fashioned wipers had been designed to remove. The wind squeezed water through all the cracks of her beloved truck; it was only slightly drier inside than outside. Wiping the moisture from her face, Josie leaned forward, clutching the steering wheel and peering out over the red hood. The road was wide, and the two cars had it to themselves. But superimposed over the white trunk of the police car was the image of the body.

It had been a male—she was sure of that. Tall, stocky, broad shoulders, wearing a navy polo shirt tucked into pressed chinos, Docksides on his feet—he was wearing the uniform of many men on the island. He lay in the middle of the floor so awkwardly, that thing pulled tightly around his neck. . . . Despite the oppressive heat, Josie shivered, remembering the scene.

She slammed on the brakes, hydroplaning across the water-covered road and coming to a stop within inches of the police cruiser.

"What the f—!"

Chief Rodney got out of his stalled car and sloshed toward her through the rising water. He ripped open the door to her passenger's seat. "Goddamn cruiser's flooded out. Get going!"

"I—"

"Josie, if this thing will pass through the water, get it in gear and get the hell out of here before we're washed off this damn island!"

She didn't waste time answering. They were only blocks from the bridge. The water was rising, now coming in through holes in the floor.

"Drive up on the median."

"We'll sink in the flower beds. . . ."

"Up on the median. It's high ground."

A wave splashed against the truck, and Josie decided she had been given some good advice—even though it came in the form of an order. Hoping for a curb cut, she steered up onto the median. While water didn't stop coming in, it didn't get any worse, and she glanced over at Chief Rodney.

He was staring straight ahead. "There's a caution sign up here somewhere—"

There was a loud clank, and something scraped across the bottom of her truck.

"I think we just found it."

"Any change in the gauges?"

"What?"

"Did it break anything? Are any of your gauges recording major new leaks?"

She took her eyes off the road long enough to be fairly sure of her answer. "I think we're okay. Anything else—Shit! What the hell was that?"

"Mailbox or something. Don't worry about it. As long as nothing essential gets broken, we're fine. Can't this thing go any faster?"

"I don't dare increase the speed. Look at that!"

"What?"

"There's a dog over there, a little brown and black thing. It's floating on some sort of plank. . . ."

"What the hell are you doing?"

"I'm just going to see if it will get in the back of the truck if I get a bit closer. . . ."

"You're worried about an ugly, wet dog at a time like this? Are you nuts?"

"I may be, but I'm also the one with the vehicle that works, so you better just let me . . . Oh, look, he did it! He jumped right in!" Josie looked over her shoulder at the small window in the rear of the cab. "Do you think he'll be okay?"

"I don't have a lot of worry to waste on a damn dog right now. I wish you'd stop paying attention to that mutt and keep your eyes on the road."

"I would if I could find it," she answered. She was aware of sweat soaking through her T-shirt and running down her forehead into her eyes. It didn't matter much because she was traveling on instinct only at this point. Each and every street had a sign, but they were all but invisible under the circumstance. Josie stared out the windshield, glancing from side to side every time she dared take her eyes off the road.

"There should be a bright pink house around here somewhere," she said.

"Right ahead on the left."

"Then we're a block away from Tenth," Josie referred to the street that led off island.

"Stay to the left. The left side is slightly higher—Watch out for that dingy!"

"I thought people were supposed to get their boats out of the water or secure them tightly," Josie muttered as the wooden boat bashed into her bumper.

"Probably wasn't even in the water until the island began to flood. Lots of people just lean those things against the sides of their houses. Turn here. Damn it, Josie, we're going to make it!"

There was no mistaking the relief in his voice, but it was nothing compared to what Josie was feeling. She knew this truck, and it wasn't accelerating normally. They traveled slowly, making their way up out of the water onto the large concrete bridge.

"I just hope this bridge was designed to withstand this wind," she announced as a particularly strong gust actually moved the truck closer to the side.

"If memory serves, it was built to withstand winds of up to ninety-five miles per hour," the police chief said grimly.

"Oh, but—"

"If you're thinking that old Agatha is a bit gustier than any ninety-five miles an hour, you're right. So don't take your foot off that accelerator until we're on dry ground."

"I think it's going to be a while before any ground we travel across might actually be considered dry," Josie suggested, tightening her grip on the steering wheel as the howling wind seemed to increase. They were approaching the highest point of the bridge, and she found herself hoping they didn't blow right off. Of course, it was always possible that the bridge would blow down first. She glanced out the back window and grinned for the first time since leaving the Point House. The dog they'd picked up, soaked and filthy, was facing right into the wind, and she could swear there was a smile on its face.

"God, look at that!" Chief Rodney wasn't pointing at the dog.

"Wha—Is that a tornado?"

"Just a small one. Sure hope it stays out over the water."

"Yeah, me, too. Damn. The mainland seems to be flooded, too."

"Did you think the storm would only hit the island?"

Josie sighed. "I guess I didn't think. Do you have any suggestion which roads we should take—if we make it to higher ground?"

"Turn left right after we get off the bridge."

"But—"

"Josie, I know these damn roads. We're here—turn left. Turn left here!"

She did as ordered, too worried to be annoyed by his treatment of her. Almost miraculously, the water seemed to stop coming up through the floorboards of the truck. "It's higher here," she breathed, amazed.

"Yes. But it won't be high enough for long. See that gas station up there on the left? Make a turn in the closest driveway and circle behind the building—"

"Behind the building?"

"High ground. Don't argue. I've been a cop on the island for years. Lots of my friends are cops off island. I know my way around—Watch out!"

Josie successfully dodged the metal Exxon sign and many of the tree branches that followed it. Two hours later, when they had traveled ten of the eleven miles between the bridge and the high school, the shelter site for island residents, she was as exhausted as she was relieved. Until her engine made a strange noise and died. She coasted over to the side of the road, turned off the ignition, put on the emergency brake, and looked at Chief Rodney.

He was scowling.

"What?"

"How many times were you told to make sure your vehicles were filled with gas?"

"I—" She looked down at the gauges, amazed. "We ran

out of gas? After all that? The truck just ran out of gas? It isn't broken?"

"Damn right. Women! Can't do a simple thing like keep their cars filled with gas in an emergency."

Josie suddenly discovered that she had enough energy to be furious. "You would still be stuck on the island if I hadn't picked you up! You have no right to complain!"

"Hey, who told you where the high ground was? You'd be floating out to sea—what are you doing now? We have about a mile to walk in this rotten storm. You won't need your purse, damn it!"

"I'm not looking for my purse!" Josie insisted, scrounging around behind the seat. "I'm looking for a piece of rope."

"What for?"

"To tie the dog to—"

"Don't tell me—"

"Chief, I'm going to take this piece of rope and walk that dog back there to the shelter with me. Period." She jumped down out of the truck, slammed the door behind her, and leaned into the wind.

The dog didn't seem happy to see her. In fact, it growled menacingly at Josie's approach.

Chief Rodney chuckled. "Probably knows you're a cat person."

Josie was surprised to discover the man beside her. "It's just scared," she replied angrily. She was terrified, wet, and exhausted. She was damned if she was going to let a little thing like a snarling strange dog stop her from what she had to do. Josie reached out and grabbed the dog by the collar and pulled it off the back of her truck. "Come on, dog. Time for walkies," she announced. Possibly the dog knew authority when it heard its voice or perhaps it was just tired of being soaking wet, but it allowed Josie to tie the rope around its collar, and the three of them started off down the road in the pouring rain.

SIX

WAVE radio . . .

A WAVE, NOT from the radio, but from a passing car, splashed Josie, Chief Rodney, and the dog as they walked by the side of the road. The dog growled.

"*. . . at the shelters . . .*" The radio signal faded as the car sped away.

"I think the shelter's about half a mile ahead," Chief Rodney said, as another wave from a car identical to the first washed over the threesome. It, too, had its radio blaring.

"*. . . and now this . . .*"

They were so wet by the time the third wave hit them that even the dog didn't bother to respond.

"You'd think one of them would stop and pick us up," Josie shouted as the rear lights from three identical Ford Expeditions vanished into the storm.

"Maybe they don't like dogs."

"Maybe they don't like cops," Josie replied angrily. She had, after all, rescued the chief from the island. The least he could do was be nice about her . . . about the dog, she corrected herself.

"Oh, thank heavens," Josie said as an island police car, lights flashing, stopped in the middle of the road.

"You folks own that red truck back a ways?" a young patrolman stuck his head out into the rain to ask them.

"Do you know who I am?"

"Is the truck okay?" Josie asked quickly before the policeman had time to answer Chief Rodney's question.

"Yeah, we're just out trying to account for the people who got lost in this storm. . . ."

"Do you know who I am?" Chief Rodney repeated his question.

"Don't have time for guessing games now. You two just get in the backseat, and I'll drive you to the nearest shelter—I said the backseat—Oh, it's you, Chief Rodney. I didn't recognize you. I guess I've never seen you when you were so . . . so wet. I guess."

Josie grinned and slid into the backseat. Chief Rodney was furious, and the young officer driving was working so hard to make up for his mistake that neither of them noticed when the dog climbed in beside her.

"So how's the evacuation going?" Josie asked when the police chief's diatribe had dwindled down to a few huffs.

"Looks like pretty much everyone is off island. We sure as sh—We couldn't find anyone there last time we swept the area. We did a house-to-house search, just like you ordered, Chief. Until the water was too high to drive through. There's a rumor that some teenagers snuck back though across the bay. They want to ride the surf or something."

"I don't give a damn about some surfer dude wannabes. Did anyone see what happened to my car?"

"Well . . ."

Josie wondered if this young man was a bit tired of being the bearer of bad news.

"Well, what?"

"Someone—I think it was one of the guys—said something about a sedan that looked something like yours being spotted near—or, actually, he said, *in* that liquor store at the north end of the island. . . ."

"That's Sam's store!" Josie cried.

"What do you mean *in*?" Chief Rodney roared.

"Not actually in. I don't think he actually said *in*. I think the word used was *through*. Yeah, he said *through* the front window. That's not exactly in, is it?"

"Sam's store," Josie repeated. "How did the chief's car get so close to Sam's store?"

"Washed in with the tide. From what I hear, lots of things are washing in with the tide, and high tide won't be for—" He glanced down at his watch. "—for at least another three hours."

"Shit."

Chief Rodney's word summed up the situation for Josie as well.

Back in the sixties someone in the nearest inland township had owned a large plot of unusable land and had had enough political clout for it to be bought by the municipality for a new regional high school. Many of the elements that made this property (a dozen acres on a rocky hillside) unsuitable for farming contributed to its desirability as an evacuation shelter: it was high above the water and had plenty of space for parking.

Right now cars covered the macadam, and parking had been extended across two soccer fields and a baseball diamond to the track.

"They were gonna park cars underneath the bleachers until the wind started moving them around a bit too much," explained their driver as he maneuvered his vehicle through the tight lanes left by parked cars.

"What bleachers?" Josie asked.

"Them over . . ." He turned to look over his shoulder. "Well, them that were over there."

Josie looked behind them and saw nothing. She had a sudden, compelling need to find shelter as fast as possible.

"I need to get to the control center," was Chief Rodney's way of stating the same thing.

"It's around back."

"I'll get out right here," the police chief announced as the car arrived at the heavy cement canopy provided to shelter youngsters being dropped off by family, friends, and buses. Today the only person about was a young man leaning against one of the posts, smoking a cigarette, and looking annoyed.

"Okeydoke, but I gotta warn you. That guy over there is a reporter . . . and a pest. If he finds out who you are and that you just left the island, he'll probably want to waste your time interviewing you."

Chief Rodney seemed to perk up a bit. "He's a reporter for one of the local papers?"

"Nope. The Weather Channel. I don't know where his crew is, but they're bound to be around somewhere. He's been trying to find what he calls 'the big story' for the past two hours."

"Well, I think he's about to find what he's been looking for. I'll give him a story." Chief Rodney climbed out of the car immediately. He strode purposefully toward the reporter, shoulders squared, a serious expression on his face. "I understand you're interested in interviewing the last people to leave the island and—Shit! . . ." The chief's words were drowned out by an astonishing crash as the far end of the canopy smashed to the ground.

Josie and her driver were stunned by the event and immediately turned to stare at the damage. Fortunately, neither man had been injured. At least not physically. Chief Rodney's expectation of fame seemed to have vanished.

"Damn! Where the hell is my cameraman when there's actually something happening!" the reporter shouted angrily, looking at the pile of rubble with disgust.

"I have a story. . . ," Chief Rodney insisted.

"Yeah, maybe we'll talk later," the reporter said, sounding like he didn't mean it and starting to dial his cell phone.

"But I was the last person to leave the island," the chief explained. "And I'm in charge of the evacuation . . . and I'm . . ." His words were lost again in the wail of the wind as he followed the reporter around the side of the building.

"Guess the chief wants to be on TV," Josie's driver said, grinning.

"Yeah. Sounds like it."

"What are you gonna do with that dog? Pets aren't allowed in the shelter, you know."

Josie looked down at the tan-and-black dog sitting by her side, still staring out the car window at the crushed canopy. "I don't know. . . ."

"Look, I shouldn't do this, but these are strange times. Why don't you leave him right here? I'm on duty inside, and if I park a ways away, no one should know. Other people have done it."

"Left their pets in their cars?"

"Yeah. Let's drive around a bit. I'll park near another car with a dog, okay? Maybe the other animal will keep yours company."

"That would be helpful," Josie said.

"You look like a nice person. You wouldn't have a dog that chewed up stuff, right?"

Josie looked doubtfully down at the animal by her side.

The dog was tense, and Josie, accustomed to life with a cat, had no idea what was normal for a canine in this situation. "No, you're right. I wouldn't want to have a dog who destroyed things." She had opened her mouth to explain that she didn't exactly own, or even know, this particular animal when she realized they were passing by three white Expeditions parked in a row.

"You don't happen to know who owns those cars, do you?" she asked, pointing.

"Sure. The Hudson sisters."

"The who?" Josie asked, thinking it sounded like a singing group from the thirties or forties. Then the name clicked. "Are they relatives of the man who bought the Point House?"

"Yeah. They're his daughters. One of the guys down at the station asked the youngest out on a date. She refused. He got the impression that she felt dating an ordinary policeman might be beneath her."

"They all drive the same car?"

"Yeah. Weird, huh? How about if I park right here? There's two golden retrievers in that Volvo, and goldens are always friendly. And there's nothing around to fall on us here, right? Would be nice if some of the police cars survive the storm, right?"

"Right!"

"I'm gonna do something I shouldn't. Here." He tossed something into the backseat and Josie, much to her amazement, actually caught it. She looked down and discovered a car key in her outstretched hand.

"Why?"

"You're gonna want to walk your dog, right?"

"Yes, I guess . . . Of course," she answered more forcefully. She reached out to scratch the dog's still damp head and was rewarded with a low growl.

"What's his name?"

"Oh . . ." she glanced at the single tag hanging off the dog's collar. "Loki," she read slowly.

"Odd name."

"Yeah, well, you know how it is."

"Sure do. My kid named my dog Bunny. I've got the only rottweiler in the goddamn world named after the Easter bunny."

"How long are you going to be parked here?" Josie asked, suddenly realizing that she hadn't found a permanent solution to the dog problem.

"I'm scheduled to be here until the storm is over. You just make sure you're one of the first out of the building when the all clear is sounded, and I'll drive you and your dog back to the island."

"Sounds good."

He locked up the cruiser, and they both ran through the storm to the shelter.

There was a desk outside the entrance to the gymnasium, and Josie stopped there to record her name and address before walking through the doorway . . . into mayhem. Every square inch of the floor seemed to be covered with people and their belongings. At second look, she realized that the crowd was fairly well organized. The gym floor, divided into rows, had informal aisles that wound through the many families and their belongings. Bedding, consisting mostly of sleeping bags, blankets, and pillows, mapped out each person or family's space, and many adults were lying down, napping or reading. Children raced up and down the bleachers, screaming gleefully at the unexpected freedom. About two dozen of the island's teenagers were slouched at one end of the room chatting and giving the assembled community scornful glances.

Above it all was an electronic hum, which Josie realized was the combination of hundreds of portable radios and boom boxes turned to stations reporting on Agatha's progress up the coast.

"Josie! Josie! Josie! Over here!"

Despite the size of the crowd, Josie immediately picked out Sam, Risa, and Basil. The trio had devised a little living area near the doorway in the second row of evacuees. Josie smiled, comparing Risa's teak deck chair piled with silk pillows and light pashmina shawls to the plastic and terry upon which most people were lounging.

She picked her way through the crowd, trying to avoid dripping on anyone. She greeted friends and neighbors as she went, many of whom had questions about their homes and property.

"I didn't see anything. The rain was too heavy," Josie assured each one, heading to the comfort of Sam's arms.

His first words, however, left something to be desired. "Where the hell have you been? I've been worried sick about you! You said you were going to leave the island as quickly as possible."

As a mother, Josie understood that worry could turn into anger once a person was assured of their loved one's safety. As a lover, she would have appreciated a less maternal response to her arrival. "My truck broke down, but it lasted longer than one of those expensive new police cruisers that Chief Rodney drives," she added quickly.

"How do you know that?"

"I rescued him," Josie explained proudly. "Do you think now I can dash all over the island this summer without worrying about getting a ticket?" She grinned up at him, crinkling her freckled nose.

Sam looked down at her, a serious expression on his face. "Josie, the predictions are getting worse. It may be

that we'll all be lucky to even have an island to live on after
Agatha gets through with it."

SEVEN

And WAVE radio would like to send this out to
all our listeners . . .

L OOKING BACK, JOSIE couldn't remember exactly when
the lights went out.

By that time, the crowd in the gym had become almost
festive. In each corner, televisions, borrowed from the
classrooms, had been set up, and students had strung wires
across bleachers, around gymnastic equipment, and under
floor mats to bring continuous cable coverage from the
Weather Channel to those interested in watching Agatha's
progress. When the storm moved out to sea, the noise increased as relieved citizens ate the food they'd brought
along and took discreet sips of forbidden alcoholic drinks.
Risa and Basil had chatted and feasted on the excellent
antipasti Risa provided. Sam, worried about the damage
to his store and the limits of his insurance coverage, had
refused even to taste the *moscardini al sedano* or the *pâté
di coniglio*—two of his favorites. Josie, her appetite af-
fected by images of the dead man and questions about
what—or who—she should tell about him, nibbled ab-

sentmindedly on focaccia covered with fresh herbs and sipped Diet Coke.

"Guess there will be lots of work for you contractors once this storm moves out to sea," her son's third-grade teacher commented as he passed by.

"I already have a full summer schedule," Josie answered, wondering immediately if that was true. If the body she had discovered turned out to be the owner of the Point House, she just might have lost the job of her dreams. She turned to ask Sam if the death of one of the signers of a contract nullified that contract and realized that their temporary neighbors in the shelter were three immaculately dressed young women—obviously the drivers of the three white Expeditions that had splashed her. She forgot her question and leaned toward the trio. All three were blond and groomed, and discussing a topic they apparently found exciting. The one with a red silk scarf tied in her hair was talking.

". . . I say we confront him now while changes can be made."

"Exactly what changes?" asked the one with the slightly darker shade of blond hair, her narrow golden glasses perched on her nose.

"The changes we agreed on!"

"What we need to change is his mind!" This from the longest, frizziest, and blondest.

"Since when does Father change his mind about anything? When he makes up his mind about someone in his family, he sticks to it—"

"I'm not talking about his family. I'm talking about the house—"

"That damn house. I wish we'd never heard of that damn house!"

"It's not the house that's the problem," the one with

glasses insisted. "I keep telling you, the house is an excellent investment. Land on the ocean within commuting distance of New York City is rare and desirable. That house can only go up in value. It's a safe place for our money, believe me."

"It's not that we don't believe you. It's just that you know what Father does. He has a good idea and then completely screws it up," the woman with the red scarf said.

"That's not quite true," objected the one with the frizzy hair.

"It doesn't matter if it's true or not. It's his money. If he wants to throw it into the ocean, he can do it. . . ." She pushed her glasses up on her nose as she spoke.

"He really can't, can he? I mean, if he did something like that, we could claim he's incompetent and get power of attorney or have him put away or . . . or something, right?" The frizzy hair bounced around as though waves of anguish were running through it.

"Beca, what's wrong with you? You're not thinking tonight. The man came to this country in the sixties, completely broke, with no education and speaking no English. In ten years, he owned his own successful business. In twenty, he was worth millions. He sells his business at a profit—a huge profit—and retires to live the good life, part of which is buying a large house on the ocean, which he plans to remodel into a family compound so that his daughters and their families can visit. What is there about that story that would make a judge declare him incompetent?" the woman wearing glasses asked the other two.

"Good question," Sam whispered.

Josie grimaced. She didn't realize he'd been eavesdropping, too. She leaned closer and whispered a question. "You know who they are?"

"No. Only that the one wearing glasses has a taste for

imported merlot. The one with her hair tied back drinks champagne cocktails made with the best bubbly from France. And the one having a bad hair day will drink almost anything as long as it's alcoholic." He didn't bother to whisper his reply, as the three women had gotten up and were headed toward one of the television monitors.

"Do you think it's possible that owning a liquor store is giving you a jaded view of the world?" Josie asked, watching them pick their way across the crowded floor.

"After twenty years working as a prosecuting attorney, my viewpoint is more than jaded—it's completely skewed—but not so much that I am comfortable with the thought that those grown women seem to feel that their father's fortune belongs to them."

"They may have serious cash-flow problems," Basil announced, moving closer to Josie and Sam. "They were in the restaurant for lunch a few days ago chatting about their lives—European vacations, exclusive camps for their kids, spas in Switzerland, and houses in Aspen and East Hampton were all mentioned. And look at their clothing, hair, and manicured toes and fingers. Those women are high maintenance. Expensive high maintenance."

Josie brushed her self-trimmed bangs off her dirty forehead. Basil's assessment didn't apply to her. "All I know is that they're inconsiderate. Each one passed Chief Rodney and me as we were walking here. Not only didn't they stop and offer us a ride, they passed so quickly that their cars splashed us. Not that that mattered much. We were already soaked. And they might not like dogs. . . ." She stopped speaking and looked down at her lap. "Speaking of dogs, do you think one would eat this?" she asked, pointing to the bread she had almost finished.

"There isn't a dog alive who would turn down Risa's cooking," Basil assured her.

Sam, who knew Josie better, only said, "Where is this dog?"

"Outside in the police cruiser."

"Why are you worried about a police dog?" Basil asked.

"It's not. It's . . . I don't know who it belongs to. It sort of adopted me."

"And it doesn't have a collar?"

"It has a collar, but there's only one tag hanging from it. It says Loki. That's all. No other name or address or anything."

"Loki?" Basil asked.

"Some sort of Norse mythological character, I think," Sam said, once again surprising Josie with his knowledge. "A trickster—like the raven in North American Indian culture. I dated a woman who was finishing up her Ph.D. in anthropology, and the trickster's impact on primitive cultures was her thesis topic," he explained, this time not surprising Josie. Mention any subject, and Sam had dated an expert in the field.

"Sounds like the dog's owner is an educated person at least," Basil commented.

"Hmm. I wonder if we could find out who it is. You know, make an announcement asking if anyone owns a dog named Loki."

"I don't think the officials in charge here would appreciate that. There were lots of people who wanted to bring animals into the shelter, and they were all turned away," Sam said.

"Yes, I notice many dogs and cats in cars," Risa added. "I just hope owners leave nice fresh water for the poor things."

Josie suddenly stood up. "Water? Do you think the dog

really needs water? I mean, we just walked through a flood."

Sam knew exactly what she was talking about. "Which was undoubtably as stressful for the dog as for you—and look how you're eating and drinking."

"Good point," Josie muttered. "I think I'd better go out and check on Loki. And bring the poor thing a snack."

"I'll come with you," Sam said. "It could be dangerous out there."

"Fine." Josie picked up scraps from their meal and wrapped them in a piece of leftover foil.

"Do you think the dog will drink from a cup?" Sam asked.

Josie shrugged. "I suppose we can give it a try."

"Good, let's get going."

"Don't you think we need to bring a bottle of water?" Josie asked.

"Unless the weather has changed a whole lot, I think we can just hold the cup up to the sky and it will fill up in no time at all."

"I suppose," Josie said, putting on her soaking jacket and flinching as cool water poured out of the crumpled hood and down her back. She hadn't been inside long enough to dry off, nor had she brought along dry clothing to change into, but what she was wearing had warmed up in the fusty space, and the contrast was surprising and chilling.

The noise level in the room increased as they made their way to the doors.

"What's going on?" Josie looked back over her shoulder.

Sam was squinting through his glasses toward the closest TV. "Sounds like Agatha has turned around and is heading in our direction again." He moved closer to the screen as though mesmerized.

"Sam, I'm going to go on out to Loki. Okay? Sam?" He wasn't the only person in the room entranced by the news, and as Josie watched, a crowd closed around Sam and the monitor. The men who had been stationed at the door to greet people as well as to keep children from dashing out were also drawn toward the television, thereby allowing Josie to leave without interference. She just shrugged, zipped up her rain gear, and pressed the bar that held the door closed.

Despite the news on the television, the storm actually seemed to have decreased. The wind was coming from behind as she walked through the rows of parked cars, stopping once in a while to tap on the window of one at a cat or dog imprisoned inside.

It was easy to locate the police cruiser, but for a moment she thought Loki had escaped. Then she heard a growl.

It came from the floor of the car. "Hi, sweetie. Are you hungry?" Josie put the key in the lock, and the noise increased. Maybe the dog would prefer her to use its name. "Hi, Loki, time for dinner. Time for a cookie."

Apparently that worked. Josie opened the door slowly and tossed a piece of the focaccia inside. The dog looked up at her and then down at the bread. Its nose twitched.

"Go ahead. You need it," Josie said encouragingly.

The dog sniffed suspiciously, took one small bite, and then another. Josie, realizing Sam still had the cup, reached in cautiously and took hold of the leash still dangling from the dog's collar. "Come on, Loki. You need water and walking. We don't want you to be responsible for staining the nice, new police car."

The dog responded to her tug and allowed itself to be pulled from the car back into the storm. The rainwater had settled in large puddles by the side of the gymnasium, and Josie led Loki over there for a drink. But this dog apparently had a mind of its own—and the curiosity usually attributed to cats. Loki yanked and tugged and managed to coax Josie around the corner of the building and right into the middle of an argument.

Two of the Hudson sisters were there, up to their ankles in water, hair flopping around their faces like strands of thick soaked yarn, makeup streaming down their cheeks, screaming at each other. Loki stopped and growled. Josie frowned and pulled the dog back from the fray.

But neither her presence nor that of the dog dampened the ardor either women felt for the fight.

"You're a fake! And when Father finds out what you've been doing, he's going to have a fit."

"You'd like that, wouldn't you? We all know you want him dead. His death would solve a lot of your problems, wouldn't it?"

"How can you possibly say that! I love Father! Who's been taking care of him all these years? Who stayed with him? Who—?"

"You weren't helping him. You were helping you. You can't afford to live like—"

Loki, blessed with an incredibly shrill yelp, stopped the fight as effectively as a referee's whistle. Both women started, then turned, and stared at Josie and the dog.

"Who are you?" one asked, wiping soaking wet hair out of her face.

"She's the carpenter. I've seen her working at the house," the other explained.

"I'm a contractor," Josie corrected them. "I own my own company. Island Contracting."

"Oh, you're the person my father hired to remodel the house. I've been wanting to talk to you. You've left out whirlpools."

They were going to stand here in the middle of a storm and discuss the details of a remodeling job? "Excuse me?"

"The bathrooms. Each one has a tub, but they aren't whirlpools. I think whirlpools are a necessity. And they add to the resale value of the house."

"I don't have anything to do with that. You'll have to talk to your father's architect."

"Well, can't you just make a substitution?"

"No, I can't."

Much to Josie's surprise, the other woman arranged a polite smile on her otherwise angry face. "But you're a woman. You understand another woman's need for these things."

The bathroom in Josie's apartment had an old stained bathtub, a pink sink that Josie had scrounged from a re-modeling job to replace an old turquoise one that had leaked for years—the improvement was functional rather than cosmetic—a fifties toilet, which worked perfectly but was stained from the rusty water the island once had, and broken tiles on the floor and walls. Josie was perfectly happy in that bathroom; she did *not* understand "another woman's need for these things."

"I cannot substitute anything without the owner's okay," she said stubbornly. "On the other hand—Ack!"

A wooden window shutter flipped around the corner and sliced the space between them. The dog barked, the women screamed, and Josie had just a moment to wonder if, perhaps, the women she was speaking to were now, in fact, the owners of all those bathrooms.

EIGHT

Well, kiddies, some of the wimpier radio stations were blown right off the air, but not your old friends at WAVE radio. Those real waves left your favorite WAVE alone, and we are here to tell you . . .

JOSIE THREW HERSELF back against the soggy seat in her truck. Just her luck. The truck wouldn't start, and the radio wouldn't stop. And there was no one around to help her.

Hurricane Agatha had passed over the island, swung around when it hit the mainland, and headed out to sea. By five A.M. the all clear had been sounded. Then it had been left up to the officials on duty to explain that citizens and vacationers would not be allowed onto the island until the police had secured the area. Evacuees were told to remain in the shelter until further notice. It was not a situation that made anyone happy. And, luckily, it was one Josie hadn't had to suffer through. She had been offered a ride home with the young police officer. She had been grateful until realizing he had had to make it—Loki wouldn't let him into his own patrol car until Josie restrained the dog. Then the officer had driven her to her truck, poured in an emergency can of gas, and left her to return home before he put up the barricades in front of the bridge.

So here she was: alone on a deserted island. Josie opened the door and jumped out of her truck and into about nine inches of sand that had been washed against the curb. She had traveled a dozen or more blocks from the bridge in stunned silence and awe. The worst destruction had happened to the buildings located in the two blocks just next to the inlet. As far as she could tell, each and every one had been seriously damaged. A few homes had vanished entirely, leaving behind the pilings they had been anchored to as sentries standing over otherwise empty lots.

Dune Drive was beneath a sand dune. Fortunately Ocean Drive turned out to be less appropriately named, and she had taken that road until her truck refused to travel any more. Then she walked.

And as she walked the thing that struck her the most was how much the island resembled one of those "What's wrong with this picture?" games her son had loved when he was little. The steeple of St. Mary's Catholic Church had been relocated atop the Dairy Queen. Boats were not merely out of water, they were upside down and buried beneath the remains of the island's now empty water tower. Cars were on lawns. Trees were on the roads. Glass, sand, and water were everywhere.

But none of this came as a surprise, she realized as she walked along. What was surprising was the oasis of property apparently avoided by the storm. After blocks of destruction where nothing over twenty feet tall was undamaged, on Eleventh Street, a half dozen of the oldest homes on the island were apparently untouched, and Josie was startled to hear the tinkling of a wind chime hanging from some decorative woodwork on a porch sodden with rain. Homes with balconies ripped off the front sported beach towels pinned neatly on the clotheslines in the backyards.

She wasn't merely wandering aimlessly. The route she had planned would take her past the buildings she was worried about the most: Sam's house, Sam's store, Risa's home, and Island Contracting's office. As she moved north to south, each building she passed increased in importance to her.

Sam lived in the dunes, in a fifties ranch house he and Josie had been remodeling for the past few years. Josie had compromised reluctantly on the design of the wrap-around deck Sam had added to his home, but she had never liked it. Apparently Agatha agreed with her. The deck was almost completely destroyed. It had been well built, but it hadn't been strong enough to withstand the weight of Sam's stone chimney falling on it. Josie knew there must be major damage on the roof, and she made a mental note to return as soon as possible with a ladder and a tarp. She then continued on down the island.

Sam's store hadn't fared much better. In fact, the entire block of stores had been seriously damaged from wind and was still flooded, but Sam's store was the only one from which the trunk of a police car protruded. But apparently that part of the island was lower than the rest. It was under what looked like a couple of feet of water. Josie was forced to remain a few blocks away. As the tide went out, she would be able to get closer.

The liquor store was miles from home, but she caught a ride in a white Jeep with some young lifeguards who had been deputized to help out in the emergency. At least, that's the story they told her. Josie, older and a bit wiser, suspected they had been given a job to keep them out of trouble.

"We're going to get out the boats and paddle around the low areas to make sure no one's stranded," a blond young man with an unhealthy and devastatingly attractive tan, explained happily.

"How much of the island is underwater?"

"About a fifth is what we were told. Mostly on the bay side . . ."

"Do you think you could drive me to Island Contracting's office? It's at 127th Street. On the bay."

"Yeah, I know where that is. How about we take you as close as we can? . . ."

"I'd really appreciate that." She leaned forward in her seat, tense with worry at what they might—or might not—find when they got there. Loki, perched beside her, growled.

Josie was transfixed by Agatha's destruction. If the homes and businesses hadn't belonged to friends and neighbors, she would have found the scene interesting rather than tragic. They were five blocks away from Island Contracting's office when the water became too deep for the Jeep to ford.

"Don't worry. I'll walk from here," she announced, jumping out into the knee-high water.

"Watch out. You don't want to get washed away."

"I'll be fine. I know where I am here. I know where the high ground is—" Her assertion would have been more effective if she hadn't, at that very moment, stepped into a hole and fallen flat on her face. Loki, apparently startled, jerked away and inadvertently pulled her up.

"Yeah, well, if you drown, don't tell anyone we had anything to do with it. We need our jobs," one of the lifeguards called over his shoulder as they drove off.

Clutching the dog's leash tightly, Josie started off. But, even on her feet and, at one point, climbing from deck to deck, she could only get to within three blocks of her office. She sat down on an overturned freezer that was resting against the curb and tried to figure out what to do. The sky was a brilliant blue, dotted with fluffy white clouds. If she kept looking up, she could imagine that there had never even been a storm. One of those small inconsistences again struck her. Whole roofs had been ripped off and shredded. So why did that house still have a wooden deck built up over its roof? It was one of those perches that were so popular with homeowners who were inland, but desired a view of the sea. She would have thought that type of structure would fall first.

On the other hand, anyone standing up there didn't have to look east to the sea. A slight turn to the west, and Island Contracting's office just might be within view. Josie scrambled to her feet and set off.

The deck had an outside stairway (although she could have walked right into the house it sat upon without any trouble—not a single window had been covered and not a single window was intact), but the bottom few feet of stairs had been ripped off. Josie looked around for something to tie the dog to before she struggled to the top. That turned out to be a completely worthless gesture—Loki, getting the idea immediately, leaped to the bottom step and pulled against its collar to continue.

"Hang on there, dog," Josie cried, and less easily and less gracefully, she scrambled to the top.

The view was amazing. Josie stared at the damage Agatha had done and slowly turned around. The ocean, the dunes, the bridge to the north outlined in the flashing lights atop police cars, the bay, her—she took a deep breath—her weathervane waving in the now light breeze. Her heart was pounding. Water surrounded her tiny building, and it was possible that the end over the bay tilted down just a bit, but it was there. She looked around for someone to share her relief and joy. "It's there, Loki, it's still there!" She put her arms out and, much to her surprise, the dog jumped right up into them. "It's still there, Loki, it's still there," she repeated, spinning around in happiness.

The storm was over, the sea was still, the dunes were . . .

She stopped so fast she almost dropped the dog. Island Contracting's tiny old building was still hanging in its precarious position over the bay, but the Point House was gone. The dune the Point House had stood on for over a century was gone, too. For a moment, she clearly understood why people have said they could not believe their own eyes. It didn't seem possible, but clearly it was. Josie put down the dog and leaned back against the railing.

She was shocked. She was astounded. She was upset. She was relieved. . . .

"Now no one will know about the body, Loki."

The dog cocked its head with what Josie interpreted as an inquisitive expression. "No one except me and the murderer," she added thoughtfully.

At five P.M. people who could prove they were residents of the island were allowed to cross the bridge. There was, in fact, only one bridge they could cross. Engineers had condemned the large new bridge until further tests could be done to determine the worthiness of the structure. The old drawbridge at the southernmost end of the island, which had been standing since the late thirties, still stood. When Sam arrived at his store, he discovered Josie sitting on a folding chair right in front of the shattered window. There was a grim expression on her normally friendly face. Loki slept by her side.

"Josie? Are you okay? Is anyone hurt?" That Sam expressed concern for Josie before saying anything about his business was a sign of how much he cared for her.

"I'm fine. Really," she added when he didn't seem reassured. "There were these kids . . . well, not kids, teenagers is more like it. I didn't recognize them. They must be tourists or something. Anyway, they were walking out of your store. Not the door," she added. "They were walking out of the window. With wine. In boxes, not bottles. I thought if I stayed here, they wouldn't come back. Oh, Sam—" She burst into tears.

"Josie, you don't have to be so upset. Boxed wine isn't exactly a high profit item." He put his arms around her.

"It's not the wine. It's the Point House."

"What about the Point House?"

"It's gone."

"Gone? You mean badly damaged?"

"No. I mean gone. Blown away! Out to sea! Vanished! Oh, Sam, I thought everything was going to be okay, but it isn't, is it?"

He pulled her tighter and kissed the top of her head before answering. "I know how much this job meant to you, but you and Island Contracting are one of the businesses that will profit from this storm. You don't have to be upset."

"I do. I really do." She sniffed a few times, wiped her eyes and nose on his shirtfront, and looked up at him. "It's not the house I'm upset about. It's what was in it. . . ." She stopped speaking.

Sam had begrudgingly helped her investigate murders in the past. But only reluctantly. And that reluctance had put a strain on their relationship. Why—now that the body as well as any evidence connecting the body with Island Contracting had disappeared—get him involved? Besides, Josie knew that concealing knowledge of a crime was illegal. Sam could lose his law license if she got him involved. Just because he didn't practice anymore didn't mean that he didn't value his profession.

"What was in it?" Sam asked.

"I . . ." She was in turmoil. Now that she had started blabbing, she had to tell him something. "There were some very valuable things in the house and . . . and I think some of them had been damaged. Badly. By Island Contracting." Well, as far as that went, it was almost true.

He gave her a strange look. "Josie, as much as I admire honesty, I can't imagine that you have to worry about anything your crew might have damaged. After all, the entire house has vanished."

Josie frowned. "Of course, but I'm afraid someone else knows about it. Someone who might hold us responsible—even though h—, even though everything washed away."

He looked down at her and up at his store. "You know, I think a glass of a nice fresh merlot might just be an excellent idea about now. Why don't we go in, see if we can find an unbroken bottle, break it open, have a glass, and you can tell me all about whatever is really bothering you."

"I . . . Okay, maybe some wine would help."

But Sam didn't answer. He had gotten up and gone over to the plate glass window the police cruiser was still sitting in. He was staring at his store. Josie looked up and saw the sad expression on his face. "Oh, Sam, I didn't realize . . ."

"Hey, glass breaks. Besides, I'm insured. *And* I'm a lawyer, so my insurance company had better not try to screw me. So I'm better off than a lot of our friends and neighbors. Let's see what there is left to drink around here." And he walked right into the most incredible mess he had ever seen.

And walked out a few minutes later with a corkscrew

and a bottle of red wine. "This one has a nice character," he commented, a smile on his face. "But we'll have to make do with paper cups. My display of Reiger wineglasses seems to have imploded."

Josie realized she was smiling. Being with Sam was such a comfort—until he started asking the hard questions.

"So tell me what's really bothering you." He started to neatly open the bottle of wine.

"Nothing, really," she lied. "I mean, there are lots of things," she added, as he looked up from his task with a skeptical expression on his face. "I really wanted to remodel that house. And . . . and there was someone else there when I was there."

"Before the storm?" he asked, filling two cups with wine.

"Yes. Someone driving a white Expedition."

"Could have been Mr. Hudson himself."

"Really? Did he drive a white Expedition, too?"

"Too?"

"His daughters—all three of them—drive white Expeditions. I was told he bought them for them."

"I heard that, too. But I have no idea what type of car he drives. It will be interesting to see how he takes what has happened to his house," Sam commented, sipping his wine.

"Yes."

"Did he make the first payment yet?"

"Yes. I was going to pick up the second one today." She paused. "Do I have any sort of legal obligation there?"

"What sort of legal obligation?"

"Well, we had a signed contract. But now that there's no house to remodel, can I just go off and get other jobs?"

"I don't see why not. From what you tell me, there's very little land left to build on even if he decides to start from scratch on a new house. And you do have a calamity clause in that contract, you know. Neither party to the contract is responsible in case of an act of God—or an act of Agatha, I suppose. I can't see any reason for Cornell Hudson to hold you to the contract. And he probably can't anyway."

That last phrase, at least, didn't surprise Josie one bit.

NINE

Good morning from WAVE radio. We bring you emergency information hourly. And golden oldies in between. Now for . . .

JOSIE WOKE UP thinking about the Point House. Sam had spent the night in her apartment. Having spent hours securing Sam's store by nailing broken shelving over the smashed window, they were too tired for a romantic interlude. They had rolled the police chief's car out into the street, activating the flashers so the few drivers on the road would see it. Risa had slept in Tyler's room because her own bed downstairs was soaking wet. Urchin, less than thrilled with Loki's company, held herself aloof on the kitchen counter. No one had seen Basil or the members of Josie's crew.

The south end of the island was above water until the block before the bay (the location of Island Contracting's office). But here, too, the wind and rain had done massive damage. Thanks to Josie's skilled carpentry, all the windows of Risa's house were intact. The front door, however, had come open during the storm, and a tall spruce had crashed through the roof of the sunporch as well, causing extensive water damage.

Risa had arrived home before they did, and all the wicker porch furniture, including the elegant Victorian chaise she favored, had been pulled off the porch and stood drying on the lawn when they arrived.

"Don't tell me Risa did this all herself," Sam said, stopping to look about.

"Probably. She may be gorgeous, but she's strong. And she's not one to let grass grow under her feet."

As if to prove her statement, Risa appeared in the doorway carrying two large plastic buckets of filthy water. "Ah, you two. Now you are here, perhaps Josie will help me and dump these in street. Just because hurricane visits is no reason to be messy."

"I can do that," Sam offered.

"No, Sam. I have other job for you to do. You need to build fireplace."

"Well, anything I can do to help out, but I must admit I don't understand your priorities. It's not going to get cold any time soon."

"Fireplace not for warm air. For cooking. And it not in house. In driveway. That ugly black stuff is flat and will not burn. I have brick and cinder things—"

"You mean cinder blocks?"

"If you say. I say you will build fireplace from those things, bricks and old crab traps. Then we have quick dinner before going to bed. Tomorrow we get up early. Much, much to do."

"I can help out," Josie offered.

"You go find wood."

"But I'm the builder," Josie protested.

"But you woman and cinder things heavy. I tell Sam how to do this. You just find wood. Dry wood."

"Dry? Nothing on this island is dry!"

"You look. You find. I get out food. Steaks, I think. And olive oil and garlic."

"Sounds good," Sam said, suddenly perking up.

"Of course," Risa replied with the confidence of a natural born chef. "You follow me. You build. Josie find fuel. I cook. We all eat."

And that was the way it had gone. Sam had built an elegant large barbecue from the materials Risa had chosen. The crab traps, cut into usable pieces, had become an efficient grill. The pine boughs Josie had laid underneath pieces of dock, home, and tree had flamed up nicely, despite the dampness. Their dinner of steak and *bruschetta* had been delicious. Eventually, they'd fallen into their beds sated and exhausted.

But Josie had awakened with only one thought on her mind—to check out the Point House. She had dreamed that the house was still perched in the dunes and that, when she drove up to the back door, Mr. Hudson was there to greet her, a big smile on his face. In her dream, Josie was driving a white Expedition, and remarkably, she was blond. Sam's snoring woke her up, and she became the redheaded owner of a broken-down red truck once again.

One glance at the window in her bedroom reminded her that she had yet to remove the wood protecting the glass. But her work had been slipshod, and she could see chinks of pale daylight. Time to hit the road. She slipped out of bed as silently as possible, got dressed in the bathroom, and managed to leave the house without waking anyone. Only to discover Risa standing in the middle of the driveway, fiddling with the barbecue.

"Good morning. You need coffee, strong coffee," Risa stated flatly, flinging one end of her shawl over her shoulder.

Josie knew better than to argue. Besides, Risa was right. She did need coffee. And only Risa could brew up delicious espresso under these conditions. "Thanks," she said, accepting a cup. "But I was wondering if I could borrow your car," she added.

"*Sí*. Of course. You borrow, but you must then shop."

"Shop? I don't have time—"

"You stop at Sam's Market. Don't go in front door. He be closed. Go around back and tell who you find there that you picking up food for Risa. Then bring back here. Okay?"

What else could she say? Especially since Risa had just passed her a paper plate of toasted bread thickly smeared with her homemade peach preserves. "No problem. But I want to—"

"You do what you have to do. Just bring food back here by time for dinner."

"I will! Thanks, Risa. Oh, and, Risa—"

"I take care of dog. You take care of food."

"You got it," Josie said, pocketing the car keys and hurrying off.

The water had receded from the blocks by the bay, but she still couldn't drive up to her office. She decided to try later at low tide. She headed up the island.

She wasn't the only person awake. In fact, she doubted if the island had ever been this busy so early in the day. Men and women were taking down the heavy boards they had put up less than forty-eight hours ago. Wet furniture was drying in the faint early morning sunlight. Home-owners were covering holes in one part of their home with pieces salvaged from another. Children were walking around, clutching favorite toys or pets.

She drove down Dune Drive as far as she could; then she parked on the side of the road—actually the side of a sand pile now—got out, and walked to what had been the bottom of the Point House driveway. Nothing. The dune had been cut in half by the storm. She started up what she thought had been the path to the house and tripped on something sticking out of the sand. She reached down and pulled out the elaborate sign. "Hudson House," she muttered the words out loud.

"Amazing, isn't it?"

The voice came from behind and startled her so that she jumped.

"Hey, it's just me."

Josie whirled around and found Betty standing in the road. She was wearing running clothes and, from the sweat on her T-shirt, was in the middle of a serious workout.

"What are you doing here?" Josie asked. "I thought you went back to New York."

"We never made it. John was so worried about getting caught in the storm that he just drove inland and checked into the first motel we found. We were glad to be out of the wind and rain, but once that passed, we realized we were in a dump. Our room reeked of mildew and years of cigarette smoke. And the Weather Channel was giving the all clear, so I talked him into coming back here. The inn doesn't have any power or water, but it did provide us with a fabulous breakfast cooked on a Weber grill, and John's willing to hang around for a while. Why are you here?"

"Here?" Josie asked.

"Yes, here instead of at the office or Risa's place. I

jogged by Sam's store and saw the damage there. How did the office make out?"

Josie updated her friend on the storm damage and then looked around. "Have you walked around at all? Is there any sign of the Point House?"

"I have no idea. Want to check it out?"

"I sure do!" They headed toward the ocean.

It was Josie's first look at the beach and she was astounded. Debris was everywhere. The sand, usually a smooth, gleaming stripe between dunes and sea, was corrugated and pockmarked with pools of slushy looking water. Gulls and other seabirds swooped down to peck at piles of dead and rotting . . .

"Are they eating fish?" Josie asked suddenly.

"I suppose."

"Do you think they'd eat anything else?"

"Seagulls? You know seagulls. They eat anything that doesn't move . . ." Betty stopped speaking and stared at her friend. "What's wrong?"

"Nothing. . . ," Josie began to protest then stopped. Betty was her friend. She could tell her the truth. "Cornell Hudson is dead."

"What happened? How do you know? Was he killed in the storm?"

"He was killed before the storm."

"He . . . how? And, Josie, how do you know?"

Josie looked around. Aside from a few beachcombers walking aimlessly by the side of the water, probably tourists who didn't have to worry about property damage, she and Betty were alone. "I was in the house before the storm," she explained. "Looking for my tool belt because a lot of my tools had been Noel's and I sure didn't want to lose them."

"Did you find it?" Betty, who knew how important Noel had been in Josie's life, asked quickly.

"Yes, but there was this man lying on the floor of the living room. He was dead."

Betty gasped. "Are you sure that he was dead? Could he have been unconscious?"

"He— he had been strangled. . . ."

"But did you pick up his wrist and check his pulse or—" Betty paused and thought for a moment. "—or anything like that?"

"Not really. You don't think he could have been alive, do you?"

"I don't know. . . . Probably not. How long were you in the room with him?"

"Less than a minute. Chief Rodney came in behind me, and I left right away. I didn't want him to see the body. It's the beginning of the season. If Chief Rodney starts investigating he'll drive us all crazy. He'll suspect me as well as every member of my crew—whether they have any connection to Cornell Hudson or not. Island Contracting will lose work. It could destroy the company and I can't allow that to happen."

"Can't argue with you there. That man can screw up the most simple thing. But—"

"But what?"

"But what are you going to do now?" Betty asked.

"I don't know! I mean, I really don't know anything. I don't know the identity of the body. . . ."

"But you must have thought about it."

"Yes, and it's probably Cornell Hudson, but how can I be sure now? The house is gone, for heaven's sake. Not just the body, the whole damn house!"

"Does anyone know about it?" Betty asked.

Josie took a deep breath. "Yes, there is someone else. At least someone else was at the house when I was there."

"Who?"

"I don't know."

"Did you see someone else?"

"No."

"Then how do you know someone else was there?"

"There was this car in the driveway—a big white Ford Expedition. It was there when I arrived and gone when I left."

"But maybe—"

"Maybe the person driving that car didn't see the body," Josie interrupted. "I know. I've thought about that."

"And?"

"And I suppose it is possible. But not likely. He was lying right in the middle of the living room. And you remember the way that house was laid out. Anyone coming in the front door, down from one of the upper floors, or from the kitchen or dining room would have to cross that area. Only by walking into the kitchen through the back door and out again could anyone in the house avoid seeing him."

"Oh. And that's what Chief Rodney did?"

"Yes."

"So you think that only you and the person or people who were in this Expedition know about the body."

"And the murderer. Unless the murderer arrived and left in the Expedition."

Betty nodded.

"I really do think the man was Cornell Hudson," Josie added.

"Why?"

"Well, I didn't see his face really well, of course. But the hair and build were the same. And Mr. Hudson could have been at the house. He has a key, of course. Maybe he wanted to see it one last time before we began demolition. Or maybe he was planning a family reunion. His daughters are all on the island—"

"His family lives with him?"

"Not really. His daughters are grown up and have their own lives—and families. Mr. Hudson was building suites for each of them with places for their children and husbands to live. But there's something really interesting, Betty. He bought them all the same car—white Ford Expeditions!"

"He bought them cars even though they're adults living on their own? They must be rich New Yorkers."

Josie was momentarily diverted. "What do you mean?"

"You'd be amazed at how rich families—quote unquote—help their grown-up children in New York. The couple who live above us, in the penthouse of our building, were given their apartment as a wedding present! It's worth millions! And it's not as though they don't make good money. They both have important jobs at Salomon Smith Barney. In a few years, they could have bought a nice place on their own. But, apparently, his family thought they shouldn't have to wait to be worth a couple of million dollars. I think it's strange, but John doesn't even notice. Believe me, my child isn't going to be spoiled like that." She patted her completely flat stomach.

Josie resisted smiling. Betty had yet to find out how difficult it was to refuse your children anything.

"How do you know that Mr. Hudson didn't drive up in the white Expedition?"

"If he did, someone was with him. Someone who drove the car away before I left the house, because it was gone when I left."

"Was it there when the chief arrived?"

"I don't know, and it's probably too late to ask him now—at least without him wondering why I want to know."

Betty looked up to where the Point House once stood. "You know, that was always my favorite house on the island. When I was a kid, the family that owned it used to spend the entire summer here. At least the kids and their mother did. Their father came down for weekends and all of August, I think. They were all tall and good-looking, and they had the latest sports equipment. They'd fly huge silk kites, set up volleyball nets on the beach, bring out the most amazing surfboards and Boogie boards, and spend entire days skimming across the waves. They seemed to have such a wonderful time. They didn't have to get summer jobs, and instead of staying on the island during the bleak winter months, they returned home to even bigger houses and more luxurious lives. At least that's what I imagined. And now that's all gone."

"But you're living that life," Josie said. "At least your child will. John's got a great job, you two seem to have lots of money . . ." She stopped speaking, wondering if she was being insensitive. The expression on Betty's face wasn't a happy one. "Betty? Is something wrong? Did I say the wrong thing? I know I sometimes really put my foot in it, but—"

"It's not you. It's me. I . . . I love John, but . . ."

"But what?" Josie cried, panicking when her friend stopped speaking. "What's wrong?"

"It's his friends. They don't like me."

"How could anyone not like you?" Josie asked sincerely.

"They . . . they think I'm a stupid hick. And I'm beginning to think they're right."

TEN

WAVE has been told that FEMA—the Federal Emergency Management Agency—will be touring the island for the next few days, so you guys turn down your radios, put away the beer, and pretend to be miserable. We wanna get as much money as possible outta those guys screwing up the country in D.C.

BEFORE JOSIE COULD protest that Betty could not possibly be right, something happened to convince Josie that she was. They were joined on the beach by a woman walking along carrying a champagne bottle in one hand and pistachio green silk sandals in the other. Josie recognized her as one of Cornell Hudson's daughters. To Betty, she was a neighbor.

"My goodness, Betty Jacobs. I never expected to find you here."

"This is my island. I mean, I grew up here," Betty said. Josie was surprised by the awkwardness of Betty's response.

"Heavens, are you telling me that this is where you worked as a carpenter? Amazing!" She seemed to notice Josie for the first time. "And I . . . I recognize you. You're the carpenter my father hired to work on Hudson House."

84

Josie didn't bother to correct her. "Josie Pigeon," was all she said.

"I'm sorry." Betty apologized in a sincere voice. "Josie Pigeon, this is Beca Bonaventure. Beca lives in my building. But I didn't know that the beach house she's been talking about recently was—that was the Point House?" Betty asked, sounding as though she couldn't believe it.

"Yeah, I guess that was its old name. Not that it needs a name anymore . . . Can you believe this? I don't know what my father is going to do when he discovers that his dream house was washed into the sea."

"It's a terrible loss," Josie said sincerely.

"Maybe for you, but as far as I'm concerned it was the best damn thing that could have happened."

"Why?" Betty and Josie asked in unison.

"This island's okay. I mean, it probably was an all right place to grow up, but it isn't the Hamptons, is it? There are only a few decent restaurants, no shopping to speak of, and I've met only one interesting single man in all the time I've been here. And trying to start up a relationship with him may turn me into a drunk. No matter how many hints I've dropped, Sam Richardson hasn't even gotten close to asking me out. And there's a limit to how many times I can stop in at the liquor store and pick up a bottle or two."

Josie realized this must be the sister who Sam had described as being willing to drink anything. Before she could comment, Betty spoke up.

"Maybe he's not as interested in you as you are in him."

Beca seemed to consider this statement seriously. "He certainly didn't strike me as gay—"

"He isn't!" Josie protested.

An amused smile flickered across Beca's face. "And just how do you know?"

"Sam and Josie are—are a couple," Betty stated flatly.

"Engaged?" Beca asked, a slow smile forming on her face.

"No, but—"

"You don't have to be engaged to be in an exclusive relationship," Betty insisted.

"I—"

"So many men are unwilling to take that final step, don't you think?" Beca's smile was becoming nasty.

"What do you think will happen to the property the Point House sat on?" Josie asked, deciding it was time they changed the subject and talked about something that interested her. Betty was so upset, she was flushed, and that certainly wasn't good for her or her baby.

"The dune is gone," Beca pointed out, looking back at the spot where the house had been.

"The land may be flat, but it's still there," Betty pointed out.

"Really. What do you think it's worth?" Beca asked quickly.

"This may not be the Hamptons, but that doesn't mean that land is cheap," Josie said, turning and staring at the property. "Possibly a couple of million dollars."

"That much?"

"Maybe even more," Josie assured her.

"Are you going to sell it?" Betty asked.

The smile that had been forming on Beca's face vanished. "I'd love to, but . . ." She paused. "It would have to be over my father's dead body."

Josie and Betty exchanged glances.

"My father loves this house. You should have seen him right before they ordered the island evacuated. He was standing up on the widow's walk, looking out to sea like some character in a movie. He's probably in his architect's office right now designing a new house."

"Do you really think so?" Josie asked intently.

Beca looked at her suspiciously. "Why not? My father believes in taking control of any situation. And he wanted a home by the sea."

"But he's dea—," Betty began.

"He's a dear, dear man," Josie interrupted.

"Yeah, well, I don't think there's anything dear about a man who's busy spending his children's money just to gratify his own ego, and, if you knew what he's been doing, you'd agree with me!"

But Betty's attention had wandered. "Are those people waving at us?" she asked, looking back toward land.

"They seem—"

"Oh, heavens, that's Win and some men I don't know. Leave it to her to find all the single guys around," Beca said.

"They're wearing uniforms. It may be the police. I think the overweight one on the end is Mike Rodney," Josie said.

"And he is single," Betty added, grinning. "Maybe you'd like to meet him."

"They're all heading this way," Josie pointed out. "I think we're going to meet them whether we want to or not. The blond woman, your sister, her name is Win?"

"Yes." She strode off to meet her sister and her companions.

"Win and Beca?" Josie said, looking at Betty, who only shrugged.

"They're both way too sophisticated to have stupid names like Betty and Josie."

"I don't think my name is stupid! Or yours either," Josie protested.

"Yeah, well, what people like us think doesn't matter all that much."

There was no time to protest. Win and three policemen

had joined them. Josie barely had time to wonder if the Hudson sisters shared the same hairdresser or if that baby-fresh blond hair could possibly be natural before Mike Rodney began to speak.

"Josie, we're looking for the father of these ladies."

"I don't understand. Why should I know where he is?" Well, she didn't actually know where he was, she reflected.

"Dad says you were the last person to leave the island and that your last stop was at the Point House. . . . Sorry, Hudson House," he apologized to the blond woman on his right, whom Josie had identified as Win.

"You were at my father's house right before the storm hit?" The information seemed to fascinate both sisters.

"I went there to find my tool belt. And that wasn't my last stop! My last stop was to pick up your father, Mike. I rescued him when his car broke down!"

"Notice how emotional she is?" Mike Rodney asked no one in particular. "Goes with red hair."

"You mean that's natural?" Beca asked, sounding surprised.

"Of course it is," Josie said, running both hands through the tangled mess.

"Well, how could we know? Not that it's exactly a color women walk out of Elizabeth Arden with," Beca said sarcastically.

Josie was beginning to understand why Betty felt the way she did. And she wasn't going to allow herself to be intimidated—at least not yet. "Sam Richardson has always liked the color of my hair," she said looking straight at Beca.

Mike Rodney interrupted the conversation. "I don't know why the hell you're talking about hair color when Cornell Hudson is missing."

"You brought it up," Josie protested.

"These ladies are worried about their father," Mike Rodney repeated.

"Why are the police involved?" Betty asked.

"He never arrived at the shelter," Win explained. "And he told Beca he would meet us there."

"Yes, that's true," Beca said.

"And you know the island police. We're always ready to help out when residents come to us with a problem."

"Especially if the problem belongs to wealthy, good-looking female residents," Betty muttered under her breath.

"Your father didn't exactly mobilize the entire force when Island Contracting's office was broken into last month," Josie said.

"As I recall that incident, nothing was taken. Although you did lose about a dozen kittens."

"The window was broken. My office was entered into. And the back door left unbolted. Three little tiger kittens were let out. They might have run into the road and been run over. . . ."

"Were they?" Betty, softhearted, asked at once.

"Well, no. In fact, they all came back in the evening, but, still—"

"Could we stop talking about cats and hair and start looking for my father?" Win protested the change of subject.

"I don't know where he is," Josie said quickly.

"But she can find him. Josie's known for her investigations—as well as for running the best contracting company on the island," Betty added.

Josie was so stunned by this statement that she could only turn and stare at her friend.

"Really?"

"So you're saying that the police don't have to worry.

That you and Josie will find Mr. Hudson and tell him his daughters are looking for him." The expression on Mike Rodney's face expressed his skepticism. He and the Hudson sisters could have formed a doubting trio.

That was probably what made Josie act so impulsively—and foolishly. "I'd be happy to find your father for you," she stated flatly.

"Really?" Win managed to add a few unnecessary and sarcastic syllables between the *r* and the *y*.

"Really. And I'd better get going. I have a job to do as well as an investigation to carry out."

It's difficult to spin on your heel and turn in sand that has been well churned up by wind, rain, and tide. Josie fell flat on her face.

"I'm sure we'll all be looking forward to seeing the results of your work," Mike Rodney said above the chuckles of the women standing by his side.

Betty helped Josie up, and without another word, the two of them walked away, Josie muttering angrily to herself.

"They make me furious, too," Betty said.

"It's not them. I'm mad at myself. I can't believe what a fool I was. How could I even think of claiming to find a man who's dead!"

"They don't know he's dead."

"But I do! And I still stupidly . . ." She stopped and looked at her friend. "Why did you say that?"

"What?"

"Why did you say they don't know he's dead?"

"Because they wouldn't be looking for him if they did, right?"

"I don't see why not. I mean, if you died and then your body disappeared I'd look for you."

"Thank you," Betty said, and then grinned.

Josie smiled back. "You know, this is really silly. I know Mr. Hudson is dead. Why don't I just go tell them what I know?"

Betty stopped walking and thought for a moment, staring out to sea. "Why didn't you tell anyone as soon as you found the body?"

"Because . . . Well, there was the storm and everything."

"And Chief Rodney is included in that everything?" Betty asked.

"I guess."

"And then, when you were at the shelter and you saw his daughters, why didn't you mention finding their father's body to one of them?"

"I don't know. It wasn't the right time. I didn't know what to say. . . . And why are you asking me all these questions?"

"Because these are the questions . . . some of the questions that everyone is going to be asking you when you explain that you saw Cornell Hudson dead on his living-room floor and that the only reason you can't find him is that he—"

"And the floor as well, remember," Josie interrupted.

Betty nodded seriously. "Is that he and his floor and his entire house were washed out to sea in Hurricane Agatha."

"Exactly." Josie nodded, her unruly hair blowing in the gentle breeze coming off the ocean.

"And you know what's going to happen?"

"What?"

"You're going to be arrested for murder . . . at the very least."

Josie didn't say anything for a few minutes. She hadn't even mentioned the one damning detail of the murder scene, and Betty still came to the conclusions she feared.

"Do you really think that might happen?"

"With the police on this island, you never know," Betty said. "After all, they arrested me for murder once, remember."

"Of course I do." Josie frowned and sighed. "But then, if you hadn't been arrested, Sam wouldn't have called John, and you wouldn't have met him and fallen in love and gotten married and gotten pregnant."

"Are you saying that being arrested for a murder you didn't commit can be a good thing?"

"In your case, it was," Josie reminded her.

"But things are different for you. You're in love with Sam, and let's face it, Josie, both Rodneys can't stand you."

"There's one other thing," Josie said.

"What?"

"If I end up in jail, Island Contracting will miss out on the best remodeling jobs on this island in decades."

ELEVEN

Water trucks will be at Twenty-first and Ocean each and every afternoon. People are reminded to bring their own clean containers. We at WAVE radio are saving up our empty beer bottles. . . .

"**B**UT WHERE DO we start?" Josie asked, rolling up the legs of her jeans and plunging right into the knee-high water.

Betty, who was wearing red gingham shorts, merely pulled off her sandals and followed Josie into the water. "The daughters are probably his beneficiaries, don't you think?"

"I suppose so. They have been complaining awfully loudly about their father spending the money they expect to inherit," Josie agreed, tripping on a curb hidden below the surface and almost falling on her face.

"Be careful," Betty urged.

"I am being careful. I thought I knew every single inch of this area, but there's junk under the water that—that doesn't belong. As well as all the junk that floats." She pushed a large chunk of Styrofoam out of their path as she spoke. "What about the mother?"

"Oh, my mother! I keep thinking about her. I haven't told my parents about the baby yet. They're coming up for a visit in August. I thought that was soon enough. . . . You know how excited Mom will be. And she'll drive me crazy— Oh, you mean Beca's mother."

"Yes."

"Dead. When Beca is looking for sympathy, she tells a sad tale of how she was shipped off to boarding school at a tender young age because of her mother's untimely and tragic death. She makes herself sound like a character out of *Jane Eyre*."

Josie, concentrating on avoiding something evil beneath the water, didn't comment on Betty's untypical lack of sympathy. "And it wasn't like that?"

"Are you kidding? In the first place, she was sixteen years old. I mean, it's tough to lose a parent, but she wasn't exactly a babe in arms. And the school was some sort of finishing school in Switzerland. I couldn't even believe places like that exist anymore! Anyway, when Beca isn't trying to get your sympathy, she's trying to impress, and that's when she tells the real story of her life. Skiing trips to the Italian Alps, tiny little boutiques in Paris where only the elite shop, crashing parties in Monaco, dates with men that John refers to as Eurotrash, but they do have titles and lots of cash. Believe me, Beca's teen years were anything but depressing."

"You really can't stand her, can you?"

"I—Ouch!" Betty picked up her foot and stared at the small cut on the bottom. "What did I step on?'

"I don't know. But it could be metal. Didn't the radio say something about free tetanus boosters being given by the Red Cross down at the lifeguard station?"

"Yes, but I had one just a few weeks ago. I stepped on a nail in the parking lot at the Montauk Yacht Club. John insisted I see a doctor immediately."

Josie grinned. "You? In Montauk where all the rich people vacation? Betty Jacobs, how you've changed!"

Betty elbowed her ex-boss and hooted with laughter. "Yeah, I used to say that, didn't I? I guess it was just my insecurities showing. After all, I grew up with nothing and I never, ever expected that to change. At least, not as dramatically as it has since I married John."

"But you always had what was important. A wonderful family. And incredibly good looks," Josie added with a wicked grin.

"Yeah, well, in the world I live in now, neither of those things is all that important. A good-looking woman without money who marries a wealthy man is just another gold digger on the Upper East Side." Betty bit her lip.

Josie realized the topic was depressing Betty, and she changed it. "You know, the water's pretty deep here and the tide should be going out. Why don't we find someplace to sit and wait until it's easier to walk?"

"Good idea. Do you think anyone would mind if we sat on those steps?" Betty pointed to a modern house they were passing.

"Hey, we built those steps! Remember? About seven years ago—"

"And the deck, too! Sure! And we did a good job. Look at the rest of the block!"

Both women looked around. The houses at this end of the island were like little islands themselves, sticking out of the water. Most of them were damaged, but the one they had worked on was only wet.

"I gather Beca was brought up with plenty of money," Josie began when they had seated themselves on the steps.

"Tons. Her father is loaded—well, you know that if you've been working for him—and apparently he loves to spend what he has on his daughters."

Josie thought for a minute. "You said apparently. What do you really know about the family?"

"A little. After all, Beca lives in our building."

"Isn't your building awfully big?"

"Actually, by New York standards, it isn't. There are twenty-one apartments and three penthouses."

"I thought there could only be one penthouse—on the top floor."

"That's what I thought, too, but it turns out that a penthouse is an apartment that takes up an entire floor—so the three top floors are penthouses. They're huge, but not as huge as the apartments of people who have bought up a second apartment and combined the two."

Josie didn't say anything. She and Betty had kept in touch since Betty's wedding, but she had been too busy to accept her friend's numerous invitations to visit her in

New York City, and until this moment, she hadn't really realized how different their lives had become. "Does Beca live in a penthouse?" she finally asked.

"Nope, but she has the biggest apartment of all—it's a breakthrough. That's part of her problem."

"What problem?" Josie asked, thinking that an extraordinarily good-looking wealthy young woman couldn't have too many problems.

"She's on the board in our building."

"Betty, you've lost me."

"We're a co-op, and the people on the board really have an incredible amount of power. You wouldn't believe!"

"Like what?"

"Well, in the first place, they decide who can and who can't buy into the building. But I guess everyone knows that. I mean, back when I lived here, I was always reading in *People* magazine about how someone famous like Madonna couldn't buy an apartment in one building or another."

"So Beca is on the board so that she can pick out who her neighbors are?"

"Partly, but the real power comes when someone wants to do something to their apartment. You know how we used to complain about the zoning rules here on the island?"

"Sure."

"Well, it's even worse in a co-op. At least, it seems worse."

"Why?"

"I guess because it's more personal."

"What do you mean?"

"In the first place, our building isn't that large, so you know the people who are telling you what you can or can't do. And their decisions are—or maybe they just seem to be—more capricious."

Josie glanced at Betty. She was impressed. Not only had her friend added a layer of sophisticated gloss, but she had improved her vocabulary. "What do you mean?"

"According to John, the people on the committee have to follow the rules of the building, but John says that interpretation is everything."

"You mean in a legal sense," Josie said.

"Yes. And we both know what that means."

"I should. Sam talks about his days as a lawyer almost as much as his precious vintages. But I don't understand what this has to do with you knowing anything about Beca."

"I told you, she's on the board—"

"But—"

"Actually she's brand-new on the board. She was elected a few months after I married John. I moved in right at the beginning of the election campaign. That's why."

"Betty, you're making no sense!"

"That's because like everything else, life in New York City is nothing like life here. Here no one wants to be on the planning committee. It's a huge bother. But in New York, those committees are power, and everyone wants power. At least everyone John's introduced me to so far . . ." She stopped talking and looked down into the water, which was slowly receding. Josie couldn't tell if Betty was just trying to give herself time to get her thoughts together or if she needed to contemplate her answer. "Not that everything's different. Where you live is extraordinarily important—just like on the island. It may not be a house on the water, but the right address and the right size apartment can have a lot to do with the impression you make when you meet people for the first time."

"That doesn't surprise me, but what I don't understand

is why her being on the board of your co-op means that you know a lot about Beca Hudson."

"Beca Bonaventure. She's gotten married—and divorced, so I've never met Mr. Bonaventure. And the reason is that a lot of residents want to be on the board, so it's always a hotly contested election, and you know how things go in a hotly contested election."

"Are you saying there's a lot of mudslinging?"

"Yeah, but I don't think *mud* is exactly the right word for it."

"Got it. So did you learn anything that might mean that Beca killed her father?"

"Probably not," Betty admitted. "Just that she's a greedy, selfish bitch who likes to get her own way."

"Boy, you really don't like her."

"I know. She made a fool out of me, and I don't like people who do that."

"No one does. What happened?"

"Well, we got back from the honeymoon, and John immediately wanted to redecorate some of the apartment. I was thrilled, of course. I mean, I never ever expected to live in a luxury apartment in Manhattan—or to have what looked to me like an unlimited budget for decorating. John suggested that I hire a decorator, but, stupid me, I told him that I wanted to do it alone."

"What's so stupid about that? It sounds like fun."

"God, just think about it, Josie. I've decorated two places in my life—my room at home where I covered the walls with photos of Sting and Peter Frampton and bought a cheap cotton bedspread. And that little apartment I had over on Fourth. Remember that? Do you think John would feel comfortable living in a place with turquoise-blue furniture from the Salvation Army store, pink walls, and that awful green indoor-outdoor carpeting on the floor?"

"I hate to tell you, Betty, but no one felt comfortable there. That was the most nauseating combination. And I admit, it doesn't sound like John. So why did you refuse to hire a decorator?"

"Because I'm stupid. At least I've been acting that way ever since I got married."

"What do you mean?"

"Oh, God, Josie, I'm always in over my head. Moving into John's world has been like moving to a foreign country—everything is different. And I'm too stupid to ask for help. I just keep saying I can do it on my own and then make the most appalling mistakes."

"Thinking the finger bowls have soup in them at dinner parties?" Josie asked, remembering a story she'd once read.

"No." Betty thought for a minute. "I don't think I've ever seen a finger bowl. Besides, I'm young and pretty. Dinner parties are easy. Men like me, and while I can't keep up my end of a conversation about current affairs, everyone seems to think it's interesting that I was a carpenter and asks me all about that. And I grew up on boats and can talk about sailing even though nothing I sailed was as ritzy as John's friends' boats. But I'm not at all sophisticated, and I don't have an interesting career—and I always end up acting like I know things I don't know."

Josie looked out at the water. She knew what Betty meant; sometimes she had the same problem. "You're smart. You'll learn. And once you have the baby, you'll have lots in common with other young mothers."

"I suppose."

"But what does this have to do with Beca?"

"Well, I met her right after I moved in. She was actually the only person in the building who dropped in to visit. I thought that meant she was the only friendly person in the building—which was my first mistake."

"She wasn't?"

"Nope. And, generally speaking, people in the building don't just drop in on each other. Not that I didn't meet people. John and I were invited to dinner parties every weekend. It turned out that there were lots of friendly people in our building. And, of course, all John's old friends were eager to meet me."

"Sounds a little stressful," Josie said.

"It was, sometimes. I know everyone wanted me to feel good and fit in, but I just ended up feeling more and more out of it. So when Beca offered to help with anything, I asked her for help with the apartment."

"Right away?"

"Well, she started telling me about her father and how his company had remodeled all these apartments and how he was going to turn the extra bedroom in her place into a walk-in closet and all and these great plans she had for putting up curtains instead of doors and—well, she sounded like she had all these great ideas, and her father was a builder. I got the impression that she wouldn't look down on me because of my job, and that she would help."

"I gather she didn't."

"Nope. I ended up helping her."

"Do what? Remodel her closet?"

"No, even Beca doesn't have that sort of nerve. She wanted me to help her campaign for the board. Not that she was quite so up front. She suggested I come to tea at her apartment the next afternoon and meet some of my neighbors. She even helped me pick out what I was going to wear, which was smart of her. My very first thought after she invited me was what to wear."

Josie nodded, thinking of her own closet full of overalls, jeans, and the casual clothing life on the island demanded.

"So I went to her apartment and found out that it was a planning meeting for Beca's campaign. Everyone there was so nice to me and so enthusiastic about Beca being on the board that I simply forgot she was going to be running against someone—someone who might be more qualified, and just plain nicer, than Beca."

"And that's what happened."

"Yeah. Big time. I really got sucked in by that bitch. I did everything she asked, stuffed flyers underneath doors, put up posters in the elevators, called people I didn't know to talk about her. By the time the election was over, I'd met everyone in the building, and half of them were barely speaking to me."

"I don't suppose you got a lot of help with your apartment either."

"None. Beca said to wait until after the election, and then, of course, she was too busy to help out. Her opponent claimed that Beca was only running so she could do what she wanted inside her own place. And it turned out that she was right. Beca had half her apartment ripped out and remodeled right after she got her seat on the board."

"She can probably get a good deal from her father."

"Maybe so, but I don't know if her father's company did the work."

"Maybe they didn't get along."

"Yeah, but did she hate him enough to kill him?" Josie asked.

"Or did she need money enough to kill him for her inheritance? There are rumors in the building that she needs an incredible amount of money to live. She sure spends enough of it."

"What do you think?" Josie asked, wondering if finding Cornell Hudson's murderer could possibly be this easy.

"I don't know. But maybe the sisters are more awful than Beca is."

Three suspects. So much for easy.

TWELVE

WAVE radio reminds its listeners that driving through water can be dangerous. So do what soggy Solly is doing. Get out of that car and swim!

"INEVER THOUGHT we'd make it!" Josie reached out and patted the sign that announced the office of Island Contracting.

"What is that on the roof?" Betty asked.

"That's the new weather vane I had made for the office. Do you like it? I couldn't believe it lasted through the storm—although I did fasten it onto the I-beam myself."

"The thing I'm talking about sure doesn't look like a weather vane. It looks more like some sort of trap . . . maybe . . . Oh, no! It's your crab trap!"

"Not on the roo— Oh, no! It is!" Josie cried, spying the large wire cage that Betty was talking about. Then she started to laugh. "You don't suppose there are still crabs inside!"

"There's something, and in this sun, if whatever it is is dead, it's sure going to smell awful pretty soon."

"You're right. Oh, hell . . ."

When Sam Richardson and John Jacobs arrived at the office of Island Contracting, they found their women up on the roof.

"Hey, the tide's going out. You can come down now," Sam called up, laughing.

"And, for God's sake, be careful!" John added.

"We're fine. We're just trying to get this trap down from the roof. It stinks!"

Josie walked over to the edge of the roof. "Maybe we could hand it to you two and—"

Sam Richardson moved away quickly. "I can smell it from here. Why don't you just drop it into the bay?"

"We can't do that," Josie answered. "Look over the deck out back. But be careful, some of the rail is missing, and one or two of the decking planks, too."

The men did as she requested but were back out front in minutes, shaking their heads. "Someone sure is going to be unhappy. That boat must have cost around a hundred thou," Sam was saying.

"Someone's insurance company, you mean," John muttered, looking up as he spoke. It was obvious he was more worried about his wife than about the large cabin cruiser that had run aground directly behind Island Contracting's office. "Betty, be careful—"

"Don't worry, sweetie. I know every lump and bump on this roof. I'm the person who put the last layer of shingles up here."

"She really is fine," Sam insisted. "Why don't we go inside and see—?"

"Oh, yeah, Sam. You two go on in. You won't believe what's in there," Josie called down to him.

"It's better than watching," Sam pointed out to his friend.

"I guess."

The time Josie had spent covering her office windows had paid off—the water had come up through the floor as waves washed up and down the bay. There was a high-water line of scum and effluence at two feet around the room and on the furniture. Until power was restored, there was no way of knowing if her computer had been damaged. And the light on her answering machine was uncharacteristically out. But, amazingly enough, the top of her desk remained relatively dry, as did the top two drawers of the file cabinets that lined one wall. Both spaces were covered with sheets of paper, held down with rocks, shells, chunks of wood, and, in one case, a large ceramic bowl with LE CHAT printed on its side.

"She doesn't keep a very neat office, does she?" John commented, glancing up as footsteps could be heard on the roof.

"Actually, it's usually worse than this." Sam picked up some of the papers and shuffled through them. "Son of a gun, these are all from people who want Island Contracting to repair their homes. Josie's going to be thrilled."

"Josie is thrilled," she said, appearing in the open doorway. "They were here when we got here. Evidently a lot of people are hoping I'll help them get back into their homes and fix their businesses."

"But how did they get here?" John asked, glancing at the muddy streets.

"Probably floated here when the water was higher," Josie said. "But, Sam, I could really use your help."

"Well, I can wield a hammer, but—"

"I'd like you to help me sort through those requests.

Figure out who to help first and who—if anyone—to refuse."

"You need to prioritize."

"Exactly."

Sam was piling up the papers before the word was out of her mouth.

"And maybe you want to help Betty," Josie suggested.

"Is she stuck up there?" The horrified expression on John's face betrayed his feelings.

"No. She's out back throwing up off the deck. The crabs had only been in the sun for a few hours, but they smelled, and the moss bunker was really disgusting. And I guess, being pregnant, it made her sick."

John dashed out the door.

"He's a good husband," Sam commented.

"Hmm. Sam, what about the Point House?"

"What about it? It's gone, isn't it?"

"Yes, but do I—does Island Contracting—have any obligation to help whoever owns the property to rebuild?" She was certain he would know the answer. Last year, he'd updated the contract that Island Contracting had been using since before Josie started working.

"I don't think anyone can deny that a hurricane is an act of God. You can consider your obligation to Cornell Hudson to be over. As long as you pay him back any prepayments."

"Oh . . . all the stuff I ordered . . ." Josie bit her lip.

"I warned you not to pick up—"

"I didn't, but . . . Sam, my suppliers are my friends. I don't want to stiff them for the cost of materials I ordered and then didn't pick up."

"Josie, their insurance companies will cover any losses. That's not your problem, believe me."

"You're sure?"

"I'm sure. As long as they've been reasonable about insuring themselves for flood damage and such. And, with the building boom that's been going on around here for the past ten years, no one has any excuses when it comes to not doing that."

"I guess . . . So, how do I go about helping out all these people?" she asked, pointing toward the pile of papers.

"You help your friends first. This friend in particular. Please."

Sam and Josie looked up and discovered Basil Tilby standing in the open doorway.

"What are those?" Josie asked, pointing to his feet.

"The only boots I own are leather, Italian leather. These were left behind at the Sea Shanty. I didn't throw them away, thinking that, with the abominable weather we have in the winter, they just might be useful. And they are. Stunning, don't you think?" He wagged his left foot in the air to better display the neon green rubber boots with bright pink eyes on the toes.

"Dreadful," Sam pronounced.

"What do you need us to do for you? Is your house okay?" Basil's house was one of Josie's favorites on the island—and one of the last that Noel Roberts had remodeled before his death.

"I haven't been home. To tell the truth, I'm afraid to go there. But the Sea Shanty and the Gull's Perch were both badly damaged, and I'd really like to get at least one of them back in action as soon as the power comes on and we get some water that's not polluted. I can keep my diners happy drinking wine and Pellegrino, but for cooking and cleaning up, I need running water."

"Do you think it's more important to repair restaurants than homes?" Josie asked seriously.

"The tourists who think Agatha was exciting will be

leaving the island pretty quickly if they find they have to cook for themselves, and that won't help the island's economy," Basil answered. "And there are people who depend on the money they make working for me in the summertime, remember."

Josie glanced at Sam.

"He's right," Sam answered her unasked question.

"So what exactly needs to be done?" Josie asked, reaching for a sheet of scrap paper.

Sam smiled. "You two figure out how to get the best dining on the island back, and I'll go through these and see what I can find out. Basil has a point. We should probably give the businesses priority."

"Just let me know what you decide, Josie," Basil said, moving toward the door. "I've got to get started cleaning up. Hey, looks like you're going to have help, whatever you decide. Good morning, ladies—" The screen door on the office slammed behind him.

"Ladies?" Josie turned to see who Basil was speaking to and then grinned. The first characteristic of a good crew was their ability to follow directions. These women had done as they were told. Sissy, Ginger, and Renee were coming up the walk, chatting and laughing. "Hi, guys. Great to see you," Josie called out.

"Hi, Josie," Renee called back.

"Hey, you're still here!" Sissy said happily.

"The miracle is that the office is still here," Ginger said, looking around at the ruined buildings nearby. "And we would have been here sooner if Sissy hadn't insisted on stopping at her place and making sure that rat of hers was alive."

"Bitsy's not a rat!" Sissy cried.

"And is Bitsy okay?" Josie asked.

"Yup. And thank heavens the office didn't get damaged," Sissy said. "I was afraid it would be gone and we'd lose our jobs. I don't mind living in a shelter for a while, but I sure can't live for long without an income."

Josie saw Sam glance at her. She knew he was thinking about Basil's request. She nodded back to him. "Okay. Businesses first. Especially those that have a lot of employees. More especially those that hire locals."

Sam smiled broadly. "You got it."

"And you, Sissy, run after the man who just left here and tell him I said for you to follow him in Risa's car. Make a list of damages and what needs to be done to get his place up and running again. Then come back here, and we'll see what sort of supplies we're going to need. Then I need you to stop at Sam's market—"

Sissy was out the door before Josie had finished speaking.

"Don't you think that, with my experience, I'm more qualified to do that?" Ginger asked.

"I need you here," Josie said, wishing it wasn't true. "You're the only one who can go through the pile of jobs after Sam has organized them and make out a supply order. But first it would be best if you could get out to the shed and see what sort of shape things are in out there." Although she had improvised the last of this, it seemed to make Ginger happy.

"No problem. I'll just make one of the cars that's going up island stop for me. Be back in a few." And Ginger then turned and dashed out the door.

"What about me?" Renee asked, sounding completely uninterested in the answer.

"I . . . um."

"Josie, John and I were just talking about the Point House," Betty announced, coming in from the back deck, "and we have a thought."

"The Point House? What? You mean that big house out at the end of the island? Our next job?" Renee asked.

"Well, it was our next job. It was swept into the sea in the storm. . . ," Josie began to explain.

"I—You're—you're kidding! It's not true. I mean, it's so big."

"It was so big, now it's gone." Josie paused. Renee seemed very upset. "Are you okay?"

"Yes, I just . . . it's a surprise is all. I—"

"You don't have to worry about having a job," Josie added quickly. "Those piles Sam is going through are requests for Island Contracting's help."

Renee looked at Sam. "That is good. I—I do need to stay employed. I mean, I need the money."

"Don't we all," Josie agreed.

"There will be a lot of money around, with insurance companies paying out what they owe. But payments may not be as . . . as timely as you would like, Josie," Sam reminded her.

"Well, if I have to wait, my suppliers will have to wait. That's all there is to it. This is an emergency, after all."

"Exactly," Sam agreed. "But it's going to mean lots of extra paperwork," he added. "Accurate paperwork."

Josie grimaced. "Ugh." She was a disaster when it came to paperwork.

"I can help with that," Renee said. "I . . . uh, I've hung around offices in my time, so I know something about things like double-entry bookkeeping."

"You're kidding! That's fantastic! I can really use your help."

"Well, sounds like you're organized," Sam said, standing up and stretching. "Good thing, too. I promised Risa we'd be at your house for lunch over an hour ago."

"I think I'd better hang out here, but you go ahead," Josie said. "I know Risa's cooking up a feast."

"No problem," Sam said.

"We'll go with you," John said.

"I . . . Josie can probably use my help here," Betty suggested.

"Only if you're feeling better and really want to help out," Josie said.

"I do. I really do," Betty insisted.

"Hon. . . ," John began.

"We'll be back in less than an hour," Sam said. "Sooner than that if we leave right away."

"Then let's get going," John suggested.

The two men were out of sight, and Josie and Renee were beginning to go through the forms Josie used to keep track of Island Contracting's financial affairs when Betty suddenly spoke.

"I love him, but he's going to drive me crazy."

THIRTEEN

Sure, we're wet. Sure we're messy. But Sea Side Miniature Golf is open for business ten A.M. to ten P.M. So bring the kiddies on by for a treat they'll never forget. Now back to WAVE radio news . . .

"I DON'T BELIEVE it! Did you see that? I don't believe it! Some people will try to make a buck out of anything."

Sam, driving, looked over his shoulder, hands firmly on the wheel. "I don't see—"

Josie pointed. "Back there on the left! There was someone selling T-shirts about the hurricane. I don't believe how commercial and crass some people can be!"

"I don't think—"

"Sam, people are suffering because of the storm. Homes have been destroyed. Lives . . . Well, I guess we don't actually know if any lives have been lost." She amended her statement, trying not to think of Cornell Hudson.

"Josie, you know Island Contracting will end up showing a healthy profit this season—just because of Agatha."

"But it's different for us! We'll stay busy, but we were going to be making money—and a lot of it—on the Point House," she reminded him.

"Of course, but you know people have lost a lot in this storm. If someone is trying to make a little extra money by having shirts printed and then selling them, I don't see anything wrong with it."

"I suppose . . . As long as it doesn't turn out to be someone off island coming in and selling those shirts and profiting. Why are you turning here?"

"The Gull's Perch is right around the corner. I thought maybe we could drive by and check out the damage. It would sure make Basil feel better."

"I suppose, but I was sort of eager to see Betty and John."

"Why?"

"Because Betty was feeling so rotten and all." Actually, she was worried about her own feelings. She was becoming increasingly uncomfortable with the knowledge of Cornell Hudson's death and hoped that talking to her old friend would help. She glanced over at Sam. It would have been such a relief to tell him what was worrying her. But she'd made her decision and she was sticking with it.

"Is there something wrong? Something you're not telling me?"

Josie was silent for a moment. Half the women she knew complained that their men were completely insensitive, but sometimes she thought that perhaps Sam was a bit too aware of her feelings. "No," she began to lie.

"If it has to do with Betty's health, John should know about it immediately," Sam continued.

Josie was flooded with relief. "Nope. She's fine, Sam. She really is. I'm just tired and worried about work. This is going to be different from our usual summer spent on a couple of big remodeling jobs. Island Contracting is going to be working all over the island on smaller projects—at least at first—and I've never organized anything like that."

"That woman—Ginger—didn't you say she had run her own company? Maybe you could ask her for help keeping some of the projects organized."

"I don't like her."

"Why not?"

"She always seems really critical of how I'm running things. She keeps talking about leadership abilities and implying that I don't have them. She started to talk about some sort of training program she'd been involved in as though she thought I should sign up," Josie added indignantly.

"So give her an extra fifty dollars a week and let her run some things for you. Maybe she'll be less critical when you give her an opportunity to prove herself."

"Yeah, maybe. Oh, look, there they are—Betty and

John—they're parking over there. Look, Betty's waving to us! Pull over! Pull over!"

"No problem. You and Betty talk, and I'll just call—"

"Phone! The phone lines are up? Already?"

"Cell phone. Mine's been working for the past few hours. Of course, some of the microwave towers are down, and the police were asking that phones only be used for emergency calls, but it will just take me a second to tell Risa that we're going to be late."

Josie was staring at Sam. "To tell you the truth, I never even thought of trying to use mine. It's at home on top of the dresser in my bedroom."

"No, it isn't. Risa is using it. She—" He stopped talking as his call was answered.

Josie got out of the car and walked toward Betty. Ocean Drive was the high part of the island, and the water seemed to have completely receded, so travel was easy on this one road. She waved to friends and neighbors as they drove by. Surprisingly, most appeared to be in good spirits.

And Betty seemed to be positively elated. She hurried up to Josie, grabbed her arm, and spun her around, away from the men.

"I'm so glad to see you! You have to stay away from Chief Rodney! It's important!"

"I . . . Why?"

"Because—oh, no!"

Josie didn't have to turn around to realize what the flashing lights behind her meant. "He's here, isn't he?" she whispered urgently.

Betty just nodded. "Sorry, we've been driving up and down Ocean hoping to run into you before he did."

"Miss Pigeon. Just the woman I've been looking for!"

Josie took a deep breath and turned around. "I can explain, Chief—"

"Josie, Chief Rodney wants—," Betty interrupted.

"No, Betty, I've been thinking about this all morning. The police can deal with this one better than—"

"Josie, the police station needs lots of work! The jail wing is completely demolished."

Josie frowned. Betty really wouldn't allow her to speak. "Just because there's no jail doesn't mean they won't arrest . . ." Then she got it. "You want Island Contracting to rebuild the jail."

"The damage is much worse than that, Miss Pigeon. And the jail is not, in fact, the real problem. You'd better come with me and see for yourself."

Josie blinked. "I . . . I'm busy. I mean, Island Contracting is busy. We have enough jobs to last well into the fall."

"The Point House is gone."

She frowned. Was he trying to tell her something? "I know that," she said slowly.

"And that Hudson guy can't rebuild."

"Why not?" Josie heard Betty snicker behind her. Of course, they both knew a dead person was unlikely to rebuild—but did anyone else know?

"Dune's gone—"

"That's not necessarily true," Sam Richardson interrupted.

"Yeah, it is. Hudson wants to build anything on the strip of land that's left, he's gonna spend at least a year trying to get approval from all the agencies involved. Not just the island, but also the state and feds would get involved. Right?"

"I suppose. But it could happen this season."

"No way." Chief Rodney seemed to think he had finished his argument with Josie and looked over at Sam.

"And since that's true, tell me, New York lawyer, Josie and Island Contracting haven't got a contract with Hudson Cornell, right?"

"You could say that."

"Then she works for the town and gets the police station back in working order."

"Hey, I decide what jobs Island Contracting accepts," Josie protested. "And I've already agreed to help a lot of friends rebuild."

"You want to get permits in what's known as a timely manner?"

"Sam, he's threatening me!" Josie cried.

"There are lots of contractors on the island," Sam reminded the police chief.

"Checked that out. They all have viable contracts."

"You checked them out before you talked to me?" Josie asked. "You preferred someone else working for the town?"

"Frankly, yes, Miss Pigeon. But since the town council insisted we hire residents instead of off islanders, you're stuck with the job."

"Sam—"

"Wait a minute, Josie." Sam turned to the police chief, his arms across his chest, a serious expression on his face. "There's no time limit on this job, right?"

"Well . . ."

"Josie has a good crew this summer. Very independent women. They will be spread out working on various homes and businesses throughout the summer—"

"Fine. Let 'em spread. But I want Josie working on the police station."

"Why? You don't even like me!"

"No, I don't. But your crews come and go. You live

here. You screw up the job, and you'll be around for me to deal with."

"I . . . Sam . . . Betty . . ." Josie looked around for help.

"I haven't seen the police station since the storm, and I don't think Josie has either," Sam said. "Maybe I should drive her over, and you two can talk there."

"Not a bad idea. But let's alter it just a tiny bit. I'll drive her over. We'll walk through the damage and assess what I think needs to be done ASAP. And then, in about an hour, you can pick her up." Chief Rodney smiled.

"I think. . . ," Josie began.

"Why don't you do as the Chief asks," Sam suggested.

"I—"

"Don't worry. I'll be along soon."

"I could go with Josie. I know the building as well as anyone, and maybe I could help out," Betty offered.

"That would be great." If only for moral support, Josie added to herself.

"Sure. Come on." Chief Rodney grinned. "No one knows the inside of a jail like an ex-jailbird."

"My wife was wrongly arrested, and while at the time she insisted that a suit for false arrest wasn't anything she was interested in pursuing, it's always possible that she might change her mind at some future date." John Jacobs's profession asserted itself.

"I just want to go with Josie," Betty said quickly, realizing the police chief was becoming angry.

"Okay, men, I guess I got me two pretty passengers today," the chief gloated.

"You'll be by to pick us up?" Josie checked with Sam.

"Of course."

"And I'll be along soon, too," John Jacobs insisted, making it sound like a threat.

"Not too soon. The police station needs lots and lots of

work," Chief Rodney reminded them as Josie and Betty followed him back to his car.

Chief Rodney hadn't lied. The police station was a wreck.

"God, it's almost as though Agatha doesn't like cops," Josie commented after they had walked the property. "The fire station and the municipal offices are fine, but this place was hit hard."

"It is strange," Betty agreed. "One of those tornadoes must have touched down here. And it's going to take all summer to rebuild . . ."

"We're not gonna rebuild right away. Just wanna get everything back here in working order. Detention cells you don't have to worry about."

"But where are you going to lock up the drunks on Saturday night?" Josie asked, surprised by his statement.

"No problem. The state is sending down trailers already altered and ready to become temporary cells. All I want you to do is get this place back in order."

"This place?" Josie looked around. "You mean the offices, the dispatcher's space, and the reception area?"

"Not even that much. We're getting another trailer for my guys to do paperwork in. But I need an office, a private office, and, of course, the dispatcher needs some place to work. Right now they're set up over in the fire station. Our generator was flooded for a bit, but I understand it's up and running again."

"So you just want this place cleaned up and turned into an office for you and one other for the dispatcher?"

Chief Rodney looked around. "And I suppose there should be some place for the public to come in. They gotta bellyache, and complain, and pay for their beach tags and fire permits," he said begrudgingly.

Josie thought for a minute. "I'll tell you what. I'll take this job, but we have to agree that I do the work alone. My crew will be busy with projects we are already committed to—although they'll be on call if I need an extra hand or two," she added quickly. "It really shouldn't take more than a few weeks to get everything up and running, and then we'll have all winter to make everything the way it was."

"I'm not looking for some sort of rinky-dink repairs here, Miss Pigeon."

"And you won't get them. My sign will be out front. Everyone on the island will know this is my project. And all the work will be up to Island Contracting's high standards!" She had kept her temper so far, but it was getting more and more difficult.

"No need to show us that your hair color is real, Miss Pigeon. Now, I figure you can start tomorrow. My office—"

But before Chief Rodney could explain yet again that his office was the most important part of this project, they were interrupted.

The three women didn't actually enter the now open doorway of the police station; it was more like an eruption of sound, energy, and blond hair.

"Who's in charge? We're looking for who is in charge!"

"We need to see someone who can do something immediately. This minute!"

"Well, I'm chief of police on this island, and if anyone can help you, I can." Chief Rodney preened.

"We're the Hudson sisters. Our father is Cornell Hudson, and he's missing."

"Not true. He's not missing. Our father would never be missing. If he's not here, he's dead."

The police chief put his hands up in the air and chuckled.

"Ladies, if you always act like this, he probably just left the island for a little peace and quiet."

The three women stopped glaring at one another and turned their hostility toward Chief Rodney.

Josie and Betty exchanged glances, thrilled by the sight.

FOURTEEN

Boys and girls, I don't know about you, but I'm sick and tired of having wet feet, cold food, and warm beer. Let's light candles and get down and boogie with that famous English rock group, The Police. . . .

POLICE CHIEF RODNEY couldn't seem to decide whether to be furious or fatuous. He was such a snob and a chauvinist that, when confronted by three very attractive and expensively dressed women, his instinct was to charm, but these women were yelling at him. Josie, recognizing his dilemma, was amused. And relieved. Now he could direct his hostility at someone else.

"Now, if these were normal times, I'd ask you ladies to step into my office. But since I don't happen to have an office right now, maybe you'd like to explain what's bothering you while sitting on that . . . on the remains of that wall over there." He turned and scowled at Josie. "And maybe Miss Pigeon will leave us alone for a bit."

"I need to take measurements," Josie lied. "If I'm going to get your office built right away, I'm going to have to bring back supplies with me in the morning . . . and Betty's here to help me now."

"I'm not—"

"Okay, just be quick about it," Chief Rodney said, not allowing Betty to finish her sentence.

Josie, who had been measuring all morning long, pulled a large tape measure from her pocket and tossed a small notebook to Betty. "Look around and find something to write with. I think I saw a pencil on the ground over near the pile of file cabinets."

Betty scowled. "Josie, I'm supposed to be meeting John—"

"I think we'd better start over there," Josie nodded toward the Hudson sisters.

"Josie, I really don't want—"

But Josie was goal oriented. "They're talking. Wait, I want to hear what they're saying . . . why they think their father's dead." She hurried off, trying to get her tape measure to unwind as she went. She heard Betty sigh loudly.

"Our father is a very important man. He runs a multimillion-dollar business," Beca was saying.

"A business he created by himself," one of her sisters added.

"I think I need to get your names, ladies," Chief Rodney said, much to Josie's relief—she was becoming confused.

"I'm Beca, and these are my sisters. That one is Pip." She nodded to the tallest and blondest. "And that's Win."

"My father would not be as successful as he is if he didn't keep his word," Pip insisted.

"He told us to meet him at that house, but then he didn't come," Win interrupted.

"By that house, you mean the Point House?" Chief Rodney asked.

"Hudson House," Pip explained.

"The people on the island call it the Point House," Beca said as though describing some sort of strange habit of the aboriginal natives to her sisters.

"Oh, then I guess the answer is yes, the Point House. That's where we were supposed to meet Father."

"But the Point House is gone. It was washed into the ocean," Chief Rodney pointed out.

"We are aware of that, but that's not what we're talking about. We're talking about before the storm," Win explained. "We were supposed to meet our father at Hudson House before the storm." She spoke slowly as though to a child or someone who didn't speak her language.

"So what? He heard that the storm was coming and decided not to come to the island until it had passed. Lots of people did that."

"My father would not tell us to meet him someplace and then not show up." Beca's statement didn't leave room for an argument.

But that didn't stop Mike Rodney, Sr. "No one doesn't ever change their plans."

"You do not know our father. . . ," Beca insisted.

"And you probably don't know many people like our father," Win added.

Chief Rodney's defense came from a surprising source. "That's not true. Many important and wealthy people vacation on this island. Chief Rodney has known many men like your father." Betty was standing nearby, the notebook Josie had passed her still unopened in her hand.

"Betty's right," Josie added, as everyone else turned and stared at her friend.

"Who are you?" Pip asked in what Josie considered a snotty tone of voice.

"Betty is a carpenter who lives in my building," Beca said.

"I—I don't—I'm not a carpenter anymore," Betty protested, uncharacteristically confused.

"Then why are you helping her?" Pip asked, pointing to Josie. "I remember her. She's the carpenter my father hired to work on Hudson House. She keeps turning up."

"My name is Josie Pigeon. I own the best contracting company on the island—"

"Of course you do. My father always hires the biggest and best." Beca agreed with what Josie was saying, but Josie had a point to make.

"—and Betty is doing me a big favor," Josie continued. "She doesn't have to work anymore. She's married to a very wealthy man."

Apparently she had said the wrong thing.

"You don't have to explain to us. We know how some women are once they find a meal ticket," Beca said nastily.

"Of course, most of the women we know didn't do manual labor for a living before they were married," Pip added.

"Betty is—was—a highly skilled—," Josie began.

"Let's just get on with our measuring," Betty interrupted loudly. Her flushed face looked miserable.

"You're sure?" Josie asked, furious with these women and their snobbery and concerned about Betty. "I can call one of my workers."

"I don't mind." Betty straightened her shoulders, apparently coming to a decision. "I'm always glad to help my friends." She looked over at Josie. "We'd better get going."

"Great." Miraculously, the tape measure untangled itself, and they were able to get on with the task of pretending to measure out walls, windows, and doorways. Josie arranged herself so that she was closest to the continuing conversation. Betty kept her back to the group.

"So you women all think it's odd that your father didn't show up as he had promised," Chief Rodney summed up, glancing over at Josie.

She ignored him, squinting down at her tape measure. This wasn't the one she usually used, and the numbers were too small to read easily.

"It's unheard of," Win insisted.

"Winnie's right!" Beca said. "Father hated people who made promises and then didn't deliver. If he made a promise, he kept it. And he promised us that he would be at Hudson House before noon the day Agatha hit."

"You all live together?" Chief Rodney sounded skeptical.

"Of course not! We're grown women!" Win protested indignantly.

"That's the point, officer," Pip said. "Win and Beca live in New York City, and I live in Westchester County—that's north of the city—"

"I know where Westchester County is," Chief Rodney growled, and Josie could tell he was losing patience.

"Well, yes, of course you do." Pip glanced at Betty. "You probably have people on the island who live there during the winter months. Although most of my friends prefer Nantucket or the Hamptons. Why father chose to buy here—"

"What my sister is trying to say is that we live in three different places and got three different phone calls from Father. He said to each of us that we were to meet him before noon at the Hudson House and—"

"And he said it was important," Beca added.

"I was getting to that," Win said, frowning at her sister.

"So you see why we're concerned," Pip said loudly. "He

called each of us, told each of us to meet him here, and then he didn't show up. It's not like him. Not like him at all."

"It may not be, but there isn't a damn thing I can do about it," Chief Rodney said. "I'd like to help out ladies, but I sure don't see how I can right now."

"Why not? We just told you—"

"What you told me is that your father said for all of you to meet him here. And, in ordinary times, if he didn't show up, I'd make a few phone calls to my friends at the state police and they'd check to see if he'd been in an accident on the way here . . ."

"And exactly why can't you do this now?" Beca was at her most imperious.

"Because there's been a hurricane, in case you haven't noticed, and everyone in any official capacity in the state is more than a little busy. Besides, I don't even know if your father actually left his home —wherever he lives—"

"He lives in New York City—on Park Avenue, if you must know. And he left his apartment before six A.M. Even if he stopped for breakfast on the way to the island, he would have been here well before noon!" Pip said.

"How do you know when he left?"

"He has a live-in housekeeper. I called and spoke to her on the phone . . . ah . . . yesterday morning."

Josie glanced up, wondering if Chief Rodney had picked up on Pip's hesitation when she explained the time of her call.

Apparently he had. "What time exactly did you call?"

"I guess . . . probably around nine or so."

"In the morning?"

"Yes."

"Why?" Josie had asked the question before she could think.

"I'm asking the questions here, Miss Pigeon. And, if you and Betty are through measuring—"

"Almost," Josie assured him, putting her head back down and pretending to get on with her task.

"Why did you call?" Chief Rodney asked.

"Why not?"

"Well, if you were going to see your father in just a few hours. . . ," Chief Rodney began.

"Oh, well . . . you see, I wanted him to bring me something from his house, and I was hoping he hadn't left yet. You see, I left a bag there a few weeks ago. . . ."

"Women. Always losing things," Chief Rodney said.

Josie opened her mouth to protest this chauvinist injustice, but Win spoke first. "Yes, of course—Pip is always leaving things places."

"Not always, but this time I did. And I wanted my father to toss it into the backseat of his car and bring . . . it . . . to the island," Pip said. "And that's why I called. Even though I was expecting to see Father in just a few hours."

"And that's why we're worried," Beca summed up. "Because we know he left. In fact, we know he left early. And he's not here."

"How do you know he didn't arrive at the Po—at Hudson House, find out that the island was being evacuated and leave, as he was supposed to?" Chief Rodney asked.

"My father was a not a man who would let a storm scare him out of his house," Win stated.

"There was a mandatory evacuation," Chief Rodney reminded her.

"He would not leave his house," Beca insisted.

Josie knew the truth behind Beca's statement. She glanced over at Betty, who was writing furiously in the notebook Josie had given her.

"A few idiots said they were going to stay," Chief Rodney admitted. "We have a list—"

"You have a list of the people who refused to leave the island?" This news was so surprising that Betty spoke up for the first time in a while.

"Yeah. Their names and the names of their next of kin."

"You're kidding."

"Nope. When some idiot says he's not going to go and are we going to arrest him, we tell him no, we're not going to arrest him. But we ask for the names of their next of kin—just in case. Usually they get the idea and leave pretty soon after that. But I don't remember any Hudson being on that list. In fact, there were only six names on the list—parents of college kids who wanted to surf the storm's waves. When they had to give us their parents' names, they left the island pretty quickly."

"So your dad probably just went to a shelter . . . like everyone else."

"My father would not leave his house," Beca said.

"Then he's at the bottom of the sea right now, because that's where his house ended up, right?"

"But if he arrived at the house, I would have seen him," Win insisted. "I was there. Right before the storm."

Josie glanced at Betty again. So at least they knew which sister had driven her white Expedition to the Point House.

"I was, too," Beca said. "And I didn't see him either."

"I arrived early," Pip announced. "And he wasn't there."

"So someone stopped him from meeting us. And the only way to stop him would have been to kidnap him," Win said.

"Or kill him," Beca suggested another solution.

Pip just nodded her agreement.

FIFTEEN

We at WAVE radio . . .

J OHN FLICKED OFF the car radio. "That station wouldn't stay in business for one hour in New York City," he muttered.

"In New York we have lots of stations. Here WAVE radio is the only place to get local news."

Riding in the backseat of John and Betty's Range Rover, Josie was relieved when Betty spoke up. Betty had been silent since leaving the police station. Josie knew she was upset—but how upset? John had arrived before they'd had an opportunity to talk privately. They were almost home; she would talk to Betty during dinner. She hadn't eaten all day and was starving.

"I sure am hungry," John commented, echoing her thought.

"Me, too," Betty agreed.

"But don't you think we should leave the island for dinner? After all, there was less destruction there and maybe we'll find a restaurant open."

"The best food on the island is at Risa's," Josie assured him.

"She's right," Betty added.

"I suppose the fact that she wanted Sam to bring wine

means something." John sounded doubtful. "But . . . oh, my God! Look at all that smoke! My cell phone is down between the seats. Call the fire department!"

"No, wait. We're already heading in that direction." Josie leaned forward. It couldn't possibly be her apartment, could it? . . . As John steered around the corner, she began to laugh. "Welcome to an island barbecue—Italian style!"

The huge grill Sam had created was smoking in the center of the driveway. Deep-red coals glowed beneath metal crab traps. Always hungry, she hopped out of the car almost before it had come to a complete stop. Risa was standing out of the swirling smoke, apparently giving someone instructions on how to baste the food.

"I hope you have lots. We're all starving," Josie called out.

"They do." The sous-chef turned around and revealed herself as Sissy. "I hope you don't mind me being here. Sam drove by the store and invited Mr. Tilby and us to dinner. I came on over after him to return Risa's car. Mr. Tilby is driving Ginger and Renee. They're going to stop at the hardware store on the way here. Ginger is going to put in . . . what she called a preliminary order."

"Ginger's going to order supplies without talking to me?"

"Yes, but as Mr. Tilby was paying, she thought you wouldn't mind."

Josie frowned.

"And they both—Mr. Tilby and Ginger—said that it would speed up the process of getting his restaurants open again," Sissy added, a worried expression on her young face.

"I suppose it might," Josie said slowly. But she sure hated anyone else assuming any of her authority. On the other hand, there were more important things, she realized as Risa handed her a tin pie plate filled with food. "Looks delicious. What is it?"

"It's fantastic!" Sissy sounded relieved to be talking about something else. "There's toast with two different toppings. One is all these mixed-up olives. It sounds weird, but it's good! And the other's made from shrimp and chopped-up peppers. And there are crabs that have this wonderful sauce on them. And there's also this tiny pasta—it looks like rice—and Risa put what she calls gravy on it. Only it's full of mussels and some other fish." Sissy was pointing at the various piles on her plate as she spoke.

But Josie wasn't interested in descriptions; she was interested in eating. She grabbed her plate and a fork and, forgoing niceties like napkins or even a proper place to sit, she plopped down on an upturned crate and started to eat.

"White or red?"

Josie looked up.

"The red wine is in the paper cup. The white is in Styrofoam," Sissy explained.

"I think I'd better stick to water or soda. . . ."

"There's only wine," Sam explained, coming up and sitting down beside her. "I forgot to bring soda or bottled water. And the rain came in the back of your home through a damaged gutter, which we didn't know about, and the top cabinet fell off the wall in the kitchen earlier today—right down onto Risa's supply of Pellegrino."

"Oh, well—white then. But I'm already so tired."

"Are you saying you're not done for the day?" Sam asked.

"No way. I've got to get the next few weeks planned out . . . supplies ordered . . . I still haven't checked to see if there's anything left at the yard. In fact, that's where I should be right now." She sniffed.

"You need to get to bed. That cold isn't getting any better," Sam reminded her.

"I know. And I will as soon as possible. . . . Are you—? Can you spend the night?"

Sam stopped eating and put his arm over her shoulder. "I don't think so. I don't feel comfortable leaving home after dark again. After all, one wall is just a tarp—"

"Sam! You didn't tell me! What happened?"

"That big white pine to the north of the house is now part of the house. It must have been more damaged during the storm than I thought. It split in half suddenly and landed right on the roof sometime today. It destroyed some of the roof and about a third of the wall of the bedroom my mother stays in when she's here—"

"I don't suppose the rain damaged that awful pink silk bedspread she loves so much."

"Destroyed it," he answered cheerfully. "And I can't imagine that more than one exists. I was thinking that I'd replace it with something plain and white and see what Mom thinks the next time she's down."

"But your house." Josie returned to the main point.

"The rest of the house is okay. The tree shattered into so many pieces that I could get it off the roof by myself. And I managed to nail up an extra tarp to keep out any more wind and rain. But . . ."

"What? What else happened?"

"The rest of the deck was destroyed. Not only did part of the tree fall on it, but the foundation pilings were pulled out of the sand when the tree was uprooted."

"I guess what they say about ill winds is true," Josie said, smiling. "They do bring a bit of good along with the bad." She had hated the fact that Sam had built that deck. After all, she hadn't hung up a shingle and started to practice law in her spare time.

Sam was looking up at Risa's house. "Your place is in pretty good shape, and since Basil's going to be sleeping here for a while and Risa won't be alone, why don't you come on over to my house later?"

"Why's Basil sleeping here? What happened to his house?"

"Gone."

"Oh, Sam, you don't mean it!"

"I stopped to see him on the way over. He'd managed to get within a block of his house, only to discover that the storm destroyed it. According to him, it doesn't look like there's anything left."

"Oh, Sam." She had stopped eating. "That was the last house Noel built before he became too ill to work."

His arm tightened around her shoulder. "I know, and it was a sensational house. Simple. Elegant. Stylish."

"Maybe Basil's wrong. Maybe he couldn't see everything."

"He saw enough. There's no land, Josie. The entire block has vanished. Completely."

She was quiet for a moment. "I guess I hadn't realized how lucky the rest of us have been. How much else—?" She was afraid to ask the question. She didn't want to hear the answer.

"From what I've heard, that's the worst block on the bay. There's other damage, of course. Most of the piers to the south are somewhat worse for wear. And, of course, the dunes up on the point were washed out to sea—along with the houses up there."

Josie was silent for a minute. "I think I know where the blues for Basil's house are. I know it won't be like remodeling a fishing shack, but he could start from scratch and produce something awfully similar."

"He'll be here in a while. It might make him feel a bit better if you tell him that."

"I will," Josie assured him as Betty and John joined them. Betty was smiling happily.

"Guess what!"

"What?"

"John's thinking about taking a short vacation here."

"That's wonderful!" said Josie.

"He is?" Sam turned to his friend. "I thought you had that big case on the schedule for early next week."

"Court delay. So this isn't a bad time to take a break."

Even Josie, who knew John only slightly, could recognize the lack of enthusiasm in his voice.

"And John can work here while I walk on the beach and get some exercise. And the inn is staying open. They have supplies being delivered from some sort of Internet source," Betty explained, breathlessly. "So . . . ." She paused and took a deep breath. "We're going to go home for a night or two and then maybe we'll be coming back to . . . to relax."

Sam looked skeptical. "You're coming back to an island recovering from a hurricane to relax?"

"It's Betty's idea of relaxing," John explained.

"But I thought you thought it was an okay idea," she protested.

"I think it might be interesting to be here. Maybe I can even help Sam clean up his store a bit. But you promised you'd relax."

"I will." Betty opened her gorgeous eyes wide, and Josie had to resist smiling. Not many men could turn down Betty when she looked like this. "You know I will. I'm taking care of this baby as well as I can, John."

He melted. "I know you are, hon."

"Well, you certainly look well," Sam said, getting up.

"Where are you going?" Josie asked him.

"To get dinner for these starving people. I want John to be well fed and hearty if he's going to come back and help me clean up the store. You've only seen the selling floor. The storeroom was flooded. Every case of wine on the floor was soaked. Stupid me, I always worried about the expensive bottles breaking, so I stored them on the floor and the bottom shelves. Turned out all I did was preserve a bunch of cases of boxed wine swill, soda, and quinine water."

"Oh, Sam." Josie got up to help him.

"John can do that," Betty said quickly.

"I sure can," he agreed. "You finish your meal."

"Okay." Betty was at Josie's side before she could say anything else.

"You could at least thank me," she whispered. "You can't imagine how difficult it was to convince John to come back here."

"Why do I have to thank you?" Josie was mystified. "I mean, I'm glad you're coming back, but it's not as though you're going to help me work on the police station, are you?"

"No, I'm going to help you find out who killed Cornell Hudson!"

"How?"

"Well, first I'm going to go back to the city and talk to everyone in our building who might have met him—when he was visiting Beca. . . ."

"Good idea!"

"And then I'm going to talk to one or two of our neighbors who hate Beca—"

"Because of her winning the election for co-op board?"

"Yeah. And because of all she's done since then!"

"Like what?"

"Like not allowing some people in the building to make minor alterations on their apartments and voting to let others change their places entirely."

"Can she really do that?"

"Heavens, you wouldn't believe how arbitrary it all is! My next-door neighbor wasn't allowed to remodel her kitchen because the board decided removing the old cabinets and putting up new ones would violate the noise standards in the building."

"Noise standards?"

"Yes. But other residents were able to cut through one apartment and into the one next door because taking out the walls only made noise in their own living space."

"What about the people living above and below them?" Josie asked.

"Exactly. That's what I mean when I say that the decisions are arbitrary—and foolish. So there are a lot of people who don't like Beca."

"I guess so. So you think you might learn something that might indicate that Beca is the murderer?" Josie asked.

"I hope so!"

"Why? Why not another sister? Pip and—and what is the other one's name?"

"Winnie . . . Win is what her sisters call her." Betty supplied the answer.

"Why do you think it's Beca rather than one of her sisters?"

But John and Sam had returned before Betty had an opportunity to answer.

"Hey, you told me you were going to relax on the island, and here you are obsessing about Beca just like you do back in the city," John said, handing his wife a Pyrex plate full of food.

"Beca?" Sam asked, handing out wine.

"She's one of the Hudson sisters," Josie explained, "Her father is Cornell Hudson. The owner of the Point House," she reminded him.

"Oh, Lord. One of the infamous Hudson sisters," Sam said. "Don't tell me you know one of them back in the city."

"Sure do. I suspect Betty was hoping she'd be swept away by Agatha the way her father's house was."

"Why don't you like her?" Sam asked, picking up his own food and starting to eat.

"Betty's afraid Beca will keep us from turning my den into a nursery for the baby," John explained.

"Maybe we won't have to worry about that happening anymore," Betty said, looking up from her meal long enough to give Josie a meaningful glance.

SIXTEEN

. . . Island Realty. Remember Island Realty when you're looking for a temporary haven, a place to spend a few idyllic summer months getting away from it all. Now back to our show . . .

"Y EAH, COME TO Island Realty to rent one of our idyllic havens temporarily knee-deep in muck without plumbing, electricity, or clean water." Every other word was accompanied by the swish of a large broom as a tiny gray-haired woman wearing filthy jeans and an equally dirty sweatshirt pushed a wall of water out the front door, off the porch, and down the three steps that led to the street. Josie stepped back to avoid being splashed.

"Do you want this?" she asked, picking a piece of paper out of the sludge.

"Does it look like anything important?"

"Looks like a contract," Josie said, holding it up to the waning sunlight.

"Toss it. . . . Oh, hell, you better give it to me. These things aren't worth a damn anymore, but maybe I should keep a record of who does what."

"What do you mean?" Josie asked, handing over the contract and then grabbing an old mop and starting to help out.

"A lot of our rental business is repeat customers," Marge Crane explained. "It won't hurt to know which ones canceled because of the storm and which ones decided to keep their commitments. You know, you don't have to do that—"

"I don't mind. I want to talk to you, and I sure can't just stand around and relax while you work."

"You look like you've been working all day."

Josie chuckled. "Sam and I decided you could tell the residents from the vacationers because the residents are all exhausted and filthy. The people on vacation look a lot better."

"Only some of them. It's amazing how many people have given up their vacation and offered to work. Two strangers helped me when I was pulling the sign from the Dairy Delight off my roof. Once they were done, they left to help out down the street and didn't even hang around long enough for me to learn their names. But why are you here instead of working at home or at the police station?"

"How do you know I'm working on the police station?"

"You know the Rodneys—can't keep their mouths shut about anything. I also heard that Betty was back in town—and pregnant. At least that's the rumor."

"She is, and she is. But she hasn't told her parents yet, so . . ."

"Oh, Josie, you know the island grapevine. And Betty's a native. Half the year-round people stay in contact with her mom and dad. News like that—even with the lines down . . . they'll have heard by now. And speaking of the island grapevine, how are you and Sam's mother getting along?"

"Sam's mother?"

"What's her name? Carol? I heard she caused a small riot at the shelter showing baby pictures of Sam."

"Sam's mother is on the island?"

"Well, apparently she was at the evacuation center."

"Sam's mother was at the high school last night?"

"No, according to the person I spoke with, she was at the county middle school."

"Why?"

"That's where they took the overflow. Apparently, they had people sleeping on the floor of the library—I'd have gone over there if I'd known. Not only is there a carpet to sleep on, but there's lots to read. I could have caught up on the latest Harry Potter."

"Are you sure? Is Sam's mother really here?" Josie couldn't imagine Carol Birnbaum being around without making her presence known—particularly to her son.

"That's what I heard."

"God, I wonder if Sam knows."

"If he doesn't now, he will soon."

"You're right about that."

"You still haven't told me why you're here. You didn't stop by just to chat."

"I want to find out more about Cornell Hudson."

"Is he trying to stiff you?"

"Stiff? No, he's not trying to stiff us . . . exactly."

"Good."

"But you said he'd paid cash for the Point House."

"Honey, that was a lot of cash. For most people there's a limit to that kind of cash. It's not as though he's one of those new dot-com multimillionaires."

"So where did his money come from?"

"Did? I hope it's still coming in, the way he's spending it."

Josie bit her lip. She was going to have to be more careful. One didn't become one of the most successful Realtors on the island by being stupid. "As far as I know, he's still making money," she muttered, looking down at the end of her mop.

"He runs a very successful company. . . ."

"How do you know? I mean, he paid cash, so there wasn't any sort of mortgage application or any other way you'd know what he's really worth, right?"

"Well, not officially, but to tell you the truth, we did run a check on him. I was nervous about whether or not he actually had as much money as he claimed to have, and I didn't want to pull the house off the market merely on his word."

"Are you saying you ran a credit check on him?" Josie would have crossed her fingers if she could have kept mopping at the same time.

"One business woman to another . . . in a word, yes."

Josie looked back toward the soppy office. "I don't suppose . . ."

"To be honest, I tossed it. That was the easiest sale I've ever made, and I didn't want any papers around that might make it appear that I'd overstepped any boundaries or anything."

"You know I won't say anything to anybody. And you must remember something—"

"Actually, I remember a lot. The man is loaded! And heavily invested in real estate. In New York City alone, he owns one townhouse worth around three million dollars and four co-op apartments valued only slightly less than four million all together. He drives a Rolls-Royce and a Lexus SUV, and when he's not driving, he flies his own twin-engine plane. Except for a few minor credit card debts, he owes no one anything. I was thrilled that he chose to buy here."

"So he didn't have to sell any of his other properties to buy the Point House?"

"Nope."

Josie was quiet, remembering the conversation she had overheard between his daughters. They had claimed he was a self-made man. Was it possible to make all this money in just one lifetime—without being involved in the computer industry? "Is it true that he's a contractor?"

"Oh, Josie, he's not just a contractor. He's one of the biggest contractors in New York City. At least that's what I understand."

"Like me? Like I am? Oh, you know what I'm trying to say."

"Well, perhaps he doesn't have the same grammar skills you do, but yes, he's a contractor like you are. Hudson Brothers is the name of his company. But there's no brother.

"That's what I heard."

"Apparently, Hudson Brothers sounded more substantial than just Hudson Contracting."

"I suppose. And more personal, of course. You know, like a family owned operation rather than one that's more corporate."

"I don't think personal is necessarily what sells in New York City."

"I'd heard he was a developer, too."

"I think he did develop some land in the city, but he referred to himself as a contractor, and he called his company a contracting company. In fact, he invited me to dinner after we signed the deal, and after a few drinks, he was referring to himself as just a carpenter. But, to be honest, I think he thought of himself as a carpenter more closely related to Jesus than to you."

"Are you saying he's religious?"

"No, but he has a very high opinion of himself."

"If he turned an ordinary contracting company into millions of dollars, he has every right to think highly of himself. Unless he did it illegally," Josie added.

"There are connections between the mob and lots of contractors in New York City. At least there are in all the mob books I've read. But there wasn't a hint of anything not above board in his financial statement. I don't subscribe to any of those Web things that check out people, but I suppose you could always do that if you're worried. You are worried, aren't you?"

"More jealous than worried," Josie said in what she hoped sounded like a lighthearted response.

"Well, if he owes you money, he can afford to pay. And, as another contractor, he's probably sympathetic to any problems you might have had collecting for work—even if the storm has prevented you from turning the Point House into Hudson House."

"I guess."

"But there is something I don't understand."

"What?"

"Why did he even need Island Contracting? Why didn't he have his own company do the remodeling?"

"I have no idea. Maybe there are licensing regulations I don't know about. Or maybe some sort of tax issue. I don't know much about rich people, but I do know they have different tax problems from the rest of us—besides the fact that they probably don't have to worry about coming up with the money to pay their taxes," Josie added ruefully.

"I know exactly what you mean. Although this year we'll probably be worrying more about taking off our losses than paying in extra taxes."

"That's what you were talking about when I came over," Josie reminded her. "Are people canceling on you?"

"No, but that's only because they can't get through yet. When the wires are up and the phones are working, they'll be calling and canceling as fast as they can dial."

"But won't that mean they're forfeiting their deposit?"

"Some of them are going to be forfeiting up to half a month's rental, but those aren't the people I'm worried about. The people I'm worried about are the ones who have rented houses that are now too damaged to be lived in. They're the folks we owe money to. We have to give back their deposits, which, at this time in the season when there's no hope of new rentals, means that we're going to be losing money."

"But the last few seasons have been great."

"Oh, we're not going to go under. But we're not going to be taking any expensive winter vacations either. Not this year." Suddenly she looked up and glanced down the deserted damaged street. "But I'm better off than a lot of others. Most of our rentals are in the beach blocks, and I spent much of the day trying to visit them all and make some sort of notes about their condition so I can report to the owners when they call. Anyway, I haven't been over to the bay side yet. I hear it's pretty bad down south. Oh, Josie, I didn't even ask how your office held up."

"It's okay. Wet, of course, and the back deck was slightly damaged, but as far as I can tell, it's in good shape. But what you heard is right. A few blocks away everything is different."

"What?"

"You know the block Basil Tilby lives on?"

"Of course, my uncle used to have his fishing shack on that block. He built it back when the regulations weren't so strict. He had the longest floating dock back then. Boats going up and down the bay had to go out and around to get by. When I was growing up, I crabbed off his dock almost every day, rain or shine, and the family spent each Fourth of July out there—a barbecue at the end of the dock. Things were quieter then. It's all different now—built up and owned by summer people. But that place was one of my first sales after I got my license. And my uncle sent all of his kids to college on the profits of that sale."

"Wow! You must have been proud."

"I was."

"I hate to be the one to tell you then, but, according to Basil, that entire block of homes was washed away completely."

"How terrible! And his restaurants didn't fare too well either, did they?"

"No. He's staying with Risa now. I have some of my workers helping him. He wants to get one restaurant up and running as soon as possible—"

"Great! There are going to be some people who either don't want to change their vacation plans or can't afford to go someplace else. When they're making their decision, they call here, and the very first question most people ask is if there are any restaurants open."

"Really?"

"Yup, even before they ask about the beach. Getting Basil's places up and running will help out the entire island."

"That's what he said," Josie said, and sneezed.

"Sounds like you've picked up a cold."

"Actually, I think I'm feeling better. But I did pick up something. And I've got to go take care of it now."

"What?"

"A bitch mutt named Loki. She attached herself to me right before the storm, and I seem to be stuck with her. She's at the office now. I was just going over to pick her up."

"A dog? That doesn't sound like you, but wait. I can help out." The Realtor went back into her office and rummaged around in the bottom drawer of her desk. She returned with a plastic bag full of what looked like—well, it looked like vomit, Josie decided.

"What is that?"

"Dog biscuits. We keep them in the office to pacify pets. But these drowned in the storm."

"Well, I just hope Loki likes them, because they're her dinner." Josie leaned her mop against the porch rail and headed back to her Jeep.

SEVENTEEN

WAVE radio has received yet another bulletin from the Humane Society. They have been collecting stray cats and dogs and are giving them shelter in a trailer down by the Municipal Center. If your precious pet is missing or if you find someone else's little treasure, stop down there and check them out. . . . Of course, if the grocery doesn't open soon, we may be going to the Humane Society for our meat. . . .

"**A**LL I WANT to know is if there's going to be a curfew on the island tonight, and you give me this sort of garbage," Josie said to the radio. Although the tide was coming back in, the storm surge seemed to have retreated, and she could drive all the way to her office. She parked Island Contracting's Jeep where she thought the curb was beneath sand and shells, and she got out.

She heard Loki before she saw the dog. The barking was loud and piercing, and Josie immediately remembered telling people that if the world was divided between cat people and dog people, she sure preferred the animal that didn't bark.

"Come on, Loki. It's been a long day, and it's bedtime,"

she said, walking in the door, swinging a flashlight around the room.

She was rewarded with a growl from under her desk. "Hey, look. I brought you dinner."

The growl continued.

"But, you know what? We're going to eat it at Sam's." She reached into the dark, found the dog's collar, and pulled.

They were on their way in less than five minutes. They would have been at Sam's just as quickly if they hadn't been stopped by a policeman.

"There's a curfew on, Miss Pigeon." Mike Rodney Jr., who had never gotten over being rejected by Josie, stood by the car's side.

"I know," Josie lied. "But I was on my way to Sam's to pick up some supplies I have stored in his garage. I'll need them at the police station early tomorrow morning. Your father seems especially interested in making sure his office is repaired quickly."

"Uh, of course. It's important to the whole town. You better get on with it."

Josie resisted making a rude comment and drove off. "You growl at me and just ignore assholes like that. You have truly lousy instincts, Loki."

But she didn't know just how lousy until Carol Birnbaum appeared in the doorway of her son's house and Loki, apparently ecstatic at the sight of the large, brassy blonde wearing a sequined bathrobe, fell over on her back and offered her stomach for scratching. Carol's scarlet nails were long enough to do a thorough job of the task.

"Carol, I didn't know you were here," Josie lied.

"I came as soon as I heard Agatha was on the way. I was sure Sammy would need me to help him after the storm passed." She hugged Josie, releasing her quickly. "But you seem to have been working overtime. I'll just take this sweet little dog to the kitchen and see what might be in the cabinets to tempt him—"

"Her."

"Her—and you might want to clean up a bit, dear. There are some Handi Wipes in my purse. . . ." She floated off toward the rear of the house as Sam appeared.

"Handi Wipes?" Josie muttered, looking down and realizing, for the first time, just how filthy she was. "What I need is a large bathtub and a case of detergent."

Sam looked her over. "You know, you may have a point. . . . And I have an idea. I think it's a great idea, maybe even a romantic idea. Go grab some beach towels from that rack by the side door and follow me."

"Sam, there's nothing romantic about swimming in the ocean at night these days. I mean, the beach is full of garbage—broken windows and—"

"We're not going to the beach. We're going to skinny-dip in my next-door neighbor's pool."

"And they won't mind?"

"They're in the city," he explained. "But I went over this morning to make sure everything was okay there, just to be neighborly, and noticed that their pool, while full of pine needles, was clear of dangerous debris. How does a quick skinny-dip sound?"

"Like heaven. Bring along some shampoo, will you?"

Sam sighed dramatically. "So much for romance."

The time spent getting clean in the pool turned out to be as romantic as their evening got. Sam's mother had moved into his bedroom, leaving Sam and Josie to choose between the fold-out bed in his study, a room without a door, or the couch in the living room, which did not fold out. They decided to split up, Sam sleeping in his study and

Josie in the living room. Apparently Loki's owners had taught her to stay off the bed. Or perhaps she just preferred to share the couch with Josie.

Josie woke up the next morning cramped, tired, and ready to get to work. She had a police department to rebuild. And a murderer to catch before the police discovered that a murder had taken place. She sure didn't want to end up in one of those new, borrowed cells. She pushed the dog off her feet and headed to the kitchen, more out of habit than because she expected to find any food there. But, remarkably enough, there was a saucepan on the counter full of what looked and smelled like strong, black coffee. Carol was seated at the table, cradling a steaming mug in her hand.

"Is that—?"

"Coffee. Have some. Sammy said he was sure you were going to run off to work early, so I filled a thermos I found under the sink for you. Black, right?"

Josie glanced around the dark room. "Is the power back on? Where did you get coffee?"

Carol smiled. "I made it."

"Without a coffeepot?"

"I gather Sam didn't mention the survival course I took last spring?"

"He said something about hiking out West somewhere," Josie answered cautiously. What he had actually told Josie was that his mother and some of her Fifth Avenue friends were playing games in Zion National Park. He had implied that Carol was using the trip as an excuse to buy expensive travel gear from a London outfitter that had begun advertising on the Internet. They had even joked about sequins on tents and whether the women were bringing along manicurists to repair their nails. But according to what Carol was saying, she had attended a real survival school, and she had learned some important life skills—including making coffee in a saucepan over an open fire, after building that fire.

"You really learned to rappel down mountains?" Josie asked, looking up from her mug.

"And up," Carol answered proudly. "In fact—" She looked over her shoulder toward Sam's office and lowered her voice. "—I was thinking of giving Sammy a two-week course as a birthday present. He's getting sluggish in his old age. And I wondered what you thought about it."

"I . . ." Fortunately Sam's entrance prevented her from saying what she was thinking.

"Good morning, Mom. Josie." He kissed them both but seemed, in fact, more interested in the coffee.

Josie got up. "I really have to go. If I don't appear down at the police station with some supplies, I may end up the first resident of their new jail trailers. Carol, I wonder if you'd mind taking care of Loki for me. The Humane Society is collecting strays down at the Municipal Center, but I have to go down to the office first—"

"Of course not. Loki and I will go for a jog on the beach as soon as you leave. I took up jogging when I came home from my course. I like to get in at least three miles a day. I'm not fast, but I'm persistent."

Sam looked at his mother as though he couldn't believe what he was hearing. "What are you going to do about lunch?" he asked, returning his attention to Josie. "Now that my car's back on the island, I could bring—"

"Oh, Sammy, I was hoping Josie and I would be able to chat when she has a free moment today," Carol interrupted.

"I don't see how I can—"

"You really must eat," Carol insisted.

"I know, but I can scarf down a—" Josie paused. "—a

sandwich while I work," she ended, wondering where she was going to find a sandwich. "But first, I absolutely have to go to the office. I told everyone to meet there at seven, and it's almost seven now. I don't know what I'm going to do about lunch, but that's a long way off."

"Thanks for the coffee, Carol. I'm glad you're here to help Sam." Grabbing the thermos, Josie fled from the room.

She had told her crew to meet at the office and, once again, they hadn't failed her.

Sissy was sitting on the porch step, using a large clamshell to scrape black tar from the bottom of her work boot. Renee was sharpening the end of a screwdriver with a whetstone. And Ginger, much to Josie's annoyance, was sitting at Josie's desk doing paperwork. She looked up as Josie entered the room.

"There you are," Ginger said, too important apparently to bother with a proper greeting. "I've been waiting for you. Basil's expecting me at the Gull's Perch in just a few minutes, but you need to sign off on a few of these orders before I go." She held out a sheaf of papers and a pen.

Josie made an effort to smile. "Just let me look . . ."

"Basil and I agreed that this is the minimum necessary in the next week. I know the lumberyards are having trouble filling orders, but it seems to me that the least we can do is try."

Josie scanned the list before answering. There was nothing on it she could find to object to. "Okay." She signed the sheet. "You'd better get going before there's nothing left."

"I was planning on it," Ginger assured her, accepting the papers back. "You don't mind if I take the Jeep—"

"Yes, I do." Josie was relieved she could deny Ginger something. "I need it."

"No problem. I just thought you preferred the truck was all."

"I do, but it's broken. I left it up on Ocean Drive."

"I know, I saw it there. So I figured out what was wrong and I fixed it," Ginger explained.

"You're kidding. . . . I . . . Thank you very much. Take the Jeep then," Josie said, thrilled.

"I will. It would be much more efficient if I dropped people off at their jobs, don't you think?"

"I'll take care of that. You go on ahead." Josie said.

"Okay. You will be stopping in before noon in case Basil insists on checking out any of the details with you?"

"Of course. Let Basil know, will you?"

"Of course."

Was it Josie's imagination or did Ginger's words, echoing Josie's, sound slightly sarcastic?

"Don't let her bother you," Renee said as the door slammed behind Ginger. "It's just the way she is."

"Yeah, she's been the boss too long to act like the rest of us," Sissy said, looking up from her task.

"I didn't think I was being quite that obvious," Josie admitted. "She's really a wonderful worker."

"So you don't have to like her," Renee said.

"That's true, of course, but it's nice when everyone gets along—makes the summer easier."

"We get along. We're just not nuts about Ginger," Renee said.

Sissy frowned. "Actually, I can't stand her. She's bossy. And she's not the boss. Josie is."

Renee shrugged. "So ignore her. If she's the worst problem you have, you should be thankful."

Josie was impressed with Renee's self-possession. She herself didn't find Ginger all that easy to ignore. She decided to change the subject. "Okay. I need a review of what you're both doing, how long you think it will take, and what you need from me for support."

"No problem," Renee said, getting up and pulling a ragged sheet of paper from her pocket. "I'm working at the bank . . . the manager is thrilled to have me but wants a signed contract from you. And I promised I'd help out at that restaurant this afternoon, too."

"And I'm fine. I'm working down at the Fish Wish right now." Sissy referred to the island's bait shop. "It was disgusting yesterday with all that fish rotting with no refrigeration. But late in the afternoon, some friends of the owners came from off island to pick up the rotten bait."

"Where were they going to take it?"

"To a farm someplace. For fertilizer—just like they taught us the Indians and the Pilgrims did—you know, in school when we were little."

Josie smiled, thinking that it hadn't been so long since Sissy was "little." "How long do you think you'll be needed at the Fish Wish?"

"Just a few more hours. Maybe even less depending on how much work the owners themselves did last night."

"Then . . ."

"But the place next door—it's a pizza place—the owner came over. He says he knows you. . . ."

"Tyler is one of their best customers when he's on the island," Josie said.

"Anyway, he came over yesterday afternoon and asked if I could go over there and help them as soon as I'm done at the bait shop. He said he'll pay you whatever you ask if the work can be done right away. They have old-fashioned ovens that burn wood, and think they can get their business going again if I help them patch the holes in their roof. . . ."

"That's great," Josie said enthusiastically. She could have pizza for lunch!

"But materials are hard to get," Sissy said. "I don't know what they'll find to patch the roof with."

Josie thought for a minute. "What size holes are we talking about?"

"I don't know. Not too big, I think. They said they had used the plastic pots cheese came in to catch water after the storm had passed. How big could those pots be?"

"True. You know there are signs down all over the island. Maybe we could collect some on the way to these jobs and you could use them, sealing the edges with bits of plastic and drop cloths, to temporarily patch the roofs."

"Great idea!"

"So let's get going," Josie said. "I'm going to be working at the police station if an emergency comes up. Otherwise I'll be checking in right before noon."

EIGHTEEN

It's a gorgeous day, boys and girls, time to get out of the house, away from the old fogies, and down to the Witch's Tit—the new place to boogie. They're dancing the night away at the Witch's Tit. And Tuesday is WAVE Night. Tell the guy at the door that you heard this message on this station and get in free. . . .

"**S**OUNDS GOOD, JOSIE. You and Sam go there? Or is he too old to boogie?" Mike Rodney, Jr., stuck his face in hers, and she grimaced.

"Sam boogies just fine, thank you. And I'd appreciate being left alone to get my work done here. Your father is very anxious to have an office again," she reminded him.

"I just thought you might be able to use some strong arms to help you . . ." He paused and leered. "You know, help you do things."

Josie hadn't had any breakfast, so she managed to resist throwing up. "You can use your strong arms to turn off that damn radio. And then you can leave," she added. She wanted to be alone. Mike's father had set up his desk behind a folding screen at the rear of the large reception room, and there, smack in the middle of his desk, was a pile of papers. The top sheet, Josie had noticed, was a missing persons report with Cornell Hudson's name written on the first line of the first page. She was dying to read the rest of it. And praying Mike Rodney hadn't come to the station to pick it up. "Why are you here?" she finally asked when he didn't seem to be going.

"Just came by to say hello. And remind you to hurry up and get a place for Dad to work. He's a little grumpy without an office, truth to tell."

"No place to lie down and sleep away the day?" Josie suggested.

"You just do your work. And, remember, it doesn't pay to make enemies of your local police department." His face scrunched up into a scowl, a weak imitation of his father's annoyed expression. Then he stomped out of the building.

Josie wasted no time. She put down her tools, dashed behind the screen, and snatched up the report.

What she found there was so interesting that she didn't hear Renee's arrival.

"Sorry to interrupt—"

Josie jumped. "I was just. . . ," she began, spinning around and seeing Renee.

"I need your signature on this." Renee held out a piece of paper to explain her presence.

Josie put down the report and took the contract from Renee. "This is great. You have lots of time to get this job done and help out at Basil's place. But you're going to have to find your own transportation."

"No problem. I'll hitch a ride from someone. People whose cars are working are picking up hitchhikers. Everyone's being wonderful."

"Great." Josie didn't like being without transportation—especially since it was so difficult to reach anybody by phone. "Renee? Are you okay?"

Renee was staring down at the papers on Chief Rodney's desk. "Yes. Of course. I just . . . I don't know. I guess I'm tired. You know."

"The entire island is tired, and it's not going to get any better," Josie stated flatly.

"Of course. Don't worry about me," Renee said, apparently getting a second wind. "I'll be back as quickly as possible."

"Good." As soon as she was alone, Josie leaned over the papers again. There was lots of interesting information here, including Cornell Hudson's various addresses in New York City, the location and phone number of his office, even a list of references—people who knew him well, women he was known to date regularly . . .

Josie gasped. She couldn't believe it. It wasn't possible. It couldn't be true. She read through the last list carefully.

Same name. Same address. Josie put the papers back on the desk.

Sam's mother had been dating Cornell Hudson—recently and regularly according to the information his daughters had supplied the police. Josie sat down. How did they know each other? Where had they met? Was it possible that the relationship was serious? Did Sam know?

The front door slammed, and she heard the tapping of high heels on the linoleum, accompanied by the clicking of untrimmed dog claws. Josie peered around the screen. The woman with the answer to her questions had just walked in the door. And Loki was with her.

"Josie?"

"Back here. I'm behind the screen, Carol."

"Oh, Josie, I'm so glad to see you. You and I really need to talk, dear."

"About Cornell Hudson?"

Carol was surprised but regained her aplomb with typical speed. "Yes, my dear, about Cornell Hudson and . . . and other things."

Josie wasn't particularly concerned about other things right now. "What about Cornell Hudson?"

"We have been . . . well, I guess the word is *involved*."

Sexually involved? The thought was so much in the front of her mind that, for a moment, Josie imagined she'd said it out loud. "Involved?" she repeated the word Carol had used.

"Why, yes. Certainly, you know I date many men. . . ."

"Yes, of course, but I guess I'm just surprised that you dated a man who ended up coming here and hiring me."

"But, my dear, I'm the reason he even came here. And, of course, I'm the reason he hired you. . . ."

"Are you saying you recommended Island Contracting?"

"Naturally! It was such a wonderful opportunity! I knew

it would really make your reputation to remodel that big old house! Everyone who walks up and down the beach knows the Point House! And word of mouth is so important, don't you think?"

"I . . ." Josie took a deep breath. This was Sam's mother, after all. "Island Contracting already has an excellent reputation—"

"Oh, please don't misunderstand. I know how proud you are of your company. How proud you deserve to be. You've done a wonderful job on many houses here. I know that. But Cornell Hudson is a mover and shaker, an important man in New York society. You could have gotten an international reputation working for him. Why, that house might have ended up on the cover of *Architectural Digest*!"

"Fame and fortune," Josie muttered.

"Exactly!" Carol beamed at her as though Josie had just said something profound. "Remodeling that house could have brought you fame and fortune."

"It's always tempting, of course. . . ," Josie said slowly.

She had a quick vision of what fame and fortune would be like—living in a penthouse in New York City, eating in the best restaurants, attending gallery openings, wearing fabulous clothes . . . It was the clothing thing that popped the bubble. To look good in those designer clothes, she was going to have to lose lots of weight, get her hair cut, go to manicurists. Ugh. Fame and fortune didn't work for her. Besides, if she lived in a penthouse, she certainly wouldn't have a landlady who cooked meals for her—meals as good as any she would find in New York City. Wasn't Sam always saying that very thing about Risa's cooking? And Josie would rather walk on the beach than go to any art gallery. Besides, if New York and fame and fortune were such a big deal, why had Sam left all that and moved here?

"... but I'm happy with the way things are now. Really. But thank you, Carol. I've always loved the Point House. Remodeling it was going to be one great job."

"What I keep wondering is, what is Cornell going to do now?"

Josie almost said *nothing*, instead she answered, "I don't know."

"I don't suppose there are any comparable houses on the island?"

"There's nothing like the Point House, but there are other wonderful homes. You know that."

"But Cornell always insists on the best. That's a thought. You are smart, Josie. With the Point House gone, what is the best house on the island?"

"I suppose one of those big ones on the beach—over on Bayberry Lane . . ."

"They're new. I mean, they probably wouldn't involve a major remodel, and I certainly don't want you to end up without work."

"You don't have to worry. Agatha has provided me with enough work for the rest of the year and then some."

"But fixing up storm damage just isn't what I was hoping for for you. . . ."

"Maybe you could convince Sam to do something dramatic when he rebuilds his store," Josie said, smiling.

Carol took her suggestion seriously. "What an interesting idea. There's that bar in New York where the wine is stored up in a tower and the wine steward has to take this little lift to collect it. Sam could have something like that. Or perhaps a really good architect could think of something even more interesting. The *Times* might do a story, and it certainly could be picked up by the glossies. . . . Maybe I should find Sammy and have a chat with him before he cleans up his place too much. . . ."

"But I wanted to talk to you," Josie cried.

"Of course, we haven't even discussed Tyler yet. Sam says he's attending a computer camp for gifted and talented young people. So wise of you to send him. It will make such a difference when he applies to college."

"It's not Tyler. I want to know more about Cornell Hudson. . . ."

"So he'll hire you to work on the next house he buys." Carol nodded seriously, a lock of hair falling across her forehead. Josie realized it was the first time in all the years she had known Carol that she had seen her hair either messy or unwashed. "I can tell you exactly the type of thing that will appeal to him," Carol assured her.

"Great. But I have to get working. If Mike Rodney comes back and it looks like I'm not working on his father's office, he'll have my as—He'll be furious!"

"The man is an ass," Carol easily spoke the word Josie had edited from her speech. "Where shall we go?"

Josie pointed out the way. "I'm going to start framing in a temporary room back there so Chief Rodney will have an office space while I work on the rest of this place."

"Can I help? I've really developed my biceps in the past few months."

"Thanks, but I think I can manage on my own. You tell me about Cornell Hudson. How did you two meet?"

"Oh, I'd seen him around for years. He's a big supporter of the arts in New York—you know, the ballet, opera—so I've seen him at various charity performances. He usually had a young girl on his arm. And, frankly, I don't relish that type of competition. So I didn't give him a thought romantically, and I was surprised when he called and asked me out to dinner."

"What about his wife? I mean, he has daughters—"

"His wife's been dead for years. I don't know anyone

who had met her. And I've never heard any of his daughters refer to her."

"You know his daughters!"

"Yes. Unfortunately."

Josie, bent over and sawing a two-by-four, was glad Carol couldn't see her smile. "I gather you don't like them?"

"Frankly, they're a little old to be depending on their father for support."

"Like those cars they drive," Josie said.

"Those cars are nothing. They're living in his apartments."

"Really?" Josie remembered the list of properties she'd heard about. "Maybe they're good investments or something."

"They probably are. Cornell isn't known for making bad investments. But he would make a lot more money if they paid him rent. Oh, I'm being foolish. He loves them to depend on him. It feeds his macho needs."

Josie frowned as a piece of wood fell to the floor. She wondered what Carol might be doing to "feed his macho needs."

"I'm sort of surprised you . . . ah, you like someone like that. I mean, you're so liberated and all."

"Oh, Josie, you darling thing. I'm dating Cornell, and I made sure he bought a house here on the island and then hired you to remodel it. But I don't have any deep feelings for the man. None at all. It's just a social thing."

"Oh, I didn't know. Really?"

"Really! So what else do you want to know?"

"What is his business?"

"Contracting. Cornell is Hudson Brothers Contracting. There's no brother."

"So why did he hire me instead of using his own company to do the work down here?"

"Oh, heavens, that's easy. He wanted a quality job and I, of course, assured him that you do quality work."

"But his own company—"

"Known for shoddy workmanship. Well, I don't suppose Cornell would put it like that, but that's the truth."

"You're kidding!"

"No, although I'm afraid I'm being a bit nasty. But I have friends who made the mistake of hiring Hudson Brothers. Their work was okay, but they had the slimiest men working in their apartments. It was terrible. And horribly expensive. I wasn't surprised at all when Cornell made a bunch of excuses about why he couldn't have his workers away from the city at this time of the year. So, naturally, I jumped in and told him all about you and Island Contracting. And I didn't really have to exaggerate all that much."

"Thank you," Josie said, remembering her manners. "Carol, when was the last time you saw Cornell Hudson?"

"Oh, I was hoping you wouldn't ask me that, Josie."

"Why?"

"Because Sammy seems to think that I came to the island just to help him clean up the damage."

"And you didn't?"

"I may have implied something like that when I saw him, but . . . well . . . but, in fact, I was on the island the entire day before Agatha."

"You were here? And you didn't call Sammy and let him know?"

"Josie, there are some things a son doesn't want to know about his mother."

NINETEEN

WAVE radio would like to announce . . .

JOSIE LOOKED UP to see who had turned off the radio and smiled. The police dispatcher was one of her favorite people on the island—as well as an unfailing source of information about everyone and everything. "Oh, I'm so glad it's you," Josie said.

"It's nice to be appreciated," Angie Clement answered, moving the radio off the console covered with buttons and a microphone, and sitting down on her only slightly damp chair. "But may I ask what you're doing?"

"Building a temporary office for Chief Rodney. Just two-by-fours and sheets of plastic. Once he has someplace to hang out, I'll get started on the rest of this work."

"Is it going to be soundproof?"

Josie squinted at the two walls she had nailed up. "I wasn't planning on it, but I could staple up insulation. It won't be pretty, but it will block some of the sound. Do you think the chief is worried about that?"

"I don't know about him, but it would be a real relief to everyone else in the building. The man is a paranoid pest. Although, frankly, he's easier to be around since Agatha passed through. The cleanup is keeping him busy."

"Then I'll just dash home at lunch time. There are a

couple of rolls of insulation in Risa's garage. I was going to lay them in her attic last winter and never got around to it. They'll do to give the chief—and everyone working out here—a little privacy."

"Thanks, Josie. He's driving me nuts. Over half the buildings on this island were damaged, there are people staying in shelters until they can find dry mattresses to put on their kids' beds, and he's panicked about what may have happened to that rich guy with the made-up name who bought the Point House."

"Cornell Hudson is a made-up name?"

"Josie, who would name a baby after a college?"

"What about that actress, Katherine Cornell?"

"That's a family name, besides Cornell Hudson's not an actor. Anyway, I'm probably wrong, and strange names just run in the family. Look what those awful daughters of his are named."

"I won't argue with you there," Josie said. She leaned against the dispatcher's desk and tried to look casual. "So I guess you've met them?"

"Oh, no, Josie. I know that expression. I've seen it before. You believe what the daughters are saying. You think their father was killed, and you're investigating, right?"

"No way! I'm just curious. And, if Cornell Hudson is around he—he owes me money," Josie explained, coming up with what she thought was a viable explanation.

"Oh, that is a real problem. Have you talked it over with his family? Those girls seem to have more than enough money. If they're convinced he's dead, maybe you can insist they begin to pay off his debts."

"That's an idea. I'd do it if I could find one of them."

"Just hang around here for an hour or two. They're always dashing in just to check on whether or not we've heard from their father . . . or found his body or something . . ."

"Did you get the impression that they really believe he's dead?"

"I have no idea what they believe, but it looks like one is coming in the door. Why don't you ask her yourself?"

"I think—I think I'd better get back to work," Josie said, turning back to a pile of supplies stacked in the corner of the room.

"Is Chief Rodney here? I'm looking for Chief Rodney."

"I'm afraid the chief is out on patrol. May I help you?"

"Well, can't you call him over that thing?" Pip waved to the console. There was still a small puddle of water on top of it.

"I'm waiting until it's drier before I plug it in."

"Then why are you sitting there?"

"I've been getting everything in place."

"There's power here?" Pip looked around.

"The police station has an emergency generator. But I understand the power on the island may be back any minute now."

"I hope it's soon. Candlelight is romantic, but I prefer real light for putting on makeup, and it would be heaven to use a blow dryer again." Pip ran her hands through her almost perfect hair and grimaced as though she had found something dreadful. When no one offered to let her plug in her personal appliance, she continued. "I told Father this was a horrible place to buy a house. Now if we were in the Hamptons, I could slip off to a day at Gurney's and be nice and relaxed." She smiled at the possibility and then looked back at the desk. "Well, just tell the chief I was in. I'm sure he'll be able to find me. It's not as though this is a big island, and I'm staying at the inn, of course."

"Of course," replied the dispatcher, but Pip had swept out the door without waiting for a reply.

"Why 'of course'?" Josie asked.

"It's the best place to stay on the island. Always has been. It was when my grandfather owned it. Back then, though, it was called the Sea Coast Inn, and it was more than a little run-down. Grandpa died, and Grannie couldn't handle it anymore. She sold it to a developer who tried to upgrade and then went bankrupt."

"I remember that, and then there was some sort of lawsuit that kept the place empty for years. I used to worry when Tyler was young that he and his friends would break in and play there. You know boys."

"Yup. It sure didn't add anything there in town. Still, I was sad to see it turned into something so different. But the new inn is definitely the best place in town. Grandpa would love it. Did you know those big white pines in front of the place were planted by him? . . . What's that expression on your face? Oh, no! They were damaged in the storm, weren't they?"

"Flattened."

"Oh, well, it's the least of it. As long as we all have our health . . . That's what my grandparents would say, and they'd be right."

"Can't argue with that," Josie said.

"You know, speaking of my grandparents, my grandmother always wanted my grandfather to buy the Point House. She thought it could be a wonderful inn."

"It was certainly big enough."

"Was that what Cornell Hudson was going to do?"

"Nope. He planned on his daughters and their families coming and staying. At least that was the design that I was going to work with." Josie looked up. "Did you hear something else?"

"No, although there are more than a few people on the island who don't understand why he bought here. His daughters don't seem to have anything good to say about the island. Always talking about fancier places."

"Did anyone ever hear him say anything negative?"

"Nope. And it was his nickel, right?"

Josie nodded. "His many, many nickels."

They had gotten back down to work when Beca walked in the door. "Has either of my sisters been in here recently?" she asked without wasting time on polite chitchat.

"Yes, in fact Pip was here just a few minutes ago looking for Chief Rodney," the dispatcher answered politely.

"I gather she didn't find him?"

"He hasn't been in all morning, but—"

"And have you called him over that thing?" Beca stared at the dispatcher's console.

"It doesn't work without electricity, and it can't be plugged in until it's dried out," Josie explained from her corner.

Beca glanced in her direction. "Who are you? Oh, you're Betty's friend. The carpenter."

Josie didn't even bother to answer.

"Do you have any idea where my sister went after leaving here?"

"To find your father, apparently."

Beca snorted. "Apparently, I will have to find my father myself." She spun around and left the building.

"Well, I've heard of leaving in a huff, but I think this is the first time I've actually seen it," the dispatcher said.

Josie giggled. "She does it so well. She must have had a lot of practice."

They had just gotten back to work when Win arrived. Win had struck Josie as the oldest and most mature of the sisters; her impression wasn't changed with this visit.

"Good morning," Win began politely, pushing her glasses up on her head. "I know you must all be busy, what with the storm and all, but I'm looking for my sisters. And they . . . well, they're looking for my father."

The dispatcher grinned broadly. "We know. They both got here before you. But I'm sorry to say no one's seen your father. At least not that I know of. The chief has the entire force looking, of course." She peered up at the woman. "I don't suppose you've heard from him."

Win sighed. "No, and I'm worried. You don't know my father, but you just have to believe that this is more than odd. It's unheard of. My father . . . well, if truth be known, he was a little possessive. Up until now, I don't think there has been a day in my life when I haven't heard from him in some way. Why, when he sent us to summer camp, he had little messages delivered from his office to each of us every day."

"I can only tell you that the police are looking for him."

"I know. And without power or water, and with all this cleanup going on, it certainly can't be easy."

Josie stood up. Win appeared to be the most intelligent of the sisters. She had a lot of questions to ask. Maybe this was the perfect opportunity. "You know, my truck's been acting up," she lied, "and now I need to go to . . . to the end of the island, and I was wondering if you could give me a lift."

"Oh, no problem." Win glanced down at the Rolex on her wrist. "And I'd better get going. I'm due to meet my husband at the house we're renting. At least I hope he's still coming down. Brad does not like roughing it without modern conveniences."

"Where is the house?" Josie asked.

"Eleventh Street. At the north end of the island . . . Oh, you said you were going to the end of the island and I just assumed—"

"The north end is where I was hoping you were going," Josie said. She would have accompanied this woman anywhere, but, in fact, north was convenient. She could always beg a ride back here from Sam.

"Then let's get going."

Ignoring the grin on the dispatcher's face, Josie followed Win outside to the large white Ford Expedition parked by the curb. "I—I'm afraid I'm dirty. I've been working," she added quickly, looking down at her clothing.

"Don't worry about it. This is our country car. It's always full of stuff like sandy sports equipment and compost for my garden."

"You have a garden down here?" Josie wiped off the seat of her pants and got into the car. It looked immaculate to her.

"Oh, no. I'm talking about our weekend place in Connecticut. We're just renting down here," Win explained, climbing into the driver's seat.

"You're renting a place on the island, and you already have a country home in Connecticut?" Apparently owning a lot of real estate was a family tradition.

"Yes, but it's only because Father bought that awful house and planned on spending the summer remodeling it." Win started the car as she spoke.

"You thought you should be around to help?" Josie suggested.

"I thought . . . well, the problem isn't really what I thought. It's my sisters. You see, I believe Father had every right to spend his money on whatever he wanted. He made it and he should have enjoyed spending it. But . . . well, my opinion isn't the majority one in the family."

"Your sisters don't agree?"

"My sisters disagree vehemently. They were totally

opposed to Father buying that house. They felt he was trying to cut them out of his life."

"I don't understand."

"You see we're a very close family. At least some of us are close."

"That's wonderful," Josie enthused.

"And we all live near each other. In New York City at first and now Pip is in Westchester, but that's because of the schools up there. Private school in the city is prohibitively expensive, and Pip has triplets so the tuition was tripled."

"Triplets? How old are they?"

"Eight. She has three eight-year-old boys—active boys."

Josie smiled, remembering Tyler at that age. "Eight years old! The island is perfect at that age. They'll be able to bike and run on the dunes, build sand castles, learn to body surf—"

"They're at camp. In the Adirondacks. I don't think Pip plans on them spending the summers here."

"Really, that's too bad. But, you know, I think their grandfather did. The remodeling plans were for four suites, and one had a large bunk room. It was going to be sensational. The bunk room was in the old attic and a circular stairway was being installed to join the two spaces together. The boys really would have loved it!"

"But Pip would have hated it. She didn't really want to come here at all. And to have her kids stomping around over her head all the time—well, that really would have been the limit. My sister is the only mother among us, but that doesn't mean she's maternal."

"But she loves her kids," Josie said. After all, she wasn't maternal, but she was nuts about Tyler.

"I doubt it, but she would never admit it. It might get

back to Father, and he was big on carrying on the Hudson name."

"But the boys—"

"Oh, they all have their father's last name. But each and every one carries Hudson as a middle name—even little Henry."

"Henry Hudson?"

"Henry Hudson Jamieson is the kid's complete name. But, as my father was always pointing out, they can drop the Jamieson when they grow up."

"How does their father feel about that?"

"Their father depends on my father's money, so he's learned to keep quiet about things that bother him."

"Oh. Your father is a very generous man, isn't he?"

Win hesitated, apparently needing to think about Josie's question before answering. "My father gave many things to his family members—that is, to the ones he believed were doing what he wished them to do."

Josie didn't know whether to ask another question or to shut up. She wanted to hear more about this subject. But Win seemed to feel she'd said enough, returning her concentration to her driving. They were almost at Eleventh Street when Josie got up the courage to ask the question she really wanted to ask.

"I don't know if you realize it," she began hesitantly, "but you keep referring to your father in the past tense. I was wondering—"

But Win answered before the question was finished. "I think he's dead, if you really want to know the truth." Josie heard the sadness in Win's voice. "And, since he was in wonderful health and no one has discovered his body, I am coming to the conclusion that he was killed. Probably by someone on this island."

TWENTY

WAVE radio, . . . the station
the island sings along to . . .

JOSIE STARED AT Win. The car's motor hummed, but the
radio could still be heard. "Someone on the island?"
she repeated.

"Who else?"

"Well, I think usually . . . I mean, isn't it true that
friends and relatives are the first suspects in a murder investigation?" Josie was hesitant. She really didn't want
this conversation to end. "Did he have friends here?
Maybe people he knew or worked with in New York?"

"Who would he know down here?" Win asked.

"I don't know, but he must know someone. I mean,
when people buy houses on the island, it's usually because
they know someone here, come to visit, like the area. On
the other hand, the Point House was advertised in the *New
York Times*, wasn't it?"

"It may have been. I don't remember seeing it."

"Did—does your father know other people on the
island?"

"Not that I know of . . . No, that's not true. He dated
someone who either lives down here . . . No, wait, I remember. This woman he dated has a relative who lives

170

here—year-round apparently." Win nodded. "You know, I should find out who that is. Beca might know. She and Father travel in the same social circles."

"But do you know the identity of the person your father is dating?" Josie asked, her fingers crossed. She hadn't realized this conversation might lead straight to Sam's mother. She really hadn't believed Carol's claim that she was the sole reason Cornell Hudson had bought the Point House. It seemed to be a remarkable thing for a man one was dating to do, and Carol was inclined to exaggerate her importance to those she dated.

Win answered slowly. "I may. There is this loud, tacky woman—I don't remember her name—something with an *S* or a *C*. Cheryl or Simone or Cynthia . . . Oh, well, it will come to me."

Josie sincerely hoped it wouldn't. "Maybe he just saw that ad in the paper."

"I don't think so. Now that you mention it, Father was looking forward to seeing this woman here—last weekend. I remember he told me about it. Even mentioned going out to eat together. Not that I was looking forward to the food available here—"

"We have some wonderful restaurants on the island," Josie protested.

"So call Zagat and tell them about it," Win suggested sarcastically. "This woman . . . You know, I think Chief Rodney should know about this woman."

Oh shit! "I don't think—I mean, with the storm and all, she probably didn't even come to the island. I was talking with some of the real-estate people, and they say that a lot of people changed their plans. . . ."

"If only Father had been one of those people. Oh, damn it!" She slammed on the brake to avoid hitting a small white VW Beetle. Josie heard the screech of the tires of the car behind them. Suddenly, they were in the middle of one of those rare island traffic jams—this one caused by a crane lifting a church steeple from where it had fallen into the road—across both lanes of traffic. Unfortunately, the crane seemed to have become tangled in some fallen electric and cable wires at the same time. Win glanced in her rearview mirror. A line of cars snaked behind them. "I guess we're stuck here for a while."

Josie thanked the stars and continued her questions. "Why wasn't he?"

"What do you mean?"

"Why wasn't he one of the people who stayed home when the storm was predicted?"

"You don't know Father. He's like that. He wouldn't let a storm keep him from doing what he wanted to do."

"What about you and your sisters? Why did you come?"

"Father. He called us all and insisted we be here."

"When?"

"When what?"

"When did he call?"

"I don't know about Beca and Pip, but he called me last Monday."

"Three days before you were to meet him here?"

"Yes. He said it was important and that my sisters were coming, too."

"Isn't that rather short notice? I mean, what about your jobs, and other obligations, and . . . and all?"

"My father never allowed those things to interfere with his wishes. When he called, he expected us to listen. I don't work these days—it was too difficult to combine my career with my husband's after we were married—so that's not a problem."

"So you really could just drop everything and come here?"

"We had been planning to come down next week anyway, and I asked Father if it was possible to put off the trip for a week. And I was actually giving a dinner party for some of my husband's colleagues this weekend. Canceling that was very embarrassing, I can tell you. And, of course, we were getting word of the storm every single time we turned on the television or the radio. I know Beca was really worried about driving down. She rarely leaves the city and doesn't like high-speed driving anyway, but the idea of hitting wind and rain had her in a panic. I think she came down early—right after Father called. And Pip always seems to have something to arrange. Even with her kids away for the summer, she has a list of obligations. Living in the suburbs seems to have complicated her life no end. And Ed—"

"Who's Ed?"

"Her husband. He's weird. I mean he's nice, but it's like he spent his whole life just waiting to move to suburbia and become involved. He coaches Little League, soccer, and hockey during the school year. And he's a deacon in their church. And he's on the Shade Tree Commission—whatever that is! And now Pip says he's planning on running for the Board of Education. He's never home, and their phone rings off the hook! It's terrible."

"What does he do? I mean, it sounds like he has lots of extra time," Josie said, wondering if Pip and Ed needed money more than the other sisters.

"He's a dentist. Has his own practice. But he doesn't practice all that much anymore. He's years older than my sister and seems to be going through some sort of second childhood by getting involved with those boys of his."

"It sounds like your sister and her husband would have a difficult time getting away at the drop of a hat."

"Of course they do. We all do. But my father was not interested in hearing any of that. He wanted me here, and I came."

"And your husband came with you?"

"No, my husband stayed home to take the people we had invited to dinner at our home out to a very expensive restaurant instead. They were eating the best French food in the world outside of Paris while I was sitting in that gym stinking from years and years of sweat and filthy sneakers."

"That must have been hard for you," Josie said. "But . . . but why did your father want you all here, anyway?"

"Who knows? Father wasn't in the habit of explaining. He just demanded and expected us to meet those demands."

"I know what you mean," Josie said sincerely. "My parents and I didn't get along for a long time. We didn't even speak for over fifteen years—"

"You don't know at all what I mean," Win interrupted bitterly. "Father and I spoke almost daily. And we did get along," she added. "I don't want you to get the wrong impression. I did what my father asked me to do out of love."

Josie wondered if Win loved her father or his money, but she knew she was treading on dangerous ground, and she really hoped Win would keep talking. "That's good of you," was all she said.

"I think so. My husband isn't always so understanding, unfortunately." She bit her crimson lips and stared out at the confusion on the road. The steeple was careening to the south and threatening to knock the cross off the top of the manse to the right of the church. Dozens of men were following its path, holding their arms up in the air as if trying to wave it in the correct direction.

"That must be difficult for you when he doesn't understand."

"Not really. I can manage him when necessary."

Win was silent and Josie wondered if Win's husband, like Pip's, put up with a lot because Cornell Hudson supported him. Before she could think of how to determine if that was true, Win had opened her door and was jumping out of the Expedition. "I'm going to see if that cop knows where Chief Rodney is," she explained.

Josie frowned. Well, she couldn't just sit here. She got out of the car, too, and followed Win toward the commotion. She didn't see any policemen, but apparently the island's lifeguards had been drafted to help with traffic control. In their navy windbreakers and matching Bermuda shorts, she wasn't surprised that Win had mistaken them for policemen. It was possible, she realized, that they might know where Chief Rodney was located. But, as much as Win wanted to find him, Josie wanted to avoid him.

Win chose the best-looking young man available to talk to, and as Josie watched, he pointed toward the church. Chief Rodney was standing at the bottom of the bell tower, arms crossed, ready to do whatever needed to be done as long as it didn't involve getting dirty or working too hard.

Josie turned her back on the chief and the crowd, and walked off. Win was busy and Josie had things to do. Traffic had been stopped in both directions. She didn't know how long it would take to find a friendly face traveling back to the police station, but she might as well try. Her best bet, she decided, was to cut through yards and try another road. Thankful that her normal working attire included heavy work boots, she started off.

The day was turning out to be hot, and the scent of dead fish rose from the ground. The ocean had washed over the island at this point leaving behind piles of sea-weed, shells, minnows, and . . . and something else, she realized, looking down.

"The sewer's backed up," commented a young woman, wearing high rubber boots and seeing what Josie was looking at. "Stuff came right out of the drains around here."

"Yuck!" Josie exclaimed.

"You think it's bad out here, you should see it inside our house. My father has had us going down to the bay and getting buckets of clean water to sluice it out ever since we got back." Josie realized she was carrying two large plastic buckets.

"How much more do you have to do?"

"Actually, we've been at it for two days now, and things are looking pretty good. Rumor has it that power should be on by nightfall. I can't wait! Well, gotta go!" She turned off toward the bay, and Josie continued on to Ocean Drive.

Traffic was moving slowly here, drivers and passengers alike pointing and staring at the worst of the damage. Josie finally spotted a familiar face and yelled.

"Basil! Basil! Over here!"

Basil Tilby saw her, waved, and turned his turquoise Jeep Ranger around to pick her up. "I gather you need a ride?" He pulled the boxes from the passenger's seat as he spoke.

"Yes, please!" Josie said, getting in.

"These are going to have to go in your lap," Basil explained, passing the boxes back to her.

"No problem," Josie said, grasping the Styrofoam boxes to her chest.

"Where do you want to go?"

"I need to get back to the police station."

"I can take you there, but first I have to drop this stuff

off at the restaurant. We're going to be open for dinner tonight—with a limited menu—and they need this."

"What is it?" Josie asked. She was beginning to feel a chill from the boxes.

"Food. Shipped from New York City this morning. I have vegetables and some staples coming in this afternoon. I drove to the airport to pick the stuff up myself. Risa inspired me. We've built a temporary grill in the parking lot of the bank next door to the Gull's Perch. I hope the smoke draws in customers. I can't keep this stuff overnight without refrigeration."

"I just talked to a young woman who says she heard the island would have power by tonight."

"Rumor or fact?"

"I don't know."

"Does she work for the power company?"

"I don't believe so."

"Rumor."

"So you don't think it's true."

"I wouldn't depend on it. I don't know what you've been hearing, but I've been told at least a dozen times that power was going to be restored momentarily, that there have been fires blazing up from the south, that another storm is coming in from the north, that there was looting all night long downtown and that looters had been shot by the new owner of the Island Inn."

"Not true?"

"Not even slightly true. Access to the island is still limited at night, and during the day, everyone is too busy cleaning up to do any looting."

"I keep hearing sirens, though."

"Yeah, so do I, but I don't think they have anything to do with looting. The man who's the wine steward at the Sea Gull stopped by this morning. He's a paramedic with the ambulance corps. He says the emergency room of the hospital has been hopping."

"Why?"

"This cleanup is hard work. Yesterday afternoon there were three heart attacks, two chain-saw accidents—"

"How awful!"

"Can't say I disagree with you there."

"Anything else?"

"So many sprained ankles from walking on slippery surfaces that they were passing out Ace bandages and instructions in RICE care, and then sending people home without bothering to X-ray them. And, of course, lots of broken bones."

"What is RICE?"

"Rest, ice, compression, elevate."

"Oh, yeah. I remember."

"Of course, the really interesting thing is that the blond brigade—"

"Who?"

"Cornell Hudson's daughters."

"What about them?"

"Well, apparently they haven't even called the emergency room. They've been all over the island talking about their missing father. I don't know about you, but I think it's a bit strange that they haven't even checked in with the emergency room."

"Are you sure?"

"I asked about it particularly."

Josie didn't say anything. But she did wonder why Basil was so interested.

TWENTY-ONE

WAVE radio is proud to provide a lost and found service for all the cool dudes on the island. So anyone looking for a cool dude, call . . .

J OSIE LOOKED AT Basil suspiciously. "Why?"
"I understood you were interested in finding out exactly where Mr. Hudson has gone."

"Yes, I am. He's an important client."

"And he's dead."

"Well, I don't . . ." Josie glanced over at Basil. She realized he wasn't fooling around. "How do you know he's dead?'

"I saw him."

"On his living-room floor?"

"On his living-room floor?" Now it was Basil's turn to look surprised. "He was in his house when you saw him?"

Josie nodded.

"And he was dead?"

"Yes."

"You're sure?"

"I really think so," Josie answered. "Are you sure he was dead when you saw him?"

"Yes. When did you see him?"

"Right before I left the island. The afternoon Agatha struck."

"What was he doing in his house?" Basil asked.

"I just told you. He was in the living room. And he wasn't doing anything. He was dead. He was just lying there."

Basil put his foot on the brake and turned to look at her. "How was he lying? On his back or his front?"

"I . . . What do you mean?"

"I mean was he lying on his stomach or on his back?"

"Well, actually on his side . . ." She thought about it for a moment. "Really. Not on his stomach or on his back. On his side."

"Which side?"

"Basil—"

"Think, Josie, it might be important. Which side?"

She did as he asked and thought. "I guess he was on his ri—no, his left side."

"You're sure?"

"Yes. I was standing in the doorway, and he was facing me. And his feet were to the left and his head to the right. I'm sure. He was on his left side."

"And how close did you get to him?"

"About fifteen . . . twenty feet . . ."

"Then how did you know he was dead?"

"His head was tilted down in this odd position— unnatural. He wasn't moving. He wasn't breathing." She stopped. "How many ways do you want?"

"Josie, I've got to get this food to the restaurant so the chef can start work. And I know this isn't making sense to you, but we have to talk."

"You're right. We do. Basil, when did you see Cornell Hudson?"

"The same day you did. But about six hours earlier."

"Six hours earlier? And why was he still lying there for me to find him?"

"Josie, he wasn't in his house when I saw him. He was in the dunes."

"And you didn't tell anyone that you'd found him?" Josie asked.

"No. Of course, you're wondering why . . ."

"Well . . ." Josie knew she wasn't in a position to criticize.

"Look, we're almost at the restaurant. Let me drop this stuff off, give a few instructions to the chef, and then I'll drive you to the police station. We can talk on the way."

"Okay, but there is one thing I have to know right away."

"What?"

"Was there something wound around Cornell Hudson's neck when you saw him?"

"No."

"You're sure?"

"Positive. I was as close to him as I am to you."

"Then how was he killed?" Josie asked as they pulled up in front of the Gull's Perch.

"He was shot," Basil said quietly, and then smiled at the young woman who was waiting in the open doorway of the restaurant.

"Sh—"

"We'll talk about it later," Basil insisted. "First, I hope you'll help me unload this stuff. We'll be able to get going more quickly—"

"Great!" Josie removed the box from her lap and handed it to the woman who came out to the Jeep.

Basil was identifying the boxes as he unloaded them. "Tuna. Scallops, lovely fresh bay scallops. Blue crab, cleaned this morning. Swordfish straight from Gloucester. Mussels. Some of the smallest, freshest clams you'll see all summer. Spinach. Carrots. Baby beets. New potatoes. Cherry tomatoes, red and yellow. Patty pan squash. Lots of lovely leaf lettuce. Think you can do anything with this?"

"Of course." The young woman was staring at the bounty spread around her feet.

"I knew you could, and I'd like to help out," Basil said. "But I have to drive Josie back to her other job right now. We can talk when I return. This should only take a few minutes."

"Josie! Wait! I need to talk to you!" The voice came from above. Josie looked up and saw Renee standing on the roof. "Josie, just a few minutes. I need some help."

Josie glanced at Basil.

"Talk to her. I can always spend some time in the kitchen. She's a good worker, by the way. I hope you can spare her to work on my other places."

"I'm glad to hear that. She's a little more artistic than most carpenters."

"You're absolutely right!" Basil was enthusiastic. "She has an eye. It's hard to believe she hasn't had any professional training."

"She has. She's a licensed carpenter. Where's the ladder?"

"Around back. I'll be in the kitchen when you're done." Josie nodded and trotted off. "Renee?"

"I'm here." Renee jumped off the ladder as Josie rounded the corner.

"I'm in a hurry, Renee. What do you need?"

"He . . . Basil wants me to do more than just keep the weather out. He's looking for restoration of the ceiling and some major work on the back wall of the women's room."

"What is he going to do about rest rooms?" Josie asked, interested.

"He rented two of those portable johns—like you see at weddings."

"And work sites," Josie added.

"Oh, of course."

"Look, do whatever Basil asks. If I need you to work on something else, you can stop here and move on."

"Great. You seemed busy, but I just wanted to check with you before I made a mistake."

"That's fine. But I do have to get going."

"No problem." Renee had stepped up on the bottom rung of the ladder before Josie turned the corner.

Basil was in the kitchen, looking into a pot simmering over one of six Weber grills set up in the middle of the room.

"Hey, this is great," Josie said enthusiastically.

"Where's a—? "Basil looked around and then grabbed a large Pyrex bowl. He filled it from the pot and passed it to Josie. "Try this."

She did. "Fabulous! This is the best chowder I've ever had!"

"When things settle down, you and Sam must come to dinner again. The rest of this woman's repertoire is exquisite. This is just a sample."

"It is wonderful," Josie assured the chef, who was busy cutting the tuna into thin slices. The young woman smiled.

"We'd better get going."

"Of course. Just let me finish this," Josie said, shoveling chowder into her mouth.

"Take it with you," Basil insisted, edging Josie toward the kitchen door.

"I will. Bye!" She waved back at the kitchen staff, most of whom were too busy to respond.

"Okay," Basil said, as he started up the Jeep again. "Now we need to talk. It's not far to the police station. Do we need to stop on the way, or is there any place private there?"

"There's no place private there. And I don't want to be accidentally overheard by either of the Rodneys."

"No, definitely not. So where can we talk?"

"Why not stop at my office? I can always make up some reason why I have to be there, and we'll be alone."

Basil turned the Jeep, and they were at Island Contracting's office in less than five minutes.

"This is amazing. You had very little damage here," Basil commented, parking next to the curb and getting out.

"I can't tell you how sorry I am about your house," Josie said, suddenly remembering his loss.

"We'll talk about fixing that up later," he said, following her up the walk to the building.

They didn't say anything until they were alone together inside the office; then Josie burst out, "I can't believe you saw him earlier in the dunes . . . that he was dead . . . that—"

"Josie, sit down, and I'll tell you everything. About that day. And about my past."

"Your past?"

"Sit."

She did, and he began to speak immediately. "You know that I go for a walk on the beach almost every morning. It helps clear my head. I plan for the day. I used to see Betty when she was running. There are still lots of runners, but none as beautiful or cheerful as Betty was." Basil paced back and forth across the small space as he spoke. "Anyway, I start from one of the restaurants usually and then cut in through the dunes, hit the road, and circle back. That morning . . . That morning I walked in the dunes in front of the Point House. I . . . ." He stopped talking and looked out the window at a truck full of teenage girls careering down the street. "If I'm going to tell you this, I'd better be honest from the beginning. I went to the Point House hoping to see Cornell Hudson. I'd been walking by there ever since I'd been told the identity of the new owner. I was hoping to run into him."

"Why?"

"I'll explain in a few minutes. Let me tell you about that day first."

"Whatever you want." It was obvious that Basil was suffering just by retelling the tale of that day. Josie didn't want to make things more difficult for him.

"Well, as I said, that morning I was getting exercise and hoping to run into Cornell Hudson, so I cut through the dunes right in front of his house. And there he was lying in the dunes. He was dead."

"Are you positive he wasn't strangled?" Josie asked, thinking Basil must have been mistaken.

"I told you. He was shot."

"Are you sure? I didn't see any wound."

"I've been thinking about that. You said Cornell was facing you, lying on his left side, right?"

"Yes. But he was strangled. I'm sure of it. There was . . . something tied around his neck."

"That may be true when you saw him, but he definitely was shot earlier. You said you weren't terribly close to him."

"Close enough," Josie muttered.

"But you stayed away. You didn't walk around him."

"No. I couldn't. And Chief Rodney came in then, so—"

"What? Chief Rodney knows about this?"

"No! He doesn't. I rushed him out of there. That's why I didn't get any closer. Well, one of the reasons."

"You were alone. No one else saw him."

"Not unless someone came in after I left . . . But, Basil, you haven't finished. You said he was shot. Where?"

"In the back of his neck. I was closer to him than I am to you. I saw the hole. Believe me, he was shot. And he was dead. And when I saw him, there wasn't anything around his neck except for his shirt collar."

"Was he bloody? I didn't see any blood."

"There was some blood around the wound, but not a lot. He wasn't a mess or anything."

"Did you touch him?"

"Yes. He was lying facedown. The first thing I did was roll him over. I wanted to check his pulse to see if he was breathing."

"And he wasn't?"

"No. His face was covered with sand. I don't know how long he'd been lying there." Basil stopped and thought for a minute. "Actually, his body wasn't cold. You have more experience with this type of thing, Josie. How long would it be after he was killed that he began to—uh, cool off?"

"I haven't the foggiest."

"I've read a lot of mystery novels, but I don't remember what they have to say on the subject either," Basil admitted. "Anyway, I realized immediately that he was dead. And . . . and then I walked away."

"Basil . . ." Josie didn't know what more to say.

"I know. I know what you're thinking. You think I should have reported the murder immediately. I should have called the police."

What could she say? It wasn't as though she had done that either.

TWENTY-TWO

The island police force would like us to remind our listeners of the dangers of walking barefoot at this time . . .

"**W**HY?"

"Why what?"

Josie looked up at Basil. She had known him for years. He was sophisticated. He was educated. He intimidated her. And he had done the same stupid thing she had done. "Why did you leave him there and . . ."

"And run away? Go ahead, Josie, say it. That's just what I did. I ran away."

"Did someone else come along?"

"Apparently someone did later—the person who moved him into the house. But no, Josie, I didn't see anyone else. I ran because Cornell Hudson was murdered, and I was afraid I'd become the primary suspect."

"Because you found him?"

"Because I hated him. With good reason," Basil added, seeing the surprised expression on Josie's face.

"How long have you known him?"

"We'd never actually met, but I've known of him for a while. In fact, Cornell Hudson is the reason I came to the island. It's possible, as things have worked out, that you

187

could say I should thank him. But, when I left New York, I didn't feel like that." He took a deep breath. "Do you remember when I came to the island?"

Josie smiled.

"I can see you do."

"You have to admit you stood out. I mean most of the islanders—at least the year-rounders—are more conservative than you are. And you were a new concept on the island."

"You mean that I'm gay."

Josie laughed out loud. "No. You certainly weren't the first gay man on this island. I meant that you were—are—more flamboyant than most. Look at the way you dress. I don't think I've ever seen you in jeans," she added, looking down at his suede—They were suede, weren't they?—slacks.

"Not true. Remember last New Year's Eve? I wore jeans to Sam's party."

"If they're covered with sequins and embroidery, they move right out of the jeans class, as far as I'm concerned," she answered. "But you were going to tell me why you came here, and what Cornell Hudson had to do with it."

"Well, you know I was in the restaurant business in New York."

"You once said you started as a chef—"

"Part of the Basil Tilby myth. I started as a bottle washer in a filthy off-Broadway Chinese place. It catered to people coming in from the suburbs who thought tacky red silk walls and Moo Shu duck were the height of sophistication. But I didn't stay there long. I worked my way up to chef in an excellent steak house on the East Side. But, as much as I like food, I don't really enjoy cooking. It's the presentation I love—the restaurant itself, the decor, the style. This was the beginning of all that wealth in the eighties, and there was lots of interest in eating in exceptional restaurants. I was savvy enough to know it was time to get in on the boom, but I didn't have the cash. That's where Cornell Hudson comes into the picture, although at the time I thought the money was coming from a restaurant supply house."

"The supply house was a front for Cornell Hudson?"

"Exactly. Unfortunately, I was too stupid to see the conditions that went along with it. . . . No, that's not true. I lied to myself back then, but I'm not going to keep doing it now. I knew damn well that I wasn't being given money just to help out. I was given cash and expected to make a healthy—and legal—profit."

"Isn't that money laundering?"

"Yes!"

"Is it legal?"

"Nope. But I wanted to start my own restaurant, and I did. I was young and absolutely confident in myself. So when my first place failed, I was convinced that the only thing to do was borrow more money, start over again, and open another bigger, better restaurant."

"And Cornell Hudson under the guise of the restaurant supply house was willing to lend you more money?"

"Yes. He practically threw the stuff at me. I thought it was amazing."

"But, wait a second. I was talking to—" Josie stopped for a moment, remembering she had assured the real-estate agent that she would not repeat what she had been told about the credit check, but as long as she didn't identify her source. . . "—to someone here in town who checked out Cornell Hudson. Supposedly, he's loaded and has a sensational credit rating."

"He probably had. But that doesn't mean he didn't also

do shady deals hoping to accumulate even more money—and in cash."

"But why would he need more money? I mean, why take a risk doing something illegal for money when, apparently, he didn't need it?"

"Who knows? Maybe he was the type of person who never thought there was enough money. Maybe he loved making money for the sake of making money. Maybe he liked living on the edge and doing illegal things."

"Why do you think he did it?"

"You know, Josie, I'm not sure. I came to hate that man. And hating someone is like loving someone in one way—it destroys your judgment. I simply can't be rational enough when thinking about him to make an accurate guess."

It made sense to Josie. "What happened next?" she asked.

"I owed money, and lots of it."

"And your restaurant wasn't making money?"

"It was turning a profit—barely—but I didn't have enough money to give back anything like what he wanted."

"So you were run out of town?"

"No, I was told I had two choices. I could either close the restaurant and sell everything and still owe a fortune. Or I could keep the place open and hope it became successful enough to allow me to repay what I owed. I had heard a rumor that I was going to get a good review in the *New York Times*. I knew what I was doing was illegal, but I just couldn't pass up that opportunity."

"You did what you were asked to do."

"Yes. And I did get that good review in the *Times*—an excellent review, really. I was on my way, or I would have been if the police hadn't gotten involved."

"You were caught?"

"And arrested and convicted and put in prison for almost three years."

"Basil . . ." In shock, Josie didn't know what to say.

"It was dreadful. I did wear jeans there, Josie." There was a crooked smile on Basil's face.

"Three years . . ."

"Three very long years. And when I got out, I came to the island to start my life over."

"But what about Cornell Hudson? Did he go to prison, too?"

"No. No one ever knew he was involved as far as I know. . . ."

"Why didn't you tell the police? Why did you—?" She paused, searching for the correct term. "Why did you take the fall yourself?"

"It wasn't quite like that. You see, everyone—and I mean everyone—I was involved with disappeared when the police started making inquiries. The restaurant supply house had existed only on paper. It was easy for it to vanish."

"What about Cornell Hudson?"

"I didn't know he was behind all the money at that time. I'm not sure I'd ever heard his name back then."

"I don't understand. Didn't the police look for the person responsible for giving you the money?"

"They claimed to. But there wasn't even a paper trail, at least none that anyone could find at the time."

"Did you investigate?"

"It turned out that all the money I had in the business was illegal. I had nothing. Nothing at all. I couldn't pay for anyone to investigate. I couldn't even pay for a lawyer. I had a public defender who couldn't spare any time to look into anything."

"So you were the only person arrested?"

"Yes. I had done all the bookkeeping for the restaurant. I had handled all the money. There was no one else."

"So how do you know about Cornell Hudson?"

"I didn't for years and years. I got out of prison and came here. I had a bit of good luck while I was in prison. An aunt of mine died. In my family, it had always been rumored that she had money, and it turned out that she did. She and I hadn't spoken in years and years. She not only disapproved of my lifestyle, she didn't want anyone to know any relative of hers had been in prison. So I was shocked when she left me money—not a fortune. I have cousins and they, rightly, were provided for first. But I had enough money to buy my little house here and start my first restaurant."

"That place on the boardwalk. What was it called?"

"Aunt Annie's. That was her name. I thought it was appropriate to name it after her. And it was a simple place— fried fish, chowders, homemade desserts with lots of whipped cream—"

"I loved it there," Josie said sincerely. "Why did you close it down?'

"It wasn't the kind of restaurant I wanted to run. I thought the island was sophisticated enough to support something more interesting. But I didn't have enough money then to open a second restaurant while the first was operating. I sold Aunt Annie's to a man who wanted to open an ice cream shop, and I used the proceeds to open the Gull. But I didn't have enough money to find out who was responsible for putting me in prison."

"But you did eventually find out."

"Yes. It cost a fortune. Not quite as much as Cornell Hudson had given me in dirty loans, but a hell of a lot."

"How did you do it?"

"I hired private investigators—more than a few, in fact."

"And then you put together what they said—?"

"Nope. In fact, most of the money I spent on them was completely wasted. I don't know if they were incompetent or if Cornell Hudson had simply managed to hide any trail from the money to him, but I didn't get anywhere until I happened on a man who had retired from the NYPD. He said Cornell Hudson's name had come up more than once in their official investigations of untraceable money over the years. It took a long time, but about a year ago, I was satisfied that Cornell Hudson had been behind the scam that put me in prison."

"What happened then?"

"Nothing."

"Nothing? You didn't go to New York City and confront him?"

"No."

"You didn't contact him?"

"No. I know it sounds odd. It was odd. I'd spent lots of money to find out who had come close to ruining my life. But once I knew, it didn't matter anymore. Well, that's not quite true. If it had been true, I probably wouldn't have been so upset when I heard he'd bought the Point House."

"What did you do?"

"Well, I didn't fly up in a rage and vow revenge, but I wasn't thrilled either. I wanted my past to stay in the past, frankly."

"I don't blame you! But I'd . . . well, I'd probably do just what you said you didn't. I think I'd want revenge."

"I was curious. I wanted to see him, true. But I knew there was nothing to be gained by confronting him. So I didn't say anything to anyone. I didn't even know if he would recognize me if he saw me—or even heard my name."

"But you said you were walking in the dunes. You said you were looking for him whe-when you found him."

"I was. You see, once I knew he might be nearby . . . on the island . . . I just couldn't resist."

TWENTY-THREE

WAVE radio has more announcements. . . .

JOSIE LOOKED AT him, astounded. "You mean you couldn't resist going to see him. Right?"

Basil smiled. "That's exactly what I meant."

"Did anyone else know how you felt about Cornell Hudson?"

"No one. I would have had to explain about my past and I didn't want to do that. Well, that's not actually true. I wouldn't have minded telling anyone what a crummy shit Cornell Hudson is. But I didn't want to talk about my involvement with him. I don't feel that knowledge of my years in prison would enhance my image."

"Your friends . . ."

"I know what you're going to say. You think my friends would understand. And I agree. Frankly, I'll be relieved when my friends know. I've had to invent more than a few stories to account for those three years—and to explain why I came to the island instead of staying in New York. I think Sam suspects something, though. We were once talking about his old job and how he felt about putting people in prison who were one-time offenders, who had gotten involved in something illegal almost accidentally, and I became a bit impassioned, I'm afraid."

"Sam would understand if he knew the entire story," Josie said, and then wondered if he would. Until retiring and coming to the island a few years ago, Sam had made his living prosecuting people who broke the law. And Basil had just admitted to breaking the law.

"Maybe. And I can live with whatever he thinks. But I can't live with going back to prison again. Prison is not a good thing for anyone. And, for me . . ." He shrugged and said nothing else.

"You think if your connection to Cornell Hudson comes out, you'll be suspected of his murder."

"I certainly think it's more than possible."

Josie turned and looked out the window at the bay. People were traveling in boats, collecting flotsam from the damaged piers and homes. It was hard work, but everyone seemed to be almost cheerful. Maybe these people were just grateful the storm hadn't been worse. Maybe they were glad to be alive. Unlike Cornell Hudson.

"It doesn't make sense," she said, turning back to Basil.

"What doesn't?"

"Look, you found the body right after he had been killed, right?"

"I think so. Certainly he hadn't begun to get stiff yet, and he was fairly warm. It's summer, but cool in the morning in the dunes—"

Josie felt herself becoming slightly ill. "I really don't want to think about that—"

"I'm sorry. What were you going to say?"

"Why was he moved?"

Basil reached over and took her hands in his. "Thank you, Josie."

She was astounded. "For what?"

"For never even thinking that I moved the body."

"Oh, Basil, I know you wouldn't have done that."

"So I thank you. And your question is the big one—why was he moved? Why not just leave him in the dunes until someone finds him?"

"Was he on one of the paths?" Josie asked.

"Not right on the path. Nearby."

"Could you have passed by without seeing him?"

"Yes. Of course. Why?"

"Maybe," Josie began slowly. "Maybe he was moved so that he would be found. Maybe whoever killed him wanted him to be found. I mean, he was in the house, but how was anyone to know that the house would be washed away."

"True." Basil looked serious. "And you said you didn't see the bullet wound, right?"

"No, I didn't, but whoever moved the body had no way of knowing I wouldn't get closer."

"That's true. In fact, the first thing anyone would do naturally when seeing a dead body on the floor would be to walk closer—"

"Which is exactly what I would have done if Chief Rodney hadn't come in behind me."

"You didn't want the chief to jump to the wrong conclusion."

"Exactly. When it comes to murder, he's always arresting the wrong person."

"Why was Chief Rodney there anyway?"

"The mandatory evacuation was in effect. I guess he saw my truck and decided to make trouble for me."

"What about Cornell Hudson? Where was his car?"

"I—I have no idea. One of his daughter's cars was in the driveway when I got there, but not when I left."

"Maybe she drove him there earlier in the day."

Josie considered the idea. That car had been bothering her ever since she found Cornell Hudson. "Maybe. I mean, that's what I had thought. But you found him earlier. And that raises other questions. Why was he at the house so early—?"

"Couldn't he have spent the night?"

"It's possible, but not likely. Very little furniture was there, but there were a few broken-down beds with old mattresses full of mildew. Still, I can't imagine him sleeping there. Cornell Hudson strikes me as a man who likes to be comfortable."

"We could check at the inn. If he didn't spend the night in his own house, he probably spent it there."

"Maybe he spent the night with someone else. Someone he took for a walk in the dunes early in the morning. Someone who killed him. A woman, maybe. Someone he brought from New York. Someone he's dating—"

"Oh, Basil, don't say that!"

"Why not?"

"He's dating Sam's mother."

"He's . . . How the hell would Cornell Hudson even know Sam's mother?"

"They met, they date. I don't know what else to say."

"Does Sam know?"

"Maybe. Carol told me that she's the reason Cornell Hudson bought property here—and the reason he hired me to remodel his house."

Basil put his elegant fingers together and rested his forehead against them. "Josie, this is a true mess."

"A mess? You want a mess, just come on down to the police station. There's a mess there like you've never seen. A mess that this young woman is supposed to be cleaning up, only she ain't there, and when I come looking for her I find her here schmoozing with friends."

Chief Rodney had made one of his infamous entrances.

"I needed to come here to pick up some stuff," Josie improvised an excuse. "I needed a good-size level," she added, spying one sitting on top of her file cabinets. "You don't want your new walls to tilt this way and that, do you?"

"What I want is for you to . . . Well, son of a bitch! It's about time!" he said as the lights began to flash on and off.

"Oh, well, it means they're working on them. We'll probably have power soon," Josie said.

Basil stood up. "That means I have to get back to the restaurant ASAP."

"Go ahead. The chief can drive me back to the station," Josie suggested.

"The squad car is not a taxi, Miss Pigeon."

"Good thing. Because I can't afford to pay for the ride," Josie wisecracked, starting for the door.

"Just one thing, Miss Pigeon."

"What, Chief Rodney?"

"You seem to be forgetting what you came here for."

"What?" Josie looked around the room.

Basil came to her aid. "Your level," he said, handing it to her. "You need this, remember?"

"Of course. I . . . Thank you." She hurried out the door. The two men followed. Neither was smiling.

By the time Josie and the chief arrived at the station, electricity had been restored to the island.

And the dispatcher's console was buzzing, beeping, and flashing. "Chief, there are some things here you might wanna know about," she said, looking up as they walked in the door.

"I'll get back to work," Josie said, hurrying to the rear of the room. But her pace slowed when she heard the word *body*.

". . . caught on the pier. They say they've got it stabilized, but they're gonna wait until low tide to bring it in. Too much junk in the water. No one wants to go wading and end up with a chunk of metal in their foot."

"Anyone have any idea who it is?" Chief Rodney asked, sounding irritated.

"They say it's a man. But that's all. Oh, and that there's something odd tied around his neck. No one can tell what it is, but maybe whatever it is will help identify him."

"Yeah, and maybe whatever it is got tangled around him as he was floating out in the ocean."

"That's right!" Josie chimed in enthusiastically.

"What?"

"I—I was just talking to myself."

"You're not supposed to be talking, Miss Pigeon. You're supposed to be working."

"Josie suggested insulating the walls around your temporary office, Chief. She thought you might want some privacy."

Josie looked gratefully at the dispatcher. "It should be walled in by this evening," she added.

"Woulda been walled in earlier if you hadn't decided to hang out with your pansy friend."

Josie opened and closed her mouth a few times, then decided not to waste her breath, and turned around. When she picked up the hammer, she found herself using a bit more force than necessary to sister some two-by-fours. Not that she was surprised by the chief's prejudice. But it made her see that Basil's worries were not unfounded. Fortunately the dispatcher's two-way radio continued to squawk, and someone on the other end demanded Chief Rodney's attention.

"Goddamn," he shouted, striding toward the doorway. "I keep telling those kids to get off the street. They need a permit to sell things like that. But do they listen to me? No, goddamn, I'll make them listen."

"What is he so upset about?" Josie asked, wondering what could attract more of the chief's attention than an unknown and possibly strangled dead body floating in the water.

The dispatcher was smiling. "Kids."

"Kids?"

"Yeah, there are kids all over the island selling 'I Survived Hurricane Agatha' T-shirts. They don't have the proper permits, and that's the type of thing that drives the chief nuts."

"I'm not crazy about it either. Oh, I don't care if they have permits or not. I just don't think it's right to be making money from a natural tragedy."

The dispatcher shrugged. "Seems innocuous enough to me. Besides, that storm might as well have brought some good to someone. . . . Josie, where are you going?"

"I have to see to something."

"What will I tell Chief Rodney if he returns and doesn't find you here?"

"Just tell him I needed to go get something."

"You know the chief. He'll ask what you needed."

"I don't know. Make something up. Any answer will do—just as long as it's not a new T-shirt or a large level."

TWENTY-FOUR

. . . Well, boys and girls, and old folks, too, WAVE radio is back. Thought we were goners for a while there, didn't you? Nope. Like rotten fish, we float to the surface. You can't get rid of us. So let's hear some oldies that aren't so golden. . . .

"DO YOU RECOGNIZE him?"

"Nope. Looks like an old geezer though. Any of the fishermen lost when Agatha hit?"

"Maybe he floated down from up north. I heard the storm hit Cape Cod worse than here."

"Nah. I'll bet he's a tourist. Look at the label on his shirt. That hanging sheep means the guy got it at Brooks Brothers. Not many fishermen shopping at Brooks Brothers."

Josie listened to the conversation, trying to edge through the crowd to see the body. She had no real doubt that she would recognize Cornell Hudson when she finally got in position to look over the rail and into the water, but she still hoped—

"Oh, my God, it's Father!"

Beca's scream even drowned out the radio. And she had the instant attention of all the bystanders—especially those in uniform.

"She says it's her father," ran through the crowd. "That woman knows the dead man."

Josie glanced around. Beca was alone, or at least none of her sisters were in sight. The police officers were speaking urgently into their two-way radios, and Josie knew it was time to leave. She didn't want Chief Rodney to find her here. Besides, she wondered where the other sisters were. And Sam's mother, come to think of it. Josie returned to her truck and headed up island. Maybe it would be best if she broke the bad news to Carol—and was the first person to see what her reaction would be.

Carol had come to the island to help her son clean up his store, and Josie knew she would find her doing exactly that—after her own fashion. And Carol's fashion was exuberant, energetic, and disorganized. Josie parked her truck next to a large pile of broken glass and jumped out only to have to leap back out of the path of a deluge of liquid, which reeked of alcohol, being swept out the front door.

"Josie! Wonderful to see you. I don't suppose you have time to help out for a bit? Sammy is holed up in his office trying to salvage paperwork, and I am having a terrible time with the refrigerators. Now that the power's come back on, I want to get the beer in cans cooling and that means getting all the broken glass out first—"

Josie, in a panic, started in the door. "They're unplugged, aren't they?"

"Josie, what sort of idiot do you think I am? Of course they're unplugged. Everything in the place was unplugged right away. Sammy did it, and I double-checked."

Josie stopped and turned around. "Of course. I wasn't thinking."

"You do have some time to help? Is that why you're here?"

"Not exactly. But, of course, I'll help out a bit." Josie

looked around the large liquor store. "You've done a lot!" she said encouragingly. Of course, there was still an incredible amount to be done.

Carol echoed her thoughts, "But so much still to do."

"Yes, still so much to do. But, Carol, I actually came here to talk to you. To tell you . . . something serious."

Much to Josie's surprise, she found herself wrapped in polyester-covered arms, being squeezed enthusiastically.

"But how wonderful! Why didn't Sammy tell me himself? Such a foolish man, he probably thought this was woman's business."

"Carol? I . . . I don't know what you're talking about."

"Oh, you don't have to be shy. If you're marrying my Sammy—"

"No, Carol, you don't understand. We're not getting married!"

"You're . . ." Carol pulled away and looked Josie straight in the eye. "You're pregnant. I thought you were looking a bit chubby. Well, I hope you and Sammy marry, and I know Sammy will want to do what used to be called the right thing, but, if you don't want to, I'll understand. Of course I will. You raised Tyler by yourself, and he's certainly an amazing child."

"No! Absolutely not!"

"You're not pregnant?"

"No—"

"Then you've . . . Oh, no, you and Sammy have broken up. Dreadful. But it's wrong to make any decisions under these circumstances. The storm. The aftermath . . . So stressful. So—"

Josie took a deep breath and interrupted. "Carol, I don't want to talk to you about my relationships. I came here to talk to you about yours."

"My what?"

"Your relationships. Or rather one of your . . . your rela-tionships." She ended slowly, hoping she hadn't been offensive.

Carol beamed. "Why, Josie, I didn't know you blushed. How charming. Now, tell me, which one of my relation-ships are you concerned about?"

"Cornell Hudson."

"You sweet thing. I was so afraid you'd feel like this. Believe me, I did it thinking only of you—"

"You—? Carol, what are you talking about?"

"Why—I thought you were upset about getting that big job from Cornell Hudson just because he and I have a relationship."

"You and Cornell Hudson have a relationship?" Sam appeared, his arms full of papers. "Dare I ask what sort of relationship?"

Carol smoothed back a lock of her platinum hair, which seemed to have escaped from the cement spray she used. "Sammy, have I ever questioned you about your numerous women friends?"

"All the time, Mother. Now what's this about you and Cornell Hudson? Promise me you're not going to marry him. I'd hate to have those three blondes as stepsisters."

Josie smothered a giggle. The news she had wasn't the least bit funny. And now she had to tell Sam as well as Carol. Might as well get it over with. At least, if Carol broke down at the news, Sam was here to comfort her. "Cornell Hudson is dead," she blurted out.

"Cornell? Dead? Are you sure?"

"Yes. His daughter identified his body."

Sam was a man of few words, but they were to the point. "When?"

"Just a few minutes ago. Down at the pier," Josie added.

"Cornell Hudson just died down on the pier?"

"Oh, Sammy, I kept telling him that he had to watch what he ate and get more exercise. The poor man. All that high living finally caught up with him. How many times I warned him . . ."

"He was floating in the water," Josie explained.

"Swimming! And in the rough current!"

"I don't think he was swimming. I think that he . . . I got the impression that he . . ." Josie glanced at Sam, who was watching her intently. "I think everyone thinks he's been dead for a . . . a while."

"Any idea how long a while?" Sam asked, picking up a broken bottle and examining what was left of the label.

His attempt at casualness didn't fool Josie. "Sam, your mother is probably very upset. . . ." She glared at him.

"Oh, heavens. You are sweet. You didn't get the impression that Corn and I had some sort of serious relationship, did you?"

"I . . . Well, he bought a house down here to be near you."

Sam looked over his horn-rimmed glasses at his mother. "Really, Mother?"

"Nonsense. He bought the house because I told him how chic the island was becoming and how he could get a wonderful deal from Josie to remodel the house. He certainly didn't buy it so he could spend summers with me. I can't believe I gave you that impression. I certainly never meant to."

"I . . . You talked him into coming here because you thought I needed the work?"

"Oh, Josie, you make it sound as though I've done something wrong. I was only trying to help out. A few months ago, Sam told me that you had hired these new carpenters even though you didn't have jobs lined up for the summer as yet, and I just happened to be going to a benefit at the New York Historical Society that very evening, where I just happened to run into Cornell in the line at the bar, and mentioned it to him and he asked me about the island, and one thing led to another, and suddenly he had a house down here, and you were scheduled to remodel it for him."

"Mother, I know I never implied that Josie was having trouble finding work."

"I didn't say you did. I was just making conversation, and Cornell picked up on it. He was so enthusiastic about the island and hiring Josie. . . . Well, I couldn't help it if he seemed to think I'd be seeing more of him in the future than I planned on, could I?"

"Mother . . ."

"So you don't care that he's been killed?" The relief Josie felt upon hearing Carol's feelings toward Cornell Hudson made her indiscreet.

Sam and Carol both picked up on it. "Killed? Did you say Cornell was killed? By someone?"

"Just when did this happen, Josie?" Sam asked.

She decided to answer Carol's question first. "I understand that something was wound around his neck. Someone said something about him being strangled. I mean, it makes sense, doesn't it?"

"Josie . . ." Sam looked over at his mother and stopped speaking.

Carol suddenly began firing a barrage of questions. "What was he strangled with? Who would have hated Cornell enough to want to kill him? Couldn't he just have fallen off the pier? There's so much stuff in the water from the storm . . . Who could possibly have done it? His daughters must be frantic. Do you think I should find them? They don't know anyone else on the island. Maybe I could be of help?"

"Mother, that's an excellent idea. Those poor women have no one to turn to in a crisis. A friendly face is just what they need right now."

Josie looked at Sam suspiciously. He seemed eager to get rid of his mother. Then she had an idea. "You know, Sam's right. Those women would probably be thrilled to see you. Why don't I drive—?"

"I think you and I need to talk, Josie."

She looked over at him. "Your mother—"

"Brought her own car to the island, knows her way around, and can go find whomever she wants to on her own."

"I—"

"And I'd like to speak to you."

Josie tried again. "I—"

"After all, we haven't really had a moment alone together since before the evacuation." He put his arm around her shoulder.

Carol perked up. "Oh, Sammy. You should have said something earlier. I'll just grab my sweater from your office and be off. Don't—uh, don't rush for me. I'll stop in and see Risa for a few, too. Don't expect me. . . ."

"You slime," Josie hissed at Sam as soon as they were alone. "You're not interested in a romantic moment. You just want to ask me a lot of questions."

Sam pulled her into a warm embrace. "How can you accuse me of such a thing?"

Josie, her face squashed against his chest, couldn't answer. Which was, she realized, the point of his gesture, as Sam called out his good-byes to his mother without releasing her.

"Now, Josie, I know you," he began before his mother was even out the door.

"Sam . . ."

"I want to know what's been going on."

"Sam, if I don't get back to the police station as soon as possible—"

"Josie, you've been keeping something from me for days. Now I discover that a man you were working for—and, dear God, my mother has been dating—was murdered. He was murdered, wasn't he?"

Josie sighed deeply. "Yes. He was."

"Strangled?"

"No, that's what it looks like from the pier, but it's not true. Someone made it look like he was strangled, but Basil says he was sho—"

"Basil says what?"

"That he was shot," Josie explained reluctantly.

"What does Basil have to do with this?"

"You see, Sam—"

"Josie Pigeon, what the hell are you doing hiding out here? My office isn't here. And you're supposed to be finishing up my office—by tonight I seem to recall you promised me. Of course, I could just arrest you and then you'd have to stay at the station. . . ."

"I doubt if you'd do that, Chief. You know the laws concerning false arrest as well as I do," Sam said, releasing Josie.

"I do. And I know that finding a man who had been strangled with Josie's property is probably just cause for bringing your girlfriend in for questioning—if not for arresting her."

"Your property?" Sam asked, looking down at Josie.

"Yes. A long strip of fabric ripped from one of my drop cloths—one of the dozen I stenciled with the name of the company just last winter," Josie admitted, looking down at the floor.

TWENTY-FIVE

WAVE radio's crack news team has learned that the body of island resident Cornell Hudson was found floating in the ocean earlier today. Chief of Police Michael Rodney, Sr., will hold a press conference at the police station at seven P.M. tonight concerning the man and rumors about how he met his death. . . .

"I GATHER THAT'S why all those chairs are set up? For the press conference they're talking about?" Josie had stopped hammering long enough to blow her nose and speak with the dispatcher.

"Sure are. Looks like they're expecting a crowd, doesn't it?"

"Yes. I didn't know there was that much press still on the island."

"There isn't—not anymore. For a few days there, all the networks and the Weather Channel were here. Then they got their three big stories about the storm: That it was coming. That it was here. That cleaning up afterwards is hard work. But there's nothing else to say now, and apparently saying over and over that the storm did hit isn't as newsworthy as saying over and over that the storm may hit. All the reporters with their brand-new expensive rain suits and big microphones have gone back home. My guess is that WAVE radio will show up. Maybe a few weekly shoppers from the mainland will send some kid they've convinced to be an unpaid summer intern. But most of those chairs will be empty. And that's fine with me. But I'll bet the chief will go nuts. He's been a real pain in the butt wandering around complaining that everyone on the island but him has been on TV in the last week."

"I wasn't on television," Josie said.

"Me neither, but you know how he is."

"Yeah, I know how he is."

Both women got back to work, but Josie had barely started when the dispatcher radio began to squawk and Josie heard her name mentioned. "Who's that?"

"Basil Tilby. He seems awfully upset. Says he has a big problem and needs to talk to you. I'm not supposed to use this as a personal message service," the dispatcher added as Josie dashed over and grabbed the headset right off her head.

"Basil? It's Josie. What's up?" She listened to his explanation, a frown deepening on her face as he spoke.

"Don't tell me you're leaving again," the dispatcher said as Josie returned the headset.

"I have to. Just for a few minutes. I'll be back . . . as soon as possible."

"Yeah, you tell that to Chief Rodney. That man loves to kill the messenger."

"Just tell him that . . . that I need help, and I'm going to pick up some of my other workers—to get things moving more quickly."

"Josie, he'll never believe that!"

"Then tell him I just took off for no reason at all and you don't know when I'll be back. He can't expect you to keep me imprisoned here until his office is finished." She heard the dispatcher's "Wanna bet" as she dashed out of the building.

Basil had promised to meet her in his office at the Gull's Perch. They needed privacy, Josie knew. She parked her truck behind the bank next door. Island Contracting's truck was well known, and she didn't want Chief Rodney to see it.

Basil was waiting, walking back and forth, an empty wineglass in one hand, an open bottle of merlot in the other. Josie hopped down from her truck and ran up to him. "Have you heard anything else?" she asked.

"No, not a word. But, to be honest, I don't expect to. She was so upset when she left here. Josie, I simply cannot understand it. We were working along, and that bit came on the radio about Cornell Hudson and . . . and she just went crazy."

"That's what you said on the phone, but what really happened?"

Basil seated himself on a convenient packing crate and poured out another glass of wine. He took a swig before answering her question. "It's difficult to describe. She started by making this choking sound, and I thought she was going to cry. Which she did—sort of."

"What do you mean 'sort of'?"

"She made some strange sobbing sounds and then choked more, and then she just dashed out of the room. Without saying anything intelligible. It was weird. Really weird." He drank more wine.

"And it's really upset you. Why?"

"She knows that Cornell Hudson and I are—were—connected."

"How do you know that? You just said she didn't say anything."

"When she heard the report on the radio, she . . . she turned and looked at me. . . ."

"You were looking at her?"

"Yes. I told you. She made this weird choking sound."

"While she was looking at you?" Josie asked.

"Yes. Straight at me. Josie, I know you're going to think I'm crazy, but I could swear that she knew about my past. Knew that I had hated Cornell Hudson." He lowered his voice and looked around to be sure they were alone before continuing. "She knew that the announcement of his death on the radio wasn't the first I'd heard of it."

"Basil, I don't think—"

"Josie, what do you know about Renee? Heavens, she's been here for two days, and I don't even know her last name."

"Jacquette. Renee Jacquette."

"Renee Jacquette—sounds like a stage name, doesn't it?"

"Funny, someone said that about Cornell Hudson. I don't remember who it was."

"So they both changed their names. It's a free country." Basil put down his glass and looked at Josie. "And they're not the only ones. Basil Tilby isn't the name I had as an infant."

"What—?"

"Butch Tyson. My mother was a sweet lady with terrible taste. But we're not talking about me. What do you know about this Renee? Where is she from? Where did she get her training? Who did she work for before coming here?"

"I . . . I don't know all that much. She worked for a builder up on Cape Cod last summer, that I do know. That was one of her references and as I knew the name . . . ah, I didn't bother to check it out. I mean, I could have, of course. And I know she spent the winter living in Boston and going to school . . . some sort of art school, I think she said."

Basil emptied his wineglass. "Josie, Sam has compl— mentioned to me how casual you are when it comes to checking out your employees, but I always thought he was exaggerating. Why don't you just tell me what you actually know about her."

Josie grimaced. "Not much beside her name, that she considers herself an artist, and she works in watercolors . . . Oh, I know where she's living on the island. She's renting that little apartment above Milt Seymour's garage on Twenty-second. Where are you going?"

"We're going over to Twenty-second. I know Milt—he's never trusted anyone since he got stiffed out of an entire summer's rent by a man I hired as sous-chef. He'll have answers to some of the questions I'm asking you."

"I don't have time—"

"If I'm right, Renee whatever her name is mixed up in this murder. I think we need to find her—or information about her—as soon as possible. Before," he added ominously, "the wrong person is arrested."

Josie sighed. She knew he was right. The problem was that she couldn't win. If she didn't find out who killed Cornell Hudson either she—or someone she cared about— might be arrested for a murder they didn't commit. And if Chief Rodney discovered her tooting around the island without a good reason for not working on his office, he might just kill her on the spot. "Okay. What are you driving?"

"My Jeep. We can take that."

"Fine, but I'm going to lie down in the backseat, and don't break any laws—I don't want to run into any cops until I've gotten Chief Rodney's office finished."

"Fine."

*   *   *

"I can't believe it."

"It's incredible, isn't it?"

"How could this happen?"

"I don't know. You would think that any gust of wind strong enough to blow the roof off a house would empty everything off the kitchen shelves, wouldn't you?"

"I sure would have until seeing this."

Milt Seymour's home had lost its roof and rear wall, leaving the kitchen and dining room completely exposed. Aside from a few missing cupboard doors and an upturned chair, it was like looking at a stage set. Not only were the tables surrounded by chairs, but china was still stacked in the cupboards.

"It looks to me like the garage was untouched, too," Josie said, walking up the driveway.

"The apartment door is open. Maybe Renee came back here. I'd sure like to talk to her," Basil said.

Josie thought that was an excellent idea. She followed Basil up the stairway that climbed the outside of the garage. But the open door revealed an unoccupied apartment.

"Renee?"

"She's not here," Josie said, walking into the room. The small space had been converted into an apartment using the cheapest materials. The walls had been paneled using fake wood paneling, the paper covering peeling at the edges of each sheet. Water-stained tiles hung from the low ceiling. Damaged linoleum had been laid on the floor. There was a single iron bedstead with a lumpy mattress covered with a torn seersucker spread, a pine dresser that had seen better days, a chipped bookshelf under the eaves, a table, and two fake Hitchcock chairs. A pullman kitchen had been placed against the far wall. Other than three suitcases in the corner, two expensive-looking halogen lamps, books, art supplies, and about fifty paintings tacked to the walls, little seemed to have been added to the original furnishings.

"So she really is an artist," Basil said, looking around.

"These are good, aren't they?" Josie turned her attention to the walls full of matted paintings.

"These are more than good. Josie, this is not the work of a weekend painter. These were done by someone who has been trained and who has worked at her art."

Josie was less interested in that than in what was on the bed—a large tote bag just like the one Sam's mother carried—only this one was newer than Carol's. "Look at this," she said to Basil. "Carol has one just like it. She always says she was given it by a very wealthy admirer."

"He would have to have been. It's Vuitton. These things cost thousands—if they're real. You can buy fakes all over New York City."

"I guess this isn't real then."

"Or else Renee has a wealthy admirer. She's gorgeous, you know."

"I guess. She's an excellent carpenter."

"And remarkably well read as well." Basil was kneeling in front of a small bookcase crammed with paperbacks. "Unless these were left by a former resident."

Josie wandered over to the one table in the small room. Apparently it functioned as Renee's art studio. There was an easel set up, a paint-covered pallet on the top covered with plastic wrap, a large mug of brushes, and piles of paper, both used and ready for paint. The top work was a dark rendition of the sea as Agatha approached.

"Basil, this painting was done in the dunes. Look at it."

"What?" Basil got the point immediately.

"Look."

They both stared at the scene. The high waves, ominous

sky, the beach grass blown so hard it was lying almost on the ground. Renee had even managed to portray the rain. "That was painted the day Agatha hit," Josie insisted.

"It sure looks like it, but couldn't it have been painted from memory?" Basil gently touched the edge of the paper. "It's dry—"

"She would have had to see it to paint it from memory. She must have been there—in the dunes. On the morning before the storm. The morning of the murder."

Basil moved away and looked over at the paintings displayed on the walls. "Maybe not."

"What do you mean?"

"Look at these. The plaza in front of the Uffizi in Florence. The Star Ferry in Hong Kong. Paris. Paris. Paris. This series looks like it was done in Cornwall. . . . I think Mousehole . . ."

"Wow. She is well traveled."

"Or maybe these weren't painted from life. Maybe she just paints from photographs, or other paintings, or her imagination," he added, kneeling down and looking at some paintings hung near the floor.

"Oh, good point. But still—"

"But still, she could have been painting in the dunes that morning. She could have seen the murderer. She could have seen me find the body. She could have seen someone move the body into the house."

"She could have a rich admirer who buys her expensive handbags. She could have a really rich admirer who pays for trips around the world. She could. She could. She could. Basil, we don't know anything about her."

"You could, of course, just ask me. Or is that too easy?"

Renee Jacquette had returned to her apartment.

TWENTY-SIX

... down on the boardwalk ...

"**J**UST LET ME turn this off, and you can ask me any questions you like." Renee ripped her Walkman off her head and pressed some buttons.

"I . . . we came here looking for you, and the door was open."

"Oh . . ." Renee looked behind her. "Well, thanks for closing it for me. My work doesn't benefit from being exposed to the elements."

"Your paintings are wonderful," Josie said enthusiastically. "Really, really wonderful."

"Thank you." Renee's response was polite but cold. "Why are you here?"

"We—"

"I know why you're here, Mr. Tilby. The question was for Josie."

"But Josie is here because of me," Basil said, apparently not intimidated by her attitude. "When you ran out of my place, I called Josie. I had no idea where you lived, but it was obvious something was wrong. I felt I had to see if I could help."

"Exactly," Josie chimed in. "And when Basil told me how upset you'd been, I insisted on coming over here with

217

him. To see if I could help. And," she added, inspired,
"when we saw the open doorway, we thought you might be
in here. Hurt or something. We just wanted to help."

"And then we saw your paintings," Basil continued their
lie. "To be honest, we simply couldn't resist looking at
them. They're brilliant."

"You . . . I . . . Thank you," Renee said finally.

"You said you were a painter, but a lot of people say
that," Josie chimed in. "I had no idea how talented you
are. Your artwork is wonderful. Why are you working as a
carpenter?"

Renee raised her eyebrows. "Do you have any idea how
difficult it is to make a living as an artist?"

"Yes, I supp—"

"But you're good," Basil interrupted. "Really good. You
should be painting, not working for Josie."

Josie scowled at Basil. Did he have any idea how difficult it was to find good carpenters in the middle of the
building season?

"I can't afford to. Oh, I can support myself and paint on
weekends and vacations, but that won't take me where I
want to go. I need to take classes. I need to study. And by
working as a carpenter in the summer and living cheaply
like this, I can afford to go to school all winter. It may not
be a life you can understand, but it works for me," she
added almost belligerently.

"We don't mean to sound critical," Josie assured her.

"Remember, the only reason we're here is because I was
worried about you," Basil added. "Are you okay? You
seemed terribly upset when you ran out of the Gull."

"I . . . It was the story on the radio. About Cornell
Hudson . . ."

Suddenly it all fell into place for Josie. "He's your
wealthy admirer. . . . I mean, you were involved with him."

Renee looked at Josie as though her boss had lost her mind. "My what?"

"Cornell Hudson. Your . . . well, what I mean is that he paid for you to travel . . . to go to all these places," Josie said, pointing at the paintings of Italy.

"I—" Renee looked at Josie in silence for a few minutes and then seemed to make up her mind. "Yes, he did. He paid for me to go to Italy and . . . and all those other places. I . . . I wouldn't call him an admirer exactly. I don't think he ever actually understood my need to paint. But he was willing to pay for me to study art. At least, he was at first."

"What changed?"

"He . . . Oh, I don't know. Men. You know."

"Yeah," Josie and Basil answered in unison.

"So what happened?" Josie asked after a moment.

"Oh, you know how those things go. One minute he was supporting me, and the next he didn't approve of me. Said that the life of an artist wasn't proper—all sorts of garbage. It was completely nuts. So I ended our relationship."

Renee's words were casual, but she looked as though she was going to cry.

Josie asked a question. "When was the last time you saw him?"

"I—a few—Months and months ago. Not recently!"

Josie glanced over at Basil. He appeared to be examining a series of tiny paintings on the wall by his side. She was convinced Renee was lying—she could not tell what Basil was thinking.

"I—"

"If you're feeling better, I think perhaps Josie and I should get back to work," Basil said, a gentle smile on his face.

"I . . . ," Josie began.

"Chief Rodney. . . ," Basil began.

Josie didn't need another hint. "Right. You are going to be okay?" she asked Renee, moving toward the doorway.

"Yes. I'll—I'll be back at the restaurant in just a few minutes. I . . . It was silly to get so upset."

"Take your time," Basil said, pushing Josie toward the door.

"I—"

"Is that a police car I see down there?" Basil asked, interrupting Josie. "Come on."

"I—"

"Get going!" Basil urged. "I know. We don't have to stay here. Get going!"

"What—?"

"Josie, just go!"

Basil didn't speak again until they were on the road.

"She was lying," he called over his shoulder at his passenger, who, once again, was crouched on the floor behind the driver's seat.

"About what?"

"About everything. Cornell Hudson wasn't just her lover. They were married—"

"What?"

"They were married!"

"How did you learn that from looking at her artwork?"

"Get down, Josie!"

She did as he ordered and repeated the question. "How do you know?"

"The paintings. Most of them were signed Renee Jacquette—with a big sloping signature. But some others— the ones from the Orient and Italy—they were signed Hudson. They must have been married."

"Maybe they were painted by someone else."

"I don't think so. I have a pretty good eye. I'd swear Renee did them all."

"Wow. Married to him. I wonder if Carol knows anything about that."

"Well, apparently, they're not married anymore. I mean, she doesn't live like someone who is married to a wealthy man."

"Actually she doesn't live like a woman who is divorced from a wealthy man either."

"She may not have gone after alimony, or perhaps she got a judge who thought that an artist with a trade really didn't deserve alimony," Basil pointed out.

"You're probably right," Josie said. "Why are we slowing down?"

"We're in front of the police station. And there isn't a soul around. If I were you, I'd hop out and get back in there."

"Basil—"

"Don't worry. I'm going to give Renee half an hour to settle down, and then I'll head back over there."

"You'll let me know what you find out."

"Of course. Now scoot."

Josie, glancing around, saw that no one was about to notice her entrance, and then she dashed into the police station.

The dispatcher was sitting on her desk, doodling on a notepad. She looked up at Josie's entrance. "You are the most popular person on the island."

"What do you mean?"

"These are your messages."

Josie looked down at the sheet of paper. "Good heavens! Do you think I could use your cell phone?"

"Be my guest. But do me a favor. Go into the ladies' room to make your calls."

"Why?"

"Because Chief Rodney carries a gun, and if he sees you here and not working, he just might use it. And frankly, Josie, I don't think he's all that good a shot. He might miss you and hit me."

Josie took the list and the phone and scurried off. Betty had made four calls from New York City. Sam had called three times. Carol twice. Sissy had called only once, but Ginger topped the list with six calls. Josie decided that the most important calls would probably take the most time, and, assuming frequency equaled urgency, she dialed the number Sissy had left first.

Sissy, it turned out, wanted permission to leave the job she had just finished and go on to something else. Josie had no trouble with that. "Why don't you go over to my apartment. I think Risa can probably use your help, and she'll feed you a wonderful dinner, too."

Sissy, perky as ever, agreed happily.

"Okay. One down. Four to go." Carol hadn't bothered to leave a number, so Josie moved on to Sam. But his line was busy. She figured she couldn't put off calling Ginger any longer.

The phone was picked up on the first ring. "Hi, Ginger. This is Josie—"

"Where have you been? I've been calling and calling!"

Josie was so startled by the vehemence of Ginger's response that she didn't say anything at first. Then, after the long, distressing day at the end of the long distressing week, she blew up. When she hung up, she still didn't know why Ginger had called so many times, but she was fairly sure she needed to hire someone to replace her. Josie sighed, regretting her temper, but knowing she wasn't going to change any time soon.

She dialed Sam's number again, and a woman answered.

"Sam?"

"Josie?"

"Who—?"

"Josie, it's Carol, dear. I'm so glad you called."

"I thought . . . Sam called me," Josie said.

"He probably just wanted to say hello, dear. You know how considerate he is. But I must see you as soon as possible. I have to talk to you . . . about Cornell."

"Great. I'm at the police station. When—?"

"I'll be right over." A loud click indicated that she'd hung up.

Josie looked at the phone. She didn't know how to reach Sam, and if Chief Rodney came back and discovered how little she'd done here, he really might kill her. She sighed and left the seclusion of the ladies' room. She barely had time to put a nail in place when Carol dashed through the doorway.

"May I help you?" the dispatcher asked.

"I'm looking for—oh, there she is! Josie!"

"It's all right," Josie called out. "This is Carol Birnbaum, Sam's mother."

"Oh, go right in. Apparently Josie is using the police station as her personal reception area. . . ."

Josie stuck out her tongue at the dispatcher, then turned, and smiled at Sam's mother. "Carol, what can I do for you? And where's Loki?"

"Sleeping on the couch. I took her for a long walk on the beach, but now I'm here to do something for you. Is there any place we can speak privately?"

Josie looked around. "No, but—"

"This is important, Josie. What are you—?"

"Get in there." Josie found herself doing something she never thought she would do to Sam's mother: Bossing her around and shoving her behind a broken chunk of ceiling.

"Josie—"

"Shhhh!"

"Jo—"

"Well, if it isn't Miss Pigeon. I thought you were going to have this done . . . Ah, let me see . . . about an hour ago. I believe that's what you said."

"There was a slight complication, Chief Rodney. The electricity came back on, and I had to reroute the lines to prevent any sort of fire danger back here. But you don't have to worry. This will be done before I go to bed tonight."

"I certainly hope so, Miss Pigeon. . . . Did you say something?"

Josie kicked Carol's ankle and smiled at Chief Rodney. "No. I'm fine, thanks."

"I'm thrilled to hear that." He wandered slowly to the door.

"Don't say anything until we're alone," Josie hissed, picking up her hammer and making as much noise as possible.

Luckily, they didn't have to wait long. A young officer called in about a film crew setting up down on the pier. They didn't have a permit, was this legal? The officer wanted to know.

Apparently this was one of those situations that needed the personal attention of Chief Rodney, and he left immediately.

"What did you want to tell me?" Josie asked when she and Carol were alone together again.

"I've been thinking about Cornell Hudson, and something struck me."

"What?"

"Josie, you know I'm not a vain person."

"Of course not!" Josie lied.

"And you know I'm not one of these women who feels

that it's better to pretend not to be your age. I mean, many of my friends tell me that I've aged gracefully."

"Of course."

"So you wouldn't say that I'm jealous of women who are younger. I'd prefer not to have to deal with wrinkles and cellulite, of course."

Josie got the impression that Carol's laugh indicated a carefree attitude to such insignificant things. "Of course," she said again.

"But I must admit I was flattered when Cornell asked me out."

"Because—?"

"Because he's known to date only younger women."

This didn't surprise Josie. "Well, I guess he recognized your youthful—ah attitude."

"That's not what I'm telling you." Carol took a deep breath and continued. "You see, the more I think about it, the more I'm convinced that he asked me out because he wanted to know more about the island. Because he wanted to know more about you."

TWENTY-SEVEN

Information coming into WAVE radio . . .

"NOT ABOUT ME," Josie corrected her, feeling she was catching on at last. "About one of my carpenters."

"One of your carpenters?"

"Yes—Renee. We . . . I just found out that she was married to Cornell Hudson at one time. Sammy probably told you her name when he was telling you about my new crew, and you must have told Cornell Hudson about her. That's why he was so interested in being here. He wanted to be near his ex-wife."

"Most of the men I know spend a fair amount of time avoiding their exes," Carol mused. "And, honestly Josie, I can't quite imagine Corn married to a carpenter. Where would he even meet a carpenter?"

"Perhaps she worked for him," Josie suggested.

"Well, I suppose that is possible. You're saying that she worked for him before . . . before she worked for you."

"Carol, Renee is more than a carpenter. She's a very talented and trained artist. You said Cornell Hudson supported the arts. Maybe he met her at a gallery or something."

"How old is she?"

Josie shrugged. "I'm not sure. Younger than I am. Maybe thirty, maybe a little younger."

"Good-looking?"

"Yes. She's a striking blonde."

"Sounds like a woman Corn would go for—but marry? I don't know. I think I would have heard if he had been married recently. Especially to an artist. You know, with his money, maybe he could sponsor shows for her at some of the minor galleries." Carol frowned.

"What's wrong?"

"Now that I think about it, I may have heard something about that. . . . Not about him being married to this woman, but I do vaguely remember that he once owned an interest in a gallery on the edge—the far edge, to put it politely— of SoHo."

"What do you mean?"

"Just that even Corn isn't rich enough to buy a gallery in SoHo."

"Oh. But he could have been married to Renee and gotten her shows for her artwork?"

"I certainly never heard about it, but I do know people who've known him longer—and better—than I do. I could call them."

"Oh, Carol, would you?"

"Of course. But I'm going to have to go back to Sam's house for the cord to his phone. The battery is almost dead. Unless you think that nice woman at the desk in the lobby would let me use—"

"I wouldn't even bother to ask. She's a sweetie, but if Chief Rodney came in and found you talking out there, I don't know what he'd do to her—or to you."

"Oh, Josie, Michael is such a sweet man. He always flirts with me. In fact, I've almost promised I'll go out on his boat with him someday. I'm sure he wouldn't mind if I just used the phones here. But I certainly wouldn't want to get you in any trouble. I'll just dash back to Sammy's house, pick up another battery, and make my calls. Will you be here when I return?"

Josie looked around. "Yes. At the rate I'm going, I may be here for the rest of the summer."

"Then I will find you here and tell you everything I've learned. Wait until my friends in New York hear about my adventures in the storm! I've been dying to call, but Sammy insisted that I not waste batteries. But now he'll have to let me. Bye-bye, Josie, darling. Have no fear. I'll find the truth!"

Josie watched Carol leave and then turned back to her work only to be stopped by the dispatcher.

"Josie, Betty's been calling and calling. She says she has something important to tell you. Very important."

"Oh, guess I'd better head back to the ladies' room and give her a call."

"I'll tell the chief you had some bad fried clams if he comes looking for you."

"Thanks."

"It might look more like you were making progress on his office if you cleaned up some of those piles of wood."

"I will as soon as I get back." Bad clams wouldn't have gotten Josie to the bathroom any faster. And she had dialed Betty's number before the door swung shut behind her. But Betty wasn't home. Disappointed, she left a message on the machine and headed back to work. Maybe Carol would come up with something significant.

But it was Sam, not his mother, who walked through the door calling her name.

"I'm back here, Sam!" she called out. She was feeling good. Cleaning up the mess had, in fact, given the impression of accomplishing a lot. Now that Sam was here to help, she might actually get these walls up before midnight.

"Josie, I've been trying to get you for over an hour. Why isn't your phone turned on?"

"I—I thought it was—" She pulled it from her back pocket. "Oh, the ring is turned off. Sorry. What's wrong?"

"Betty has found out some very interesting things about Cornell Hudson and his family. She says you didn't answer her calls and didn't call her back after she left lots of messages here. So she called me, and I volunteered to pass on the information."

"What did she say?" Josie asked.

Sam was busy taking a notebook from the back pocket of his chinos. "I want to get this right," he explained peering through his glasses. "Now it seems to me that the most interesting thing is that Cornell Hudson was not born Cornell Hudson. He was born in one of the Baltic states and had one of those terribly unpronounceable names—at least to Americans. He chose to change his name to Cornell Hudson because he thought it sounded American."

"Why?"

"The college. The river." Sam shrugged. "I'm only telling you what Betty was told he thought. Names were very important to him. English was not his native language. He learned to speak it in ESL classes when he was in his twenties. The students learned English by reading children's books. It made quite an impression on him. He named his children after famous characters in those books."

"What famous characters in children's books are called Win, Beca, or Pip . . . not Pippie Longstocking?" Josie asked, thrilled with the possibility.

"You got it."

"And . . . and . . ." Josie racked her brain, but the other answers eluded her.

"Try Winnie the Pooh and Rebecca of Sunnybrook Farm."

"You're kidding!" Josie had thought Beca such a sophisticated name, but Rebecca of Sunnybrook Farm . . . She couldn't believe it!

"And one other thing. There's another daughter: Her name is—"

"Renee!"

Sam seemed startled. "No, her name is Dorothy. After the little girl in *The Wonderful Wizard of Oz*," he added when Josie didn't comment. "Who is Renee?"

"She's Cornell Hudson's fourth daughter. Not his wife. Not his ex-wife. But his daughter. Who is probably going to inherit one quarter of his large estate."

"Josie . . ."

"You know, now that I think about it, she actually looks

like her sisters. The blond hair, smooth skin, her eyes . . . I should have seen the resemblance before this."

"Josie, you're really leaping to conclusions here."

"No, Sam. It all makes sense. She . . . she might have killed him! She was in the dunes the morning he died. Really! She was there! Painting the storm and . . . and then her father came out to see her. Something must have happened, and she hated him—"

"Why?" Sam asked in a quiet voice.

"I don't know why! Sam, just listen to me! She and her father hated each other, and they hadn't seen each other in years. She . . ." Josie stopped.

"What's wrong?"

"She would have to have had a gun. . . . Why would an artist be carrying a gun with her when she goes to paint on the beach?"

"Good question, Josie. I think—"

"But just because we don't know why she was carrying a gun doesn't mean she wasn't. That's logical, right?"

"No, but I know that won't stop you."

Josie grimaced and continued. "Okay. So she's painting away, and her father comes out, startles her, they argue, she shoots him and dashes away . . . No, she doesn't. She has to pack up her watercolors and all first. Then she dashes into the dunes . . . And Basil comes along . . . and someone else who moves the body—"

"Why?"

"Why what?"

"Why move the body?"

"I don't know. The weather was terrible. There was lots of wind and rain . . . maybe . . . well, I don't know why anyone would move the body—or tie my drop cloth around his neck. But someone must have, right?" She looked up at

Sam, who had a familiar doubting look on his face. "Sam, I could be right, right?"

"Do people paint with watercolors outside when it's raining? Wouldn't the paints run?"

"I . . . I suppose . . . Are you telling me you never dated an artist?" she asked hopefully.

"Actually I did. Two women. One was a sculptor, and the other worked in oils. I never dated anyone whose chosen medium was watercolor."

She didn't bother to comment. "Well, maybe you're wrong. Or maybe she was just sketching out what she planned to paint later. Right?"

"Could be."

"You don't think I'm right about all this—"

"Josie, it doesn't matter what I think. Go on. Speculate."

"Well, so Renee killed her father and ran away—after packing up her paints and all. And then . . . well, then nothing. She didn't go back and see the body because the body was moved, and then the house and the dunes vanished. She must have thought she'd gotten off free. That must be why she was so startled and upset when she heard about the body being found."

"Josie, you have really gone over the top this time. You don't know anything at all about this. You don't know that this Renee is Cornell Hudson's youngest daughter."

"But she looks just like him, Sam! You have to admit that!"

"I don't even know . . . Are you talking about that lovely young carpenter? Is that the Renee we're talking about?"

"Yes. She looks like Beca and Win and Pip, doesn't she?"

Sam considered Josie's statement. "In fact, she does. And she does seem to be different from most of your carpenters—more sophisticated or something. I noticed that the first time I met her—back in the spring."

"Did you happen to mention her to anyone—like your mother?"

"My mother?"

"Yeah. I think your mother told Cornell Hudson that Renee was working here, and that's why he came to the island, bought the Point House, and then hired us to remodel it for him. He was trying to reconnect with his daughter."

Sam was silent.

"Well, did you?"

"You know, I might have. I . . . Mom . . . Mom and I did have a conversation about your new crew and the summer season. . . ." He stopped speaking.

"Sam, no matter what sort of lousy thing you said about me, I'd really like to know what it is. I promise not to be mad."

"I don't believe that for a second, but I guess you do have to know." Sam took a deep breath. "Do you remember when you let me help you with your tax forms last spring?"

Oh, boy, did she. That weekend had definitely marked a low point in their relationship. "Yes."

"Well. To be absolutely honest, I worried a lot about Island Contracting after that."

"Why?"

"Josie, you run your business so . . . so casually . . . so hand-to-mouth. If you don't get a good job each summer, you are in danger of folding up."

"But, Sam, we always get what you're calling 'a good job'—each summer for as long as I've had the business. We've had summers when we had to turn down good jobs. Why were you worried all of a sudden?"

"I guess I'd just never realized how close to the edge you worked. I worried."

Josie stopped thinking about Cornell Hudson's murder for the first time all day. "You think I'm incompetent."

"That's not it at all! Believe me, that's not it!"

"Then what?"

"I think you're a miracle worker. I couldn't believe it! You start out so many seasons with a completely new crew. Each job is completely different—new building, new blueprints, new financial situation. Josie, I don't know how you do it. I don't know how Island Contracting stays solvent. And I can't tell you how much I admire you for it."

"Oh." She looked at him suspiciously. "Thank you. So why did you tell your mother about Renee?"

"Josie, I was worried . . . About you. About Island Contracting. And probably I was feeling a little . . . a little extraneous."

"A little what?"

"As though you were doing just fine on your own. Look, I'm accustomed to dating women who can take care of themselves. But I've always been able to understand their lives—their professional lives, that is. But you and Island Contracting—frankly, it's a mystery to me how you do it. There are so many variables and so many things that can go wrong, but you not only survive, you thrive. Anyway, I probably mentioned this to my mother last spring. I was calling her daily because I was worried about her after that awful time she had with the flu, and she kept talking about taking another survival course. Anyway, I told her more about your company and your employees and . . . more than I should have, I realize now. I was just trying to amuse her. Frankly, it's easier to talk to her about your business than about me—or mine."

"So you may have mentioned Renee?"

"Josie, I may have related the bios of everyone who ever worked for you." He removed his glasses and cleaned them on the tail of his chambray shirt. "And I am sincerely sorry for any problem I caused you."

"Not for me. You may have been the reason I got the best job of my life."

"But, if what you're thinking is true, I may be the reason Cornell Hudson was murdered."

TWENTY-EIGHT

Good morning, boys and girls. For those of you who haven't been able to find an "I Survived Hurricane Agatha" T-shirt, WAVE radio has been assured a new shipment should be on the island before noon. . . .

"**C**OFFEE, DEAR?"

Josie opened one eye. Carol was hovering by the couch, a steaming mug in her hand. "Yes. Just put it down on the coffee table there. Thank you," she managed to add before closing her eyes again.

"You said you had to be at work before six A.M., dear. That's why we set the clock radio, remember?"

"The power's back on."

"Yes, it came on around two A.M. Don't you remember? The lights all went on, and Sam's computer made that strange noise, and then Loki—"

"Discovered that she needed to go out," Josie muttered. "Yes, I do remember now."

"You were gone quite a while," Carol said, pushing the coffee closer to her.

"Yes. Loki seemed to feel that she had to protect the house from the various little creatures running around the dunes. It took me almost half an hour to convince her to come back in. And by then I was awake."

"You didn't get much sleep, did you? You look a little tired, especially around the eyes."

Josie reached out for her coffee. "I don't suppose you'd watch Loki for me again today? I'll be at the police station all day long and—"

"Don't worry about it. That dog and I get along just fine. I would have gotten up with her last night, but you know what a sound sleeper I am." Carol drifted out of the room, and her son wandered in.

"Josie, you look exhausted." Sam sat down beside her and confirmed what his mother had just said.

"Thank you. I had trouble sleeping."

"What is all this?" Sam picked up a pile of papers off the coffee table.

"My thoughts on the murder . . . Don't look at them, Sam. They probably don't make any sense at all."

"This one sure doesn't." He held up a sheet of paper covered with lines and rectangles.

"You're holding it upside down. It's a sketch of the Point House. That's pretty much the way it was supposed to look when we finished with it." She squinted at the paper. "At least that's how I remember it. It does seem as though there's been a room or two added. I thought there were four suites—one master suite and three for the three girls. But these rooms over here—" She pointed. "—are a puzzle."

"Why?"

"Well, I assumed they were for the children of the family in this suite. See, like this one. This is where Pip and her husband were to sleep. There's a stairway from here to more rooms in the attic. The attic rooms were for Pip's children."

"So?"

"So neither Beca nor Win have children. And, you know what?"

"What?"

"These are great rooms. They have the best view in the house." Josie picked up the drawing and examined it more carefully. "Sam, I'll bet these rooms were for Renee. I'll bet Cornell Hudson thought she was going to live in them—or at least visit. Maybe they were closer than she's admitted!"

"Josie, why don't you just ask her about all this?"

"But she lied to me about her father . . . she claimed he was her wealthy admirer. . . ." Josie frowned.

"What's wrong?"

"Sam, promise you won't tell me that I'm a complete idiot."

"Josie, I promise I won't tell you you're a complete idiot."

She decided she would have to be satisfied with that. "Okay, I have something to admit to you."

"Go ahead."

"Renee didn't say that Cornell Hudson was her lover. I told her. And she didn't disagree."

"You told her?"

"Yes. I was talking to her about him, and I said that he had paid for her to go to Europe and that he was . . . I think I said that he was her wealthy lover—or something like that—and she didn't disagree with me. But she didn't say that it was true either."

"Josie, what are you trying to tell me?"

"That I screwed up. I didn't ask questions as much as I told her the answers—the wrong answers."

"You mean inaccurate answers."

"Yes."

"So . . ."

"So even though Basil and I asked her a bunch of questions, we didn't learn a damn thing."

"What are you thinking about doing?"

"I need to talk to her again. Without Basil this time. I know he doesn't want to be involved. I only hope she will answer questions for me."

"If you'd like, I'd be happy to go with you."

Josie bounced over and put her arms around Sam. "Oh, Sam, thank you!"

He had just begun to hug her properly when his mother returned, cell phone dangling from her hand. "Josie, Chief Rodney just called. He says he wants to see you down at the station in fifteen minutes. He said, no excuses, dear."

Josie doubted if the endearment had come from the police chief.

"You promised me this would be done yesterday. Now what the hell happened?"

"I—"

"You are not to leave here until I have walls. Do you understand?"

"I—"

"And, since I can't trust you to do what I tell you, there is going to be an officer posted right outside the front door—"

"Are you arresting Josie?" Sam spoke up.

"No, I'm not arresting Josie. I'm just seeing to it that she keeps her word. There will be an officer sitting at a table outside the station all day long. He will be helping those FEMA guys out. And that officer has orders to call me immediately if he notices Josie leaving the building."

Josie turned to Sam. "Can he do that?"

"Don't see why not. As long has he doesn't actually try to prevent you from leaving, he can call anyone he wants."

Josie frowned. "So what about when I get finished here?"

"Then you will tell that officer, and he will call me, and I will come back here—when I have the time—and examine your work."

"What if I have to go out and get—?"

"You've used that excuse one too many times, Miss Pigeon. If you need anything, you call one of your employees and tell her to bring whatever you need. Understand?"

"Josie understands completely, Chief. She'll be done here as soon as possible."

"She better be!" Chief Rodney turned and stamped off.

"Why were you so nice to him? He's bullying me! And—"

"Josie, call Renee, make up some excuse, and get her over here."

"This place isn't exactly private," Josie said.

"True. But if you make enough noise and mess, everyone will stay away."

"If you say so . . . Sam, look who's coming in the door!"

He turned, and the two of them watched Renee walk across the foyer toward them, a toolbox in one hand and a huge level in the other. "Hi, Josie. I brought the level you asked for."

Josie and Sam both glanced at the level leaning against the back wall of the room. "I'll just put that one . . . uh, away," Sam suggested.

"Good idea," Josie muttered. "Hi, Renee. Good to see you! I've been wanting to talk to you," she added quietly.

"I thought you might." Renee looked around. "Maybe we should go someplace where there's more privacy. . . ."

"I can't leave here. Look, why don't we put together that

wall over there? Sam can pretend to help out, and we can talk while we work. If we make enough noise, no one will know what we're talking about."

Renee looked doubtful, but she did as her boss directed, and in a few minutes, Josie was asking the first question.

"I was wrong about Cornell Hudson being your lover, wasn't I?"

"He's my father." The answer was almost a whisper.

"I'm so sorry about . . . about his murder."

"Thank you. I—I've been lying to you. Ever since I applied for the job. What I wrote down on my application—it's all lies."

"That doesn't matter," Josie said sincerely.

"But you want to know about me now."

"I think I need to. I don't want to cause you more pain, of course. Losing your father—"

"I lost my father over a year ago," Renee said, using unnecessary force to hammer in a nail.

"But—"

"He disinherited me."

"Is that really possible? I mean, it sounds so . . . so old-fashioned."

"For my father, it was the worst thing he could do."

"What exactly did he do? Take you out of his will?" Josie glanced at Sam as she asked this question. He was listening intently as he pretended to sort lumber, and she knew he would understand how important the answer to this question was.

"No, that was the problem. He left me in his will against my wishes. He wanted to punish me—"

"Leaving you money is punishment?"

"I know, it sounds odd, but you don't know what being the daughter of Cornell Hudson meant. . . . Look, why don't I start at the beginning?"

"Sounds like a very good idea."

Apparently when Renee said "the beginning," she really meant the beginning. "My mother died when I was born," she explained. "My father hired a nanny immediately, but he spent a lot of time with me. I was the youngest, of course, and he was successful professionally by the time I came along. He had the time to spend with me, so my upbringing was different from my sisters'. My first memories are of sitting under the desk in Father's office, drawing pictures on the heavy white bond he used for business letters. He had a very formal office with dark chestnut-paneled walls, and he taped my drawings up all over the place." Renee smiled wistfully. "My first art show."

"It sounds as though he was proud of you."

"He was . . . back then." She'd added the final two words bitterly. "But I'm getting ahead of myself.

"Anyway, I grew up with lots of money and lots of love. But the love was conditional. Father believed he knew what was best for his daughters, and he expected them to go along with him. When I was nine years old, Win came home from college with a young man my father didn't like. There was no question in Father's mind that she would stop seeing this guy—and she did! I remember being impressed by that. But maybe, also, a little uncomfortable. I was so young, and I believed that everything Father did was right, but still . . . I liked the man Win had been dating. It was my first inkling that Father and I didn't share the same opinion about everything. But then, of course, I didn't see where that could lead."

"What happened?"

"Nothing right away. I wasn't a terribly rebellious adolescent. My father didn't ask a whole lot of me. I fit into the world he was working to belong to. I went to an excellent and exclusive private school in the city, to camp in Maine in the summer, where I chose art over sailing lessons, and I was invited to an appropriate number of coming-out parties when I turned eighteen." She shrugged. "Life was easy. And, for me, most of it was trivial. I cared about my artwork. I had improved, and by the time I was ready to graduate from high school, Father was having my paintings framed professionally before he hung them on his office walls.

"When the time came to choose a college, I was steered toward majoring in art at a university instead of going to an art school by my very best art teacher. I took his advice, and I've never regretted it. Father didn't care what I majored in and bragged about my good grades at Brown to everyone he knew. And then—two years ago last month—I graduated. My graduation present was a trip. I was to go wherever I wanted for up to a year—all expenses paid. I was thrilled. I'd been to Europe, but always on tours with fellow students. This time I was going to be on my own. I'd go where I wanted, live like I wanted, and I'd paint. I couldn't sleep for weeks. Planning the trip was so exciting."

"What happened?" Josie asked when Renee's pause extended into silence.

"Father. He planned on going with me. He said he wouldn't bother me. We would have two rooms, I could spend my days painting, and we would meet for dinner in the evening."

"And did that work out?"

"Not for long. We began in Italy. The first day was just fine. Father had picked a fabulous hotel on the Arno in Florence. We were tired after our flight, so we checked in to our hotel, walked up and down the river for about an hour, ate dinner at a small restaurant, and went straight back to the hotel and to bed. I was up before five the next morning and was sketching the view from my balcony as soon as there was any sunlight at all. That was the last peaceful moment I had the entire trip.

"Oh, of course, it was partially my fault. Father just didn't understand that my work was my work, not a hobby that could be picked up and dropped like a piece of knitting."

"What do you mean?"

"Well, he planned his days around what he thought I would like to see—famous works of art as well as all the tourist things. And each and every morning he told me where he was going and asked if I would like to accompany him. He tried to find things I would like to do, but . . . it just didn't work. I like to get up and get going. And I'm a little intense. I don't even hear people talking to me when I'm painting. I have to be alone, and when things aren't going well, I take a break—go for a walk, have a meal, take a nap, whatever. The problem is that I cannot predict when I'm going to want to stop. Father wanted a schedule, wanted to know when I was going to be free. And I tried to go along with it. I began to schedule my time. And my painting suffered. I was going nuts. I thought maybe a change of scene would help, so I suggested we head to Greece."

"Was that successful?"

"It was even worse. There was less for Father to do. He really depended on me to amuse him. I was dying to paint Greece, and I still am. I did one or two little things, but what a country. I . . . I suppose I'll get back there someday."

"So you and your father came home early."

"No, he came home early. I stayed on. But I stayed as Renee Jacquette, not as Dorothy Hudson."

"So you and your father had a falling out."

"We had the fight to end all fights. I swore I'd never see him again. He swore he didn't care. I told him I was changing my name. He told me that I was no longer a

Hudson as far as he was concerned. I told him I would never take any money from him again. And he said, yes, I would. That, in fact, is the last thing he ever said to me. He took the last flight out of Athens that day. And I stayed on . . . traveled on."

"You went to the Orient," Josie said.

"How did you—? Oh, the paintings in my room."

"Yes."

"Yes. I traveled on until I ran out of money, and then I came home and realized just how difficult it was going to be to support myself. And then I had the brilliant idea of becoming a carpenter. I'd been around carpenters all my life and . . . well, to be honest, I knew it would really upset my father." She took a deep breath and continued. "So I got myself trained, got my first job, and . . . well, here I am."

"And here's where your father came looking for you," Sam said, putting down his work and joining them.

"Yes, he must have hired a private detective," Renee said.

"He didn't need one," Sam said. "He had my mother."

TWENTY-NINE

And now WAVE radio brings you answers to
the questions everyone is asking. . . .

"**W**HEN WAS THE last time you saw your father?"
Josie asked.

"He was driving down Ocean Drive a few weeks ago. He was going up island, and I was heading down to the office. He . . . I don't think he saw me."

"So you really haven't spoken to your father since Greece," Sam said.

"Yes. But he has contacted me—through his lawyer."

"To tell you he'd taken you out of his will?"

"To tell me I was still in his will and always would be."

"What?"

"Interesting," Sam said. "You want to be independent, and he refuses to let you be."

"Exactly."

"That's truly mean," Josie said.

"Only if you see it that way. It could also be construed as being truly generous," Sam suggested.

"You don't know my father—"

"No, but he's been dating my mother, and I can't imagine that she would date a person without any positive characteristics."

"He wouldn't be the only person who treats his family differently than his dates," Josie suggested.

"Father likes to get his own way. Period."

Josie and Sam exchanged looks. "Are you in contact with the rest of your family?" Sam asked finally.

"My sisters are my only family. And the answer to your question is not anymore. Father told them what had happened before I got back to the States. Maybe it was because they heard his side of the story first, but it turned out that they were completely unsympathetic to my point of view. I don't mean to sound intolerant, but I just didn't need anyone else's disapproval. It's not as though I'm doing anything illegal or even questionable. I just want to live my own life. For some reason, they refuse to understand. Father insisted that they take sides, and they did—

his. I send Pip's boys birthday and Christmas presents, but that's the only contact."

"That is sad," Josie commented, remembering the years she and her family had been estranged.

"And it must have made your father's death more difficult for you," Sam added.

"Yes. I guess. It seems strange to be mourning someone I've been angry at for so long. And it's almost weird to think of him being murdered and not just dying in his sleep or in an accident like most people."

"Where were you when he was killed?" Sam asked directly.

"On the island." Renee looked at Josie. "You know the answer to this one, don't you?"

"I saw the painting that you did in the dunes the morning before Agatha hit. It looked to me like it was done in the area just outside the Point House."

"When I was up on the deck the day before the storm, I realized what a fantastic setting that was. And, when I woke up that morning, I realized the sky was spectacular. I just had to get out there and work."

"You really caught the violence of the storm's approach."

"Actually it's not finished."

"Why not?" Sam asked quickly.

"My father—" Renee stopped and looked guilty. "I guess that morning is really the last time I saw him. When you asked . . . I just didn't think . . ."

"So you did see him in the dunes that morning," Josie said.

"I . . . Yes. I did."

"When?" Sam asked Renee the question, but it was Josie he was looking at—scowling at, really.

"Well, after I'd finished painting, of course. I can't tell you what time it was, but I was there early—before it was

fully light. But I had to get to work, so I quit before I
wanted to and packed everything up and . . . and as I was
walking back to the house I saw something in the dunes.
It . . . it was my father lying on the ground. I . . ." She
looked from Josie to Sam. "I know this sounds stupid. I
knew I'd see him sometime, but this was so unexpected.
I panicked or something, took off and just kept going."

"You didn't stop to see if he was just lying there hurt?"
Sam asked what Josie thought was an insensitive question.

"No. I told you. I panicked."

Josie waited for Sam to ask another question, but he remained silent. "Well, I guess it's time for me to get back to
work. Are you going to stay on the island?"

"I need to stay busy. I honestly don't know what I'm
going to do with my life now. I have the money I need to
just take off and paint again. And I really did think that was
what I wanted, but . . ." She sighed. "I just don't know
what to do. There is going to be a memorial service in New
York next week, and I'll go up for that and the reading of
the will, but . . ." She looked at Josie. "Would you mind if I
just kept working for you? I promise I won't leave without
giving you time to find a replacement."

"I don't mind at all. In fact, I'd appreciate it," Josie said.

"It's an excellent idea," Sam agreed, looking depressed.

"Then, unless you need me for something, I'll go back
to Basil's place."

"That's fine."

Sam didn't say anything until he and Josie were alone
together. And then, only with her prompting.

"What's wrong? Do you think I shouldn't have let her
keep working for me? I really don't think she did it and—"

"Josie, I don't know if Renee killed her father or not, but
I do know that you have to stop answering questions for
other people."

"When did I do that?"

"When you told Renee that you knew she was in the dunes the morning her father was killed there. Until that point, she didn't know if you knew. And she might have lied, but you told her and . . . and all she had to do was agree and continue to lie from there."

"Why do you think she's lying, Sam?"

"I don't think she's lying. I know she is. Otherwise she would just answer the questions rather than waiting for you to do it for her. But that's not what worries me," he added, pulling off his glasses and wiping the lenses on his shirttail.

"What worries you?"

"My mother. Every time we turn around, she pops up as part of the story. Frankly, Josie, I'm afraid my mother is going to end up being the major suspect in Cornell Hudson's murder."

"That sweet woman murder anyone?"

Both Josie and Sam turned quickly to see who could possibly describe Carol Birnbaum as sweet.

The answer was Chief Rodney. And, for what was the first time since Josie had started working (or not working) on his office, he didn't look angry. He looked, Josie thought, concerned.

"Of course, we know Mother would never do anything like that," Sam assured him. "Our concern is that some people, who don't know her—"

"I know her, and I'm the law on this island."

Josie tried not to smile at this dramatic statement. Sam didn't seem to be having any problem looking serious. "Chief, it was my mother who told Cornell Hudson about this island, about the Point House, about—all that."

Josie knew Sam was struggling to talk about his concerns while keeping Island Contracting out of the picture.

"I do not want that lovely woman involved in this investigation in any way. Do you understand?"

"Why are you looking at me?" Josie squeaked.

"You don't think I'm stupid enough to believe that it's taking you so much time to do so little?" Chief Rodney waved his arms around the room. "You don't think I realize that you're gallivanting around on errands of your own? You think I'm stupid?"

Josie knew better than to tell the truth. "Cornell Hudson was strangled with a piece of my drop cloth," was all she said.

"That shows how little you know about it. He was shot. He was shot, and it was the bullet that killed him. Your dinky little drop cloth musta gotten wound around him when he was in the sea."

"Oh, then I guess I'm not connected to this at all."

"Yeah, right. Josie Pigeon's not connected to a murder on the island. That'll be the day."

"May I remind you that Josie has solved some of the murders that have taken place on this island," Sam said.

"And she's gonna do it again. Is that what you're telling me?"

"I—"

"She—"

"Well, this time's gonna be different." Chief Rodney glared at Josie. "This time I'm gonna help her."

"I . . . What did you say?"

"She . . . Excuse me?"

"You both go deaf in the storm? I said this time I'm gonna help her."

Josie was the first to recover from this amazing statement. "How?" she asked suspiciously.

"I got papers. I got reports. I got information. And it's all yours to look at."

"Are you referring to information such as autopsy results?"

"I mean exactly like autopsy results. Well, preliminary autopsy results. I'll get 'em for you." He turned to leave.

"Chief, your desk is over there," Josie said.

"You think I keep things I don't want the general public to see in my desk? You gotta think I'm nuts."

"So where—?"

"In the men's room, if you gotta know."

Josie watched as he headed toward the rest rooms. "Who would have thought that Chief Rodney and I would have the same idea?" she muttered.

"What?"

"Nothing. Sam, isn't this incredible?"

"What? The fact that Chief Rodney is willing to help you solve a murder so my mother doesn't get hurt or the fact that he seems to believe Mother is a sweet woman?"

"Both, I guess."

Josie put the papers back in the manila folder Chief Rodney had given her. "Well, that didn't help." She looked over at Sam, who was sitting on a sawhorse, staring off into space. "I've always assumed that it would be easier to solve a crime if I had access to the information the police have, but, in this case at least, it doesn't seem to be true."

"To be honest, it looks to me as though the logical suspects are either Basil or Renee. They both admit to us that they were on the scene, and I suppose you could say they both have motives."

"What?"

"Well, for Basil it would be revenge. And you'd be amazed how many murders are committed out of revenge. And Renee, of course, would get the money she needs to live the life she wants."

"But Renee doesn't want her father's money."

"Renee *says* she doesn't want her father's money."

"That's true. . . . But all of the sisters benefit equally from his death—that we do know from all this—so they are excellent suspects, too."

"Not really."

"Why not?"

"Because they don't need for Cornell Hudson to be dead to get at his money. He's supporting them generously right now."

"That's a good point. In fact, the only complaint they seem to have is whether or not they have whirlpools or regular bathtubs."

"And then there's always Mother."

"Your mother doesn't have any reason to kill Cornell Hudson. Think about it. He preferred her to beautiful young women. And there must be lots of beautiful young women in New York City who would get involved with a rich man like Cornell Hudson."

"That doesn't really make me feel better, Josie. He must have dated her because of her connection to the island. But why?"

"Because he wanted information about Renee."

"Why didn't he just hire a private investigator? Why my mother?"

"Because he . . ." Josie ran out of ideas. "I have no idea." She got up.

"Where are you going?"

"To finish up Chief Rodney's office. He's being nice to me, I'll be nice to him. And, I have to admit, it's important to have an office. I can't tell you how thrilled I was when I saw Island Contracting's building standing . . ."

"Josie? Is something wrong?"

"No. I just remembered something. Sam, do you have your cell phone with you? I need to call Betty again."

THIRTY

The Gull's Perch, Dairy Delight, Pizza on the Sand, Sullivan's, and the Pancake Hut all announce that they have resumed normal opening hours. At WAVE radio, we wanna know when the bars are gonna get back on line. . . .

"WHY YOU LISTEN to that station when you hate it so much is beyond me," Sam said, walking in the door of Josie's office.

"It's growing on me, I guess." She looked up from the papers on her desk. "I thought you were going to bring your mother with you."

"She'll be along in a bit. Is there any particular reason you wanted to see her, or were you just being friendly when you suggested we stop in this afternoon?"

"There is a reason, but . . . well, things don't seem to be working out exactly the way I planned."

"Do they ever?"

"No, in fact, I was just sitting here thinking about it."

Sam looked down at the blues on her desk. "Whose house is that?"

"It's the Point House—before and after. This is what

started me thinking about plans." She pointed to the pile of papers.

"Any particular reason?"

"Well, I was really looking forward to remodeling that house, but, to be honest, I think I preferred the building when it was the plain old rackety Point House rather than what I was going to be part of turning it into."

"Well, if you killed Cornell Hudson so the Point House could remain intact, I gotta tell you, you blew it."

Josie smiled. "I didn't, but you're close."

"You think Cornell Hudson was killed so that he wouldn't remodel this house?"

"No, but I think he was killed to maintain the status quo."

"What do you mean?"

"Sam, I've really screwed up this entire investigation—if you can even call it an investigation. You were right when you said I was asking questions and then answering them myself. And I was stupid in other ways. Agatha washed away the body, but I let the storm obliterate other clues as well."

"What do you mean?" Sam repeated.

"I—Oh, this may be Betty. I've been hoping she'd call." Josie picked up the ringing phone on her desk. "It's almost a miracle that things are working again, isn't it?" she added before speaking into the receiver. "Hello? Oh, Betty, hi! What did you find out?"

She listened for a few minutes and then spoke again. "You're sure?" She picked up a pen and scribbled on a notepad. "And this woman is positive? She knows it for a fact?" She wrote *Hudson Brothers* down on the edge of the pad and then began to scribble darts around it. "So . . ."

Sam walked around Josie and out to the deck that ran across the rear of the building. Someone had taken the time to replace the damaged boards in the floor. The boat had been removed from the bay. On the deck next door, small boys were pulling up crab traps and waving their contents in the faces of squealing small girls. Kayakers paddled by and waved. Josie walked out behind Sam and, putting her arms around his waist, gave him a big hug.

"Things are getting back to normal," Sam said.

"Yes, we're lucky Agatha wasn't a bigger storm."

"Definitely. So what did you find out from Betty?"

"I—Oh, there's the phone again. I hope it's Chief Rodney."

"I never thought I'd hear you say that," Sam said, and followed Josie back inside.

"Hi, Chief. Thanks for calling back so promptly. I was just telling Sam that I hoped you were on the other end of the line. . . ." She listened for a bit, and her smile turned into a frown. "You know I would never do that! Whatever you tell me will be held in strictest . . . And when I know what's going on, of course you'll be the first to know. . . . Of course. Of course. Of course. Of course. Yes, of course! Oh, I do appreciate it. I do understand. I do . . . I do . . . I do . . . I really do. Thank you. I think I'd better go now. . . ." She hung up and looked at Sam.

He grinned. "I thought for a minute there, you were going to end up married to him."

"The man's an idiot." Her frown turned into a smile. "But he called the New York Police Department and got the information I needed. And I know who did it."

"And you're going to tell me?"

"Yes. Just as soon as your mother's here. And I called in the rest of the crew about ten minutes ago—but not Renee. I don't think we need her right now, but Sissy and Ginger should be along anytime now."

Sam was focused on her first statement. "Mother? Why do we need my mother?"

Josie resisted making a sarcastic answer and sat back down at her desk. "Actually, your mother is a key person in this whole thing."

"Because she inadvertently told Cornell Hudson that his daughter was working on the island for you?"

"Her involvement began a bit before that. Oh, here they are!"

Ginger entered the room, the usual scowl on her face. "We're not getting our work done by stopping over here in the middle of the day," she said flatly.

Sissy followed close behind, perky as ever. "Hi, Josie. Hi, Mr. Richardson. Your mother just drove up."

But when Carol came into the room, it wasn't her son she greeted. "Ginger? What are you doing here?" She backed away and leaned against the wall. "I never thought I'd see you again."

"Well, Carol. You look like you've gained a bit around the hips. Not keeping up those promises you made to yourself, are you?"

"I . . . I'm still running. And I've been working very, very hard helping Sammy clean up his store. . . ."

Josie was trying not to smile at the situation.

Sam was looking for clarification. "Mother, how do you know this woman?"

"Ginger works as a . . . a leader in a wilderness training program in the winter," Josie answered his question.

"Inspirational leadership mediator," Ginger corrected her. "Your mother and some of her friends attended one of my programs early last spring."

"I'm afraid we were not her favorite campers," Carol spoke up.

"Nonsense. Liking has nothing to do with it. You need

to stop caring whether or not people like you and start living your life. You and your friends join a gym, lose some weight, and get into shape, and maybe next year we'll be able to concentrate on some wilderness skills rather than outdoor cooking."

"Are you telling me that my mother didn't spend a week rappelling up and down the peaks of Zion National Park?"

"Rappelling? Are you kidding? I couldn't even get that group out of their tents before nine A.M."

Sam looked away, and Josie could see he was enjoying these revelations, but she knew what she had to say now might not please him. "Carol told you about Island Contracting, didn't she?"

"Yeah. She said you were always looking for new people. Thought maybe you had some sort of problem getting along with people from what she said. Learned that wasn't true though. In fact, you're one of the most popular people on this little island. Can't imagine why you'd want to leave it."

"I don't!" Josie protested.

"She doesn't!" Sam added. "Mother?"

"I thought you might not want Josie to work when—if—you got married. And I knew Island Contracting would need someone to lead it. And Ginger can lead most anything."

"Mother! I know you have the best intentions, but—"

"But nothing. If you're going to be upset, I'll just leave."

"I need to ask you one more question," Josie said quickly.

"Josie, I know you wouldn't embarrass me in front of all these people. What do you want to know?"

"Did Cornell Hudson ever ask any questions about my office?"

"You mean about this building?" Sam asked, when his mother didn't answer right away.

"Yeah. Did he?"

"You know, he may have . . . We were talking about his security problems and I started talking about Sammy's security system. He—he changed the subject and asked about Island Contracting. I remember because I thought it was odd. I mean, Sammy has all those wonderful wines and imported liquors and things to protect, and you . . . I mean, Josie . . ."

"You're right. Except for a stray cat or two, a bunch of blueprints, and personnel files, there isn't much here that would interest anyone. I remember Chief Rodney saying that when we were broken into last spring."

"Cornell Hudson did it. He was trying to find out if his daughter was working here disguised as Renee?" Sam exclaimed.

"Renee is Cornell Hudson's daughter? The man who owned that house we were going to remodel?"

"Renee is the daughter of a rich man? And she works as a carpenter?" Ginger asked.

"Yes, she is. And no, Cornell Hudson didn't break in. And he didn't hire anyone to do it," Josie added as Carol opened her mouth to ask a question. "Cornell wouldn't hesitate to do something illegal to get what he wanted, and apparently he passed that particular trait on to one of his daughters."

"You weren't alone when you were talking about security, were you?" she asked Carol.

"No, his family was there. Those awful daughters . . ." Carol sighed.

Sam, the ex-lawyer, asked a direct question: "Who did it, Josie? Who broke in, and who killed Cornell Hudson?"

"Beca. And she did both. She broke in here, and a few months later, on the day of Hurricane Agatha, she killed her father."

"How horrible!" Carol said.

"The worst part of it is that she was hoping Renee would be blamed—and arrested."

"What a bitch!"

No one argued with Ginger's assessment.

THIRTY-ONE

"**W**HEN DID YOU figure it out?" Sam asked.

"I had my suspicions, but I wasn't sure until I checked with Betty. And, although I hate to admit this, Chief Rodney was more than a little helpful."

"But Betty's living in New York with that wonderful John Jacobs," Carol protested.

"Yes. And Beca lives in her building. Betty hated Beca because Beca used her, and, in fact, Beca isn't very popular in her building, so it was easy to get neighbors to gossip about her. And more than a few of those neighbors were well aware of the fact that her father's company, Hudson Brothers, had done all the work on her apartment. But I'm getting ahead of myself.

"The story begins with Cornell Hudson learning that his daughter was working as a carpenter here on the island . . . that she was working for me. I don't doubt that he wanted to reconcile with Renee—"

"Call me Dot. He always did." Renee appeared in the doorway.

"Oh," Sissy gasped.

"Speak of the devil," Ginger muttered.

"Come on in," Josie spoke up. "Since you're here, you're probably the best person to tell this part of the story."

"I heard you say you thought my father wanted to reconcile with me," Renee admitted.

"Do you think I'm right?" Josie asked. "I mean, Sam thought it was mean of your father to let you know you were still in his will, but that's not the only interpretation of that fact."

"You're right. Father used his wealth to manipulate us, but we accepted it—all of us. And I would have, too, but I found out that my art mattered more to me than my lifestyle. Father was, I think, quite simply, trying to be nice to me. He never thought we would be estranged forever. When I saw the blueprints and I realized he was planning a suite for me—one with north light and a fabulous view of the ocean . . . Well, then I knew." Renee was obviously having trouble holding back tears.

"I think he was planning a reconciliation. That's why he wanted your sisters on the island the day that we were due to begin work. Your father hoped you'd all get back together."

"I . . . That makes sense," Renee said, brightening a bit and then frowning. "But then he was killed—"

"You know, I think maybe it's time we got back to work." Ginger made the statement and stood up.

"I . . . ," Sissy began.

"We can hear whatever this is later. Sometime when we're more prepared . . . ," Ginger added.

Renee looked doubtful, but Sissy, glancing over at her,

got the point. "Sounds good to me," she said heading for the door.

"If you're sure you don't need me. . . ," Renee began.

"I'm sure," Josie said. "I'll be out later to check on you all—and—and all."

No one said anything more until the sound of work boots tramping away on the boardwalk to the street had ceased.

"Ginger's good," Sam said, when the roar of engines indicated that the crew was on their way to their respective work sites.

"She is," Josie agreed. "I didn't want Renee to hear that her sister was a murderer like this either, but I didn't know what to do about it."

"Did you have any idea at all that Renee wasn't who she claimed to be?" Sam asked.

"There probably were signs, but I didn't see them at the time."

"Like what?"

"Well, no one likes filling out all those stupid forms from my insurance company, but not only did she protest more than anyone else, she made many of her answers impossible to read. I should have realized she might be hiding something then. And, when she realized it was her father we were going to be working for, she was very concerned that he might show up at the work site until I told her that he had said it would be the architect who would be checking out the house from time to time, not her father or one of her sisters. And, finally, she was the only person on the entire island who didn't want to be on television. I should have realized then that she had something—her identity—to hide."

"I don't particularly like Beca, but are you sure she

killed her father?" Carol asked. "It seems so . . . so dreadful."

"It is, but Beca was just doing what she always did apparently. Doing and using whatever she needed to to make sure she had the life she wanted," Josie said.

"Why don't you let us in on the gory details," Sam suggested.

"What we didn't know is that the police were investigating Cornell Hudson and his company. And they were going to be making some arrests. Chief Rodney checked that out for me."

"Corn was going to be arrested? How embarrassing for him!" Carol cried.

"And for his family. Especially for the family member who was the most concerned about her position in society."

"Beca," Sam said.

"Yup. Beca cared about what people thought about her so much that she talked about her mother's death in an attempt to gain sympathy years after the event when the pain had dulled—if it hadn't vanished completely. Beca used whatever and whomever she needed to get what she wanted. Beca was not going to be the daughter of a felon without trying to do something about it. What she did was kill her father."

"But why did she think her sister would end up as a suspect?" Carol asked.

"Cornell Hudson was shot. He was a big man, and Beca—well, Beca hadn't taken any survival training and would never have managed to overpower him. So she shot him. It's strange that Renee didn't hear the shot, but she told me that when she was painting, she concentrated so much that she didn't hear things. As the storm was getting closer, the high winds and the waves would probably drown out most noises. But Beca wanted Renee blamed for the murder and couldn't depend on the body being found immediately. And she certainly couldn't have had any idea that the house was going to be washed away. So she used the drop cloths we'd left on site to drag the body back to the house—so it would be found."

Josie glanced over at Sam. "You're always complaining that I'm not organized, but this time you were wrong. If I hadn't carefully marked those cloths with Island Contracting's name, I wouldn't have been connected to the murder. And if it hadn't been for that strip of muslin, I probably would have told Chief Rodney about the body before the storm took it away."

"Which you should have done anyway."

Josie didn't even bother to turn around this time. "Hello, Chief Rodney."

"Hello, Josie. Sam. I hope I'm not interrupting anything. I thought I'd pick up Carol a bit early—"

Sam jumped up. "For what reason? If you're arresting her—"

"Sammy, you cute thing. Michael's not arresting me. He's picking me up for our date. We're going out to dinner together."

Sam looked from his mother to the police chief and then back again. "I—You—He—" He seemed unable to finish a sentence.

"I'm sure he just wants to wish us a nice time. Come on, Michael. I'm starving, and I understand Basil has bay scallops on special tonight."

Sam didn't speak until the couple had departed. And then he looked over at Josie. "Did you know anything about this?"

"Your mother did mention something to me," she admitted, and then grinned. "At least you don't have to worry about her being involved with Cornell Hudson anymore."

"Fine, instead of those blondes for stepsisters, Mike Rodney, Jr., will be my stepbrother."

Josie shuddered. "Don't even joke about it."

In return for providing the ingredients for the delicious meal Risa had just cooked them, Basil had been filled in with all the details of the story. "What I don't understand . . ." he said now, leaning back in his plastic beach chair and reaching for a jelly jar filled with wine, "What I don't understand is why you called Betty, why you needed to know if Cornell Hudson's company was remodeling his daughter's co-op."

"Because if they were competent, there had to be a reason for him to hire Island Contracting to redo the Point House."

"He did it to get to know his daughter again," Sam suggested.

"Exactly."

"But we heard they were incompetent. At least that's what John and Betty were saying."

"I know answer to that," Risa said. "People always complain about people who work on their homes. I notice this. And it makes me mad."

"Thank you, Risa," Josie said. "I—Sam, isn't that your mother's car coming down the road?"

"Looks like it. I wonder why she's here?" he said, getting to his feet.

"She's probably coming for dessert," Basil said. "Chief Rodney was probably too cheap to buy her one. That man is one of our worst customers. Always wanting discounts or free courses. Your mother can do better."

"I just hope nothing's happened—"

Carol parked and got out of the car before there was time for more speculation. Loki walked by her side as she marched up to join them.

"What happened to your date?" Sam asked.

"It's over. We came home for a little . . ." She paused. "For a sip of that brandy you keep in the kitchen. And this dog bit him. I couldn't believe it. She just jumped up and bit Michael on the hip." She turned to Josie. "You're going to have to take this dog back, Josie. I can't take her back to the city with me. She will bite all my dates."

"I . . . Urchin . . . I have cats."

Sam reached out and took the leash. "Don't worry, Mom. I'll keep her. I'll put an ad in the paper and notices up on bulletin boards around the island. If the owner claims her, fine, if not, she can live with me."

The phone rang from inside the house.

"Don't get up," Josie insisted as Risa started to rise gracefully. "I'll get it." She ran into the house and reappeared about two minutes later, shaking her head.

"Who was it?" Sam asked.

"Tyler. Finally he calls, and all he says is to be sure to listen to WAVE radio's news at eight. He says everything is fine, and he'll call back tomorrow, but—"

"It's almost eight now," Sam said, pulling a small transistor radio from his jacket pocket. After fiddling around with the tiny dials, Tyler's voice filled the air.

". . . We made over two thousand dollars profit in just three days. . . . I can't imagine how we could have made so much so quickly doing anything else."

The deep voice of the interviewer came on. "So you think you came up with a viable marketing plan."

"Yes, sir!"

All the listeners smiled at Tyler's youthful enthusiasm.

"I did the research. Created the perfect product. Hired a sales force. And got the product out on time."

"Sounds like you have a fine future in merchandising."

"Thank you, sir. But I'm planning on a career in computers. Or maybe oceanic research."

"Well, that's island resident Tyler Clay Pigeon. I'm sure all of WAVE radio's listeners wish him well and thank him for the opportunity to buy the wonderful 'I Survived Hurricane Agatha' T-shirts his friends have been selling for the past few days. Now back—"

Sam clicked off the radio and looked up at Josie. "Where are you going?"

"If he can call me, I can call him," she said, starting back to the house.

"Don't get mad at the sweetie," Carol said.

"*Sì, mio caro* Tyler was doing a good thing. Making money so he not have to depend on his mother forever," Risa added.

"Don't worry," Josie said with a smile. "I'm just going to find out exactly why the mother of the successful entrepreneur doesn't deserve at least a few free samples. After all, my friends and I survived Hurricane Agatha, too."

© Stephanie Violette

Valerie Wolzien is the author of the Susan Henshaw suburban mysteries and the Josie Pigeon seashore mysteries. Ms. Wolzien lives in an old house overlooking the Hudson River. She loves to hear from readers and can be reached online at valerie@wolzien.com.